a PATH less traveled

A MILLER'S CREEK NOVEL

Book Two

CATHY
BRYANT

WordVessel Press

Books by Cathy Bryant

MILLER'S CREEK NOVELS

Texas Roads

A Path Less Traveled

WV

Published by WordVessel Press
P.O. Box 971
New Boston, TX 75570

Library of Congress Control Number: 2010938823

ISBN: 978-0-9844311-2-0 (pbk.)

In honor of my mom,

Carolyn England,

who always encourages
and inspires me on the path.

"Trust in the LORD with all your heart,
and lean not on your own understanding;
in all your ways acknowledge Him,
and He shall direct your paths."
~Proverbs 3:5-6

Special Thanks To . . .

. . . my beta readers, crit partners, and proofreaders: Barbie B., Barbie Y., Carolyn, Hilary, Jimmie, Linda D., Linda W., Michelle, Molly, Ralene, Travis, and Virginia. Words can't express my gratitude for your invaluable help. Thanks for bearing with me.

. . . Kellie Southerland for the awesome cover design. Your magic touch helped bring this book to life.

. . . numerous online friends and blog readers who encouraged me and kept me laughing through the ups and downs of writing this book.

. . . to my church family. I love and appreciate you more than words can express.

. . . to Mom for your willingness to help in whatever way you could. I love you.

. . . to my awesome family: Josh, Jase, Megan, and Harrisen. I'm so incredibly blessed by each of you.

. . . to my awesome husband and first reader, Travis, for giving me wings. I wouldn't want to walk this path with anyone but you.

. . . to my Lord and Savior, Jesus Christ. You are the reason for it all. Soli Deo Gloria.

1

In spite of the thousands of winking lights surrounding Trish James, a wedding somehow lost its luster in the wake of death. She nudged her shucked shoes out of the way with her big toe and adjusted the tulle on the wedding arch, the soft netlike fabric billowing beneath her fingertips as she encased the twinkle lights. The church sanctuary, with its white pews, stained-glass windows, and smoky blue carpet, served as the perfect backdrop to her design.

"This wedding must be hard on you after Doc's death." Dani spoke the words as if uncertain she should speak at all.

The ache in Trish's heart started afresh, a wound that never healed, but she pushed it aside with practiced expertise. This wedding wasn't about her. "I'm fine. It's not every day my brother marries the most wonderful woman in the world." She forced a bright smile. "I've never seen Steve so happy." Mom would've loved this wedding.

Her sister-in-law-to-be didn't return the smile. Instead, the area above her clear blue eyes creased. "You sure you're okay?"

"Yep." Trish snipped the word and bent low to snag a sprig of silk ivy, then inserted it in the proper place and blinked away tears. In truth, it would be great to have someone to share her concerns with, but within boundaries—not right before the wedding, not with anyone who lived in Miller's Creek, and *definitely* not with family members. The last thing she wanted was for them to come to her rescue.

She'd told Delaine some of the situation, but her best friend since high school now lived the fast-paced, Austin lifestyle, their conversations limited to when Delaine didn't have something else on her agenda.

"I can't imagine how difficult it is to be both mother and father to Little Bo." Dani lowered her head, blonde ringlets framing her face. "And then trying to start a business on top of everything else."

Oh, no. She wasn't going there. Trish clenched her teeth. Steve had already given her this lecture. With his best brotherly concern, he'd told her she didn't have to be Superwoman. Yeah, right. Try telling that to her empty checkbook and refrigerator. She glanced at Dani, who sat atop the piano railing, swinging her legs. "Are you ready for the big day tomorrow?"

A happy glow wreathed her friend's face. "And the day after, and the day after that. I think I've been getting ready to marry Steve my entire life."

"I'm happy for you both." Though it hurt to speak the words, she meant it. It wasn't their fault her life was in the doldrums.

Dani sprang from her perch and trotted down the steps to view the stage. "You have such a gift, Trish. Everything looks magical."

Trish gazed at the curly willow branches she'd ordered and spray-painted white, now wrapped with tiny sparks of light. The fairy tale forest blanketed the stage and meandered down the side aisles in an aura of enchantment. Once the ribbons and flowers were placed, and candles inserted into globes and nestled among the boughs, her vision would be complete. "I hope it's what you wanted."

"It's better than I could've ever imagined." Dani hurried over and draped an arm across her shoulder. "Once everyone in Miller's Creek see this, you're gonna get loads of business."

A heavy sigh whooshed from her before she could contain it. "From your lips to my bank account."

Dani's eyes clouded. "I don't know how to say this, so I'm just going to say it and get it over with. Are you okay? I mean . . . do you need to borrow money or something?"

No. Yes. Yes. She wasn't okay. She needed money. She needed . . . something. "I'm fine." The lie popped out as she stepped to the box perched on the piano bench. With care she lifted two delicate cracked-glass globes and moved to the candle stands. The words "I'm fine" were her constant mantra these days, like saying them made everything all right. Who was she kidding?

She closed her eyes and reopened them with a slow blink, weary of pretending. But what choice did she have? Her brother's wedding wasn't the time or place to air her personal problems. Besides, she was thirty-two years old, more than old enough to handle life on her own. A glance at her wristwatch sent her pulse on a stampede. Still so much to do to make the decorations perfect. *God, please let this bring me business.*

Dani plopped back onto the railing. "Is Little Bo doing better?"

How could he be? "Sure, if you don't count the nightmares and barely letting me out of his sight." She omitted the fact that he was a hairsbreadth away from flunking kindergarten, unless she could help him catch up before the school year ended.

"So the psychologist is helping?"

Before Trish could respond, the double white doors at the rear of the church burst open. Incessant rain poured from the April sky and silhouetted a person's form. Dani let out a squeal. "Andy!"

The petite blonde flew down the steps toward her friend.

Trish vaguely remembered the man from the time he'd spent in Miller's Creek during the downtown renovation, though she didn't recall ever having met him. Today he wore a lightweight suit with a loosened necktie, and had an easy-going smile that brightened the room. "Hey, girl. How's the bride?"

Dani looked up at him, her face radiant. "Never better."

"Yeah, I can see that."

She tugged his arm. "Come here. I want you to meet someone."

His loose-limbed gait gave the impression of someone always relaxed, like he'd just returned from a vacation at the beach.

"This is Andy Tyler, my friend and attorney from Dallas. Andy, this is Steve's sister."

Sea-green eyes sparkled. "Well, does Steve's sister have a name?" He jogged up the steps and held out a hand, his smile still bright.

Trish laughed and took his hand. "I'm Trish James. Nice to meet you."

Dani's face took on a crimson hue. "Sorry. Guess my mind is elsewhere."

Andy's gaze rested on Trish's bare feet. "Glad to know you have a name. What about shoes?"

She couldn't help but smile. "I got rid of them hours ago."

The hall door squeaked behind them, and Mama Beth, the mother figure of all of Miller's Creek and Dani's biological mother, bustled into the room. Along with her came the smell of fresh-baked bread wafting from the fellowship hall. Trish could almost taste the melt-in-your-mouth rolls. Maybe she could sneak a few leftovers for her and Bo to nibble on next week.

The older woman gazed around the room. "My goodness, Trish, if this isn't the most gorgeous thing I've ever seen." Mama Beth hugged Andy's neck. "Hi, Andy."

A tender gleam lit his eyes as he wrapped his arms around the older woman's shoulders and kissed her cheek. "Hi, sweet lady." He turned raised eyebrows to Trish. "You did all this?"

She ducked her head and pushed a silky strand of hair behind one ear.

"All of it," gushed Dani, "and wait until you see the fellowship hall."

"Speaking of fellowship hall, I could sure use your help in the kitchen." Mama Beth's voice took on a commanding tone as she scuttled to the door. "We've got enough work to do for this rehearsal dinner to keep an entire army busy."

Dani looked torn. "But I can't leave Trish down here to do all this by herself."

Trish wrestled the wieldy greenery in place, longing to comment that she didn't need help. It would suit her just fine if they'd all go away and leave her alone.

Andy rested his hands on his hips in mock protest, his tan jacket pulled back. "What am I? Pork belly? I'll help Trish. You go help Mama Beth." He held up a hand. "Trust me when I say I'll be more help here than in the kitchen."

"Good point. I've had your cooking." Dani grinned and rushed after Mama Beth. "Y'all know where to find us if you need help."

Andy chuckled and shed his jacket, then laid it across the front pew and turned her way. "What can I do to help?"

Trish mentally checked her to-do list. "I was actually waiting for someone with more muscles than me to come around. There's a box full of candles I need brought in from my Suburban." She pointed toward the side door. "It's out there and it's unlocked."

He gave a mock salute that bounced his sandy curls. "Yes ma'am." Andy's stocky frame loped down the steps and disappeared through the doorway.

Her eyebrows rose as she made her way to the pile of greenery on the front pew. Dani's friend was more handsome than she'd remembered. Trish burrowed through the tangled mess, remembering the promise she'd made Dani to help Andy feel welcome. As if she needed a man to take care of along with her other responsibilities.

The door slammed, Andy's eyes and forehead barely visible above the box he white-knuckled. She ran to him. "Let me help. I know that's heavy. I loaded it this morning."

"Nah, I got it." The words wheezed out. "You loaded this by yourself?"

She ignored the question and pointed to the stage. "Can you bring it up the steps?"

He shot her a you've-got-to-be-kidding glare then labored up the steps, his face red, his breath coming in agonized spurts. As he reached the last step, the toe of his leather lace-ups snagged the extension cord snaking along the edge of the stage.

Trish tried to speak, but the words congregated behind her locked lips.

Andy stumbled, and the box flew from his arms, the candles launching like small missiles. He hit the floor with a thud, the box crash-landing at the base of the first tree.

In slow motion, like carefully-placed dominos, the trees rippled to the floor in a sickening staccato of crashes and breaking glass. As if to punctuate the effect, the white metal archway in the center creaked and leaned, as it teetered, then toppled forward with a bang.

Her mouth hinged open, and her hands flew to her cheeks. All her hard work . . . ruined. In her shock, it took a moment to realize Andy still lay face down on the carpet. She hurried over to him. "Are you all right?"

He pushed himself up on all fours and surveyed the devastation.

Assured he was okay, she moved to the top step and slung herself down. The scene replayed in her mind. A giggle gurgled out, and then burst forth in an almost-maniacal laugh.

Andy chuckled and crawled to sit beside her.

Without warning, her laughter turned to sobs. She covered her face with trembling hands, rage surging at yet another unexpected crying jag. Now she'd never be ready on time. No one would be impressed. No one would want her services. No business. No money.

"I'm sorry. I'm so sorry." Andy slid a hand down her arm. "I'll fix it, Trish, I promise. I'm so sorry."

Trish fisted her hands, then straightened her spine and swatted at the tears on her cheeks. "Will you *please* stop apologizing?" There was no controlling her snappish tone. "For Pete's sake, it was an accident. I'm not gonna sue." She clamped her lips, rose to her feet, and waded through the ruins. Fingers against her lips, she knelt to retrieve shattered slivers of glass from the broken globes. These weren't even paid for.

Andy stooped beside her, his eyes boring a hole into her skull. "Here, let me get that. You start putting things back where you want them."

Trish could only nod at his softly-spoken words, a knot wedged in her windpipe. She lifted a tree into position, the light strands dripping from the branches like a child had thrown them in place. So far her determination to prove herself capable had been met with nothing but industrial-strength resistance.

It's all your fault. The familiar words in Andy's head relentlessly accused, ushering forth memories and ghosts from the past. Trish obviously had spent hours on the wedding decorations, and he'd managed to undo her work with one false step. He forced the finger-pointing voice to the back of his mind and attempted to burn off the chill that now hung in the room. “You live here in Miller’s Creek?”

“Yes.” She pinched off the word. “My son and I live here. At least for now.” She didn’t look at him while she maneuvered the lights back on the branches with agile fingers.

Son? Now he remembered. Dani had mentioned something about Steve’s sister losing her husband in a freak accident. A cow kick—or was it a horse? And how long ago? “You’re leaving town?”

“I don’t want to, but we don’t always get what we want, do we?”

True, but sometimes what you thought you wanted wasn’t what you needed. Andy rose to his feet, his hands cupped to contain the glass shards. “No, we don’t. You have a trash can?”

Trish’s tawny eyes looked his way. She grabbed an empty box and hurried to him. “Here.” She glanced around the stage, her face gloomy, her shoulders slumped. “Are they all broken?”

“Don’t know.” He dumped the pieces in the box, where they pinged against each other. “Is there some place I can buy replacements?”

She rubbed one arm and shook her head. “No. I had them shipped. I’ll drive to Morganville tonight after the rehearsal to see if I can find something that’ll work.”

The sadness on her face made his breath stick in his throat. He’d been in Miller’s Creek less than an hour and had already goofed things up. “I’ll go with you and pay for them since it’s my fault.”

Trish’s shoulders rose, then fell. “It’s no one’s fault. It’s just something that happened.” Her tone was flat and lifeless. She returned to the branches and hoisted another one back into position.

Just something that happened. A shaft of light streamed through the stained glass windows and rested on her, and she slumped over like she couldn't bear the weight of the world any longer. Was she remembering the accident? He removed a pack of peppermint gum from his shirt pocket and popped a piece in his mouth. Her problems made the mess with Sheila seem trivial in comparison. What could he do to make things better?

She turned her gaze his way. "Dani told me you're engaged. When's the big day?" Trish strung lights along a tree branch. Perfectly.

He shifted his weight to the other leg, then squatted to pluck glass from the carpet. "Uh, we're not . . . I mean . . . well, it's over between us."

She raised her head, and her brown hair shimmered under the light. "I'm sorry. I didn't know."

"Don't be." He stood. "It's for the best."

"How so?"

Andy let out a half-laugh. "Turns out she still had a thing for her ex-boyfriend." Thank the Lord he'd found out in time. A wife would be wonderful, but not the wrong wife.

For a moment she didn't speak, but her face took on a knowing look. "That must've been painful."

He nodded, his lips pressed together. "It was hard, but God can bring good from hurt."

Trish stared at him like she was trying to get a read on him, and then turned back to the lights. "So neither one of us is really in the mood to celebrate—especially a wedding." Her expression matched her cynical tone.

Out in the hallway, muffled voices grew closer. The hall door swung open, and the smell of Mama Beth's home-cooking made his mouth water. A little boy who looked like Trish raced toward them, then stopped, his dark eyes round. "Whoa! What happened here?"

Dani and Mama Beth followed, their mouths ajar. After them came Steve Miller, the mayor of Miller's Creek, and Dani's soon-to-be husband.

"It's all right. Don't worry." Trish rushed to the two women and laid a hand on each of their arms. "It's nothing that can't be fixed, I promise. We just had a little accident."

Andy watched through narrowed eyes at how Trish comforted the two women, when just a few minutes before she'd been in tears. A good way to get a severe case of whiplash.

Steve sauntered toward him, his boots scuffing against the carpet, a friendly grin on his face.

He shook Steve's hand. "How you doing, Mayor?"

The other man's grin expanded as he tucked his fingers in his jean pockets. "I'll be doing a lot better in a couple of days." The little boy streaked by. Lightning fast, Steve untucked one hand and grabbed his arm. "Hold on, tiger. I don't think you have any business up there. Have you met Aunt Dani's friend?"

The boy skewed his lips in a thoughtful pose and shook his head.

"This is my nephew, Bo."

Andy stretched out a palm. "Give me five, buddy."

Bo reared back and delivered a hearty slap.

"Ouch!" Andy pretended to shake off the sting. "Man, I'll bet you can throw a baseball really far with that kind of muscle power."

The boy nodded, his face creased with a grin. "Yep, but I can't catch so good."

"Well," corrected Trish as she came to stand with them. "You can't catch well."

Andy assumed a catcher's position beside him. The little guy had to be missing his daddy. Maybe he could help. "I used to be a catcher, so I can give you some pointers later. Would you like that?"

Bo's eyes lit. "Yeah."

"Yes, sir." Trish's tone held a warning.

"I mean, yes, sir." He looked toward his Mama. "Is it okay if we play catch, Mom?"

She sent Andy a tight-lipped smile, her expression cloaked with reserve, but when she turned toward her son her face softened, and she tousled her son's hair. "Of course, but it might be tomorrow since Mr. Tyler's already promised to help me clean up this mess."

"Almost looks like a tornado touched down in here." Steve rocked back on his heels and jangled the coins in his pocket.

"A tornado named Andy." Trish gave a play-by-play account.

Steve laughed at the story, but Mama Beth and Dani still fussed about like a couple of hens. "That's one way to get out of carrying more boxes." Steve winked. "I'll have to remember that move."

"Hey, look at me!" Little Bo perched on the piano railing, one foot in front of the other, his arms out to balance. Andy's heart moved to his throat. One wrong step would hurdle him toward the slivers of glass still embedded in the carpet.

All of them raced for the railing, but Andy arrived first. He grabbed Bo by the waist and slung him over one shoulder, amused at the boy's contagious belly laugh. "Come here, buddy, before you fall and hurt that amazing pitching arm."

Trish joined them, eyes wide with panic, her face pale and strained. She gripped Little Bo's arms. "How many times do I have to tell you not to pull stunts like that?" Her voice shook as she knelt, her face inches from his.

The boy said nothing, and his lips stuck out in a pout.

Steve laid a hand on her shoulder. "Sis."

Volumes passed between the brother and sister before Little Bo bolted for the door. Trish raced after him, her dark eyes full of hurt.

Both men faced the door, an awkward silence between them. Steve cleared his throat and turned, his eyes fixed on the floor. “Sorry about that. Trish is . . . uh . . . going through a rough time.”

Andy nodded. An understatement if he’d ever heard one. Based on what he’d seen, he was pretty sure not even Steve knew exactly how rough.

2

"We're in trouble, Sis." Steve peered at Trish, his voice edged with fatigue.

She released a sigh and leaned back against the cool metal chair to view the crowded room. The outdated church parlor hadn't been her first choice for the rehearsal dinner, but with elaborate reception decorations already in place in the fellowship hall, the parlor won by default. Mom would've insisted on redecorating the place before she'd have allowed one of her children to have a rehearsal dinner here. In fact, she probably would've insisted that it be held at the ranch.

At least there would've been more space. The room swarmed with people, and from the look of things, everyone had already finished eating while she'd barely had time to fix her plate.

The aroma of brisket, mashed potatoes, and homemade bread rose from the table and set off a long grumble in her belly. She could taste the delicious food from the aroma alone, but the pleasing smells did nothing to relieve her nothing-since-breakfast hunger.

Trish winced when Steve sat down to her right and bumped against her sore feet with his boots. She steeled herself against his news. "What kind of trouble?"

"I just got a call from Jake. He can't make it."

A cold chill scuttled up her arms. "What do you mean he can't make it? He's a groomsman, for Pete's sake!"

"He broke his ankle in three places in a four-wheeler accident. He's having an operation tomorrow to put in pins."

"Great. Just great." Trish's fork dropped to the plate with a clang. She brought one hand to the bridge of her nose, aware of Little Bo's eyes on her. Why couldn't she have just one normal, uneventful day? She and Andy had finished the sanctuary less than an hour ago, and now this.

Mama Beth scurried by, breathless. "Trish, will you check to see if anyone needs more tea?" She walked backwards, one finger in the air. "Oh, and I almost forgot. Is the groom's room ready? If not, would you take care of it?" Without missing a step or a word, the older woman pivoted and continued to chat with the people milling about, like a bee buzzing between blossoms.

Trish took a cleansing breath and looked at Steve. "Well, we'll just have to find a replacement, won't we?"

Her brother's expression was incredulous. "Any idea who?"

Conversation and laughter bounced off the painted brick walls. Her eyes rested on Andy, deep in discussion with J. C. and Coot, two of Steve's old geezer buddies. Andy had been a big help with the wedding decorations, but even better, he was easy to talk to. "What about Andy?"

Steve shook his head. "Don't know if the tux will fit. Jake's a big guy, but compared to Andy, he's scrawny-looking."

"Well, there's only one way to find out." She slapped her napkin down on the table beside the plate she hadn't had time to touch, pushed her chair out with instructions to Little Bo to finish his food, and made her way through the crowd, Steve on her heels.

Andy frowned when she approached. "What did I do this time?"

Trish arched an eyebrow. "Guilty conscience?"

"Not at all, but by the look on your face I'd say you're looking for someone to kill. Just wanted to make sure it wasn't me."

Before she could answer, Coot spoke, his thumbs hooked beneath his bright-orange suspenders. "Don't worry. Her bark's worse than her bite." He bellowed the words, then wheezed his way into a hearty round of laughter, as if his words were A) original, and B) funny. Trish bit back a snarky retort and silently checked C) none of the above.

"Actually, we have a favor to ask." Steve explained the situation.

A good-natured grin emerged on Andy's face. "You know I'll be glad to help. You have the tux here?"

"Yes." Trish grabbed his arm and herded him and Steve to the hallway, almost certain she'd logged a million miles in one day's time. "It's in the music suite, also known as the groom's room."

Once in the choir room, Trish moved to the first level of chairs, grabbed the plastic-encased tuxedo, and swished it toward Andy. "There's a restroom through those doors, on the right."

A few minutes later, Andy waddled into the room like a penguin, his purple face reminding her of an over-ripe grape. "This outfit was meant for someone a little less healthy than me."

Trish rolled her lips together to contain a smirk. "You think?"

Andy assumed a cocky stance. "You're making fun of me after I spent all afternoon helping you?"

"You mean helping me re-do—"

He held up his hands, the jacket sleeves near his elbows. "Okay, okay, don't remind me." Andy tugged at the collar of the shirt. "I think the tux will work, except for cutting off my air supply."

Relief spilled from Steve's eyes. "You'll do it then?"

"Of course." He spoke as if there'd never been a doubt.

"Thanks, pal. I owe you." Steve slapped him on the back. "I'd better pass the news on to Dani before she hyperventilates." He strode from the room with a happy whistle.

Trish smiled her appreciation. "Another crisis averted, thanks to you."

"Just remind me not to bend over tomorrow, or we'll have an even bigger crisis on our hands." He winked and disappeared through the doorway.

Trish laughed and busied herself with preparing the room. She emptied the plastic grocery sacks she'd dropped off earlier, set water and soft drinks on one counter, and arranged the snacks in a separate location. The door creaked, and she whirled around as Andy sauntered over to view her work. "You never stop, do you?"

The soft tone of his voice flustered her, but she ignored the feeling and returned to her task. "Who has time to stop?"

Andy laid an arm across her busy hands. "You do. Did you stop long enough to eat supper?"

Trish frowned. "Does fixing a plate count?"

"No." He steered her out the door and down the fluorescent-lit hallway. "I can tell I'm going to have to keep an eye out for you, lady."

"I can take care of myself."

"Um-hmm." His tone held doubt. "I'm sure you can, but will you?" Back in the parlor, Andy guided her to the table, pulled out a metal folding chair, and motioned for her to sit. Then he grabbed another chair, straddled it backwards, and rested his chin on one fist.

A creamy pile of mashed potatoes beckoned from her plate. She stuffed a forkful in her mouth and closed her eyes in rapture. Mama Beth made the best mashed potatoes in all of Texas—even if they were now cold.

"How long since you've eaten—two weeks?" Andy's eyes held a bemused twinkle.

"I had breakfast." She opted not to elaborate.

"Today?"

Trish glared. "Yes, today." She stuck another bite of potatoes in her mouth and swallowed, already revived. "Are you going to sit there and stare at me while I eat? 'Cause I'm pretty sure it's not good for my digestion."

Andy's cheeks dimpled in a way that made her insides churn. "I promise not to stare if you promise to eat all that food before you head down to the sanctuary for the rehearsal." He pointed to the plate to emphasize his words.

She raised her gaze to the ceiling and sighed. "All right. Now go pester someone else so I can eat in peace."

He stood, whirled the chair around to scoot it under the table, and moved a few feet away where a group of men congregated.

She basked in the momentary opportunity to relax, but also did a quick check of the room to locate Little Bo. He stood nearby with Dad and J. C., so she returned her focus to Andy. Completely relaxed, he chatted like he'd known these people his entire life. The return to Miller's Creek must be difficult for him considering the false accusations leveled at him during his first stay. Within her, interest and admiration arose as he relayed a story, the dimple on his left cheek winking. He finished his tale, and the men around him burst into laughter.

Mama Beth hurried past again. "Trish, dear, don't forget about the tea."

Trish huffed out a sigh, shot an acidic arrow into the imaginary bull's eye on the older woman's retreating back, and made a move to stand.

Andy caught her attention with a stern shake of his head. "Got it. You eat." He grabbed a metal pitcher from the drink table and started making the rounds.

Out of the corner of one eye, she noticed Dani headed toward her, a determined set to her chin. Sheesh, couldn't she have a few minutes to eat?

Like a frog devouring a fly, Andy snagged Dani's arm as she passed. She made a one-eighty and faced the table where he poured tea. Within a minute, the guests had her engaged in conversation. Andy pointed to Trish's plate and gestured with a fist to his mouth, then finished the game of charades with a wink.

A smile curved her lips. She hated to admit it, but having someone look out for her felt good. Addicting good.

3

Andy's blood pressure climbed through the roof, along with a Texas-sized hankering for his boxing gloves and punching bag. He folded his arms, leaned against the back wall of the church, and crunched the peppermint he'd discovered in his pocket. The rehearsal was scheduled to start at 7:00, and his watch now read 7:20. He'd been in no-telling how many weddings, so it wasn't like he didn't already know the routine. Walk in, assume the fig-leaf stance, walk out. Nothing complicated. So why did wedding rehearsals have to take longer than a baseball game in extra innings?

A hen party gathered to his right, their voices lowered. At the mention of Trish's name his radar zoomed to high alert. He leaned closer.

"Trish did all the decorating. I'm sure she's trying to drum up business for that interior design shop she has downtown." The muscled woman with shiny blue eye makeup and forearms bigger than his snickered. "Like she's gonna be able to make a go of that in Miller's Creek."

"Why did she start a business in the first place?" asked another member of the group.

A third woman jumped in. "Seriously. Her Daddy's got enough money to take care of her and Little Bo for life. Then with Doc being a vet, and her selling his practice. He prob'ly left a chunk of life insurance when he died."

Andy's blood boiled. Who gave them the right to make assumptions about the private details of someone else's life? Didn't they realize how hurtful it was? Sounded like jealousy and spite to him. He still bore the scars of small-town gossip from his childhood, but thankfully, he'd proved them all wrong and risen above their gloomy forecasts.

Down in front, Trish finished talking to Dani and headed toward them.

"Shh," one of them hissed, "here she comes with that phony baloney smile."

Trish gave Andy a little wave as she passed, then moved on to the women. "Hi, y'all. Mama Beth told me you'll be serving the food for the reception tomorrow. We sure appreciate your help. Let's go to the kitchen." She motioned for them to follow. "I'll show you where everything is and talk you through the plans. Carla, Mama Beth asked that you run the kitchen tomorrow, but if you hit any snags just come find me and I'll do what I can to help."

An urge to protect Trish rose inside him. A big part of him longed to run after her and beg her to be careful. Why? He rubbed down the creepy-crawly feeling on the back of his neck and thought about the question. He knew how it hurt to lose those you loved. Then to have to deal not only with the loss, but also people's hurtful words.

Dani edged up and elbowed him in the ribs. "Hey, guy. Sorry I haven't been able to spend more time with you. How are you doing?"

"Better than the last wedding rehearsal I attended." Sheila's image rose to his mind.

"Glad to hear it. When I think about how Sheila treated you, I still get livid."

"Please don't. I'm just glad I found out before it was too late." He watched Trish and the other women exit the sanctuary. "Tell me about Trish."

Her eyes grew troubled. "I'm really worried about her, Andy. She lost her mother a little less than a year ago. I think I told you about the accident?"

"Yeah."

"Trish and Little Bo witnessed the whole thing, and they're having a difficult time getting past it." She knotted her forehead. "And there's something else. Something I can't quite put my finger on. She should be doing okay financially, but I guess her business has taken a lot of money to get off the ground . . ."

"Dani, you ready to get the rehearsal under way?" The preacher called from the front, his microphone ringing.

"Definitely." She shouted, then stepped past Andy, her eyes sparkling. "Later, 'gator."

Andy wandered to the front and sprawled out in a pew, his thoughts on the young widow and her son. She appeared to be doing okay, but things weren't always what they seemed on the surface.

Trish entered the hall door, her son's hand tucked in hers. "Have I missed anything?" She slid in beside Andy and pulled Little Bo into her lap, where he snuggled into her chest with a thumb in his mouth.

"Yeah, it's over. Already gone through it a couple of times."

Her wry expression brought a grin to his face, but the gold specks in her tawny eyes made his heart race. He forced his attention to the instructions the preacher spouted.

A few minutes later, the wedding party lined up at the back of the sanctuary to go through the ceremony. Dani had the groomsmen walk the bridesmaids down the aisle, and Andy was glad to be paired with Trish.

After making sure everyone was in the right place, Trish hooked her arm through his and turned toward Little Bo and the flower girl who stood behind them. "Hold her hand, Bo."

Her son let out a disgusted sigh and wrinkled his nose. "Mo-o-om." He stretched the word out in a pleading tone.

"It's almost over, sweetie. Then you can go with Papaw to his house." Trish turned her head back Andy's way. "Ready?"

He glanced down at her bare feet. A grin spread across his face to match the one in his heart. "Yeah, as a matter of fact, I am." Past ready.

Trish and Little Bo caught Andy's attention throughout the rehearsal. The boy had endured as much as he could take and was low on energy and patience. He yawned, and then looked at Trish with begging eyes. She met his unspoken pleas with encouraging smiles.

The silent communication between them stirred something inside him. This woman had lost the person she loved most. She could've emotionally abandoned her son and curled up in her grief. But she hadn't deserted her little boy, like . . . Familiar thoughts tangled in his brain. He snatched a ragged breath to muster his strength and, like he'd done so many times before, stuffed the thoughts deep.

After they practiced the ceremony a second time, the preacher announced the end of the rehearsal. Andy plopped down on the front pew and yawned, the fatigue of a long day catching up to him.

Trish, still barefoot, climbed the steps to give directions for the following day, and then took time to answer questions. She continued to smile and joke, gifted with the rare ability to make each person feel important and recognized. But in one second, as a group moved away, her game face slipped, and she raised fingertips to rub her forehead. She was exhausted. To make matters worse, after everyone else left, she still had more to do. Time to come to her rescue.

Andy took a roundabout way to get up the steps, and moved in behind her to place a hand on her elbow. “You look ready to topple. Let’s go buy those globes so you can get home and rest.”

Weary lines wrinkled her forehead. “I’ll get my purse and meet you in the hall.”

Andy told Mama Beth his plans so she wouldn’t worry and left to find Trish. He spied her off to one side, wistful eyes trained on Dani and Steve as they exited the building, holding hands.

She turned as he approached and quickly plastered on the breath-taking smile she could make appear at a moment’s notice. “There you are. Ready?” She jangled her keys.

“I’m driving. You need the rest.”

“But—”

“But nothing.” He sent her a stern look.” You’ve spent all day helping everyone else. Let me help you for a change.”

Her lips opened like she wanted to say something, but then she clamped them shut. “Okay. Thanks.”

Andy pushed against the heavy wooden door and led the way through the honeysuckle-scented night to his BMW Z3, his mind on the woman at his side. The woman who lugged around a mountainous hurt and tried to pretend it didn’t exist.

“This is your car?” Her voice held surprise, and in the moonlight he saw her eyes grow round.

“Yes, ma’am.” He opened her door and waited while she took a seat, then stepped to the other side.

Trish ran her fingers over the leather seat and ogled the dashboard. “It’s beautiful.”

“Thanks. You want the top up or down?”

"Down, of course." Her face lit as he lowered the canopy, a starry Texas night above them. "The heavens declare the glory of God."

"Huh?" Andy started the car, put it in gear, and backed out of the parking space.

"A Bible verse I learned as a child. It always comes to mind when I see daybreak, a sunset, a rainbow, or the stars." She tilted her head back against the seat and fastened her eyes on the night sky, the fascination with his car long forgotten.

Andy chuckled to himself. Pretty cool that the stars impressed her more than the Z. With the people he ran with, that kind of woman was a rare find.

Beside him she sighed, her face contented. "Thanks, Andy. I needed this. I can't even express how much." She spoke the words so softly the wind almost whisked them away.

"Glad to come to your rescue."

Her shoulders stiffened, and she wiggled up in the seat, the air suddenly charged with tension. "What's that supposed to mean?"

Uh oh, whatever he'd said had triggered some kind of female automatic-response mechanism. He was in big-time trouble judging by her scowl and clamped jaw. "Nothing at all."

In the near darkness, her eyes glinted jet-black. Finally she spoke, anxiety loosening its grip on his windpipe. "Why do guys always think they have to fix things?"

His eyebrows notched up. "Fix things?"

"You know, the old rescue-the-damsel syndrome."

He chuckled. "You mean the damsel in distress."

"What makes you think I'm in distress?"

Great. Another impossible-to-answer question. "I think you do a marvelous job at covering up, but—"

"Covering up?" Her voice elevated.

"Your pain. Dani told me about the accident." Andy racked his brain for a way out of this mess. The best thing to do was apologize. Even if you weren't sure what you were apologizing for. "Sorry if I said something to upset you. If you need to vent, I'm a good listener."

She didn't answer at once, but her stiff shoulders soon sagged. "I'm the one who should apologize. I guess the stress of this wedding must be getting to me. But I have to ask. What did I do to deserve this special treatment?"

"You were born." Her eyes held questions, so he continued. "I think God brings us what we need at the right time. Maybe He allowed our paths to cross so I could help. And I mean help, not rescue, if that's what set you off."

Her gaze softened as he spoke, then she laughed and closed her eyes. For a while she didn't speak, but then released a sigh. "Doc was the love of my life. I knew the first time I met him he was the man I wanted to marry. He was good and godly, everything I'd always dreamed of in a husband."

"So you asked him instead of the other way around?"

She smiled. "Let's just say I convinced him I was the right woman."

Andy chuckled, but didn't comment.

"Early last fall, we bought a new stallion." She hugged her arms close to her body, shuddered, and released a breath, her voice strained. "We both cautioned Little Bo to stay away from the horse, but we turned around for one second and he was in the pen. Doc hurtled the fence to step between the horse and Bo." Her breathing became shallow, and her face twisted in torment. "The horse spooked and kicked . . ."

His heart ached. *God, help her speak the words.*

Her expression contorted, but she continued. "Doc was in a coma the last month of his life, struggling to live, but the doctors told me he'd never get better, so I gave them permission to unplug the machines and told him it was okay to go on home." She brought fingers to her face, then eyed her hand, seemingly surprised by the tears she found there. "A few minutes later he took his last breath."

"No he didn't, Trish."

She cocked her head, her eyes questioning.

He sent a soft smile. "He didn't take his last breath that day. Your husband took his first real breath. In heaven."

The silence resumed. Had he upset her again? "I hope I didn't offend you—"

"Not at all. I believe with all my heart that Doc's in heaven, but . . ."

"But what?"

She tossed her head, her hair glinting with moonbeams. "I just can't figure out why God took him. We need him." Her simple words carried an ocean of heartbreak, and the waves crashed against his soul.

4

Saturday afternoon before the wedding, Andy stood in the church parlor and studied a large-scaled painting. The piece of art was the one redeeming feature of the room, a diamond in the midst of dusty knick-knacks and avocado velvet.

In the painting, a battered cowboy hat rested on a cedar post. Bluebonnets grew along a barely-traveled rocky path, and the nearby barbed-wire fence was in sore need of mending. He cupped his chin. Something about the painting reminded him of his childhood at Grandpa's farm.

"It's beautiful, isn't it?" Steve moved up beside him and sipped steamy coffee from a white Styrofoam cup, his gaze on the artwork.

"Not sure beautiful is a strong enough term." Andy monotoned the words and turned back to the painting to take in the intricate detail, down to the clump of prickly pear cactus in the left foreground. The painting was definitely an original, but there was no name, just an initial. "You know who painted this?"

"As a matter of fact, I do."

Andy's interest ratcheted up a notch, and his eyebrows followed. "Really? Will you share the contact info? I'd like something similar for my office."

Steve smiled. "I can do better than that. I'll introduce you to the artist."

"Awesome."

Steve's grin morphed into a chuckle. "Trish painted the picture. I'm sure she'd be happy to give you one, since she's given her artwork to people around here for years."

His eyes widened. Trish? A painter, too?

The tall cowboy blew on his coffee, a whooshing sound that sent the smell spiraling toward Andy. Then Steve took another sip and checked his watch. "Guess I'd better high-tail it outta here. Dani informed me not to be any place where I might see her today. Stupid rule, if you ask me."

Andy laughed. "Yeah, I think the guy consensus on the you-can't-see-me-before-the-wedding rule is pretty much the same wherever you live." As Steve left the room, Andy sauntered to the nearby coffee pot to pour a cup of coffee.

Trish entered, chatting with a group of women, her hair done up with a few loose strands curling down her neck.

He blinked. She looked drop-dead gorgeous. With his eyes intent on trailing her, he over-filled his cup and sloshed the burning liquid down one arm. *Ow!* He danced in place, then grabbed a napkin, his attention back on Trish. He'd known her less than twenty-four hours, and already he was so impressed it scared him spitless.

But why was he so afraid? For one thing, he'd never met anyone so talented. Plus his last venture into the world of women hadn't worked out so well, leaving him more than a little gun-shy. But scariest of all was the load of hurt she shouldered. How could he help her through it without losing himself?

She met his gaze and sent a charming smile that made his own lips curve upward. Then her expression converted to a light scowl, and she turned her back. What had he done this time?

Without thinking, Andy slurped in a deep drink, the scalding coffee setting the top of his mouth on fire. He resisted the urge to wave a hand in front of his mouth and sauntered back to the painting, intent on not looking too dorky, or worse, too interested. Better to play it cool. He swallowed, trying to rid the tinny taste from what was left of his tongue.

Trish drifted over to him. "You look a little more refreshed than you did last night. Mama Beth's bed and breakfast agrees with you."

"I'm not the only one who looks refreshed. Or should I say gorgeous?"

Her cheeks colored to a dusky pink. "Thanks."

Andy angled his head toward the painting. "I understand you painted this."

She nodded.

"Would you be interested in painting one for me? I'd be happy to pay you well for your time."

Her eyes clouded and a vertical wrinkle appeared between her eyebrows. "Look, I truly appreciate all you did for me yesterday, but you've atoned for your mistake."

"Excuse me?"

Trish crossed her arms and gave him a hard stare. "Knocking over the decorations was just something that happened. You helped make it right, so don't feel obligated."

A short laugh ripped from his throat. "Don't flatter yourself, lady. I helped because it looked like you needed help. Not because I was trying to make up for anything."

"That's not a good reason either." She shifted her weight to the other leg, her lips pinched.

Did girls attend a special class to learn the ancient and indecipherable language of womanese? "You're mad 'cause I helped? Wanna clue me in?"

Trish's eyes flashed like gold-flecked daggers. "I don't want sympathy. From you or anyone else." She spat out the words, then spun around on one foot and marched from the room.

Mouth hanging open and hands on his hips, he stood there trying to decide his best course of action. The group of women she'd chatted with a few minutes earlier had grown silent and now stared. He let out a snort and stomped after Trish.

Out in the hall, he found her by the sound of her shoes clicking against the floor. Stiff-armed, she slung open the double doors with a bang that echoed down the empty tiled halls.

He raced down the corridor and out into the light. "Trish, wait up!"

She kept walking.

Andy quickened his pace to reach her and latched onto her bare arm. "Hey, what's this all about?"

She stopped and cocked her head to one side, missiling a sideways glare. "I don't want people to feel like they have to come to my rescue."

"Is that what you think I was doing?" He matched her gaze, squelching his desire to holler the words. "Truth is, I enjoy your company. Truth is, I actually happen to love your artwork. Truth is, you need to learn to let people help you instead of pretending you've got your act together."

Her eyes widened like she'd been slapped, then took on an icy coldness. She pivoted and headed back to the church.

Him and his big mouth. Once again he chased after her.

"Trish, I'm sorry. I shouldn't have made that last remark."

Her shoulders sagged. "The truth hurts."

Andy didn't know how to respond, especially since he kept inserting his size 11s in his yapper.

Trish continued to walk, but crossed her arms and looked away, her lower lip tucked between her teeth. She took a ragged breath and faced forward. "I want so badly to prove I can take care of myself and my son. I know there are lots of single parents out there who are facing the same challenges as I am, but I never imagined it would be this hard." She hoisted her chin, but still didn't meet his gaze, her eyes filled with tears.

The sorrow on her face yanked at his gut. She was trying her best, even if her reasoning was a little skewed. He longed to tell her that she didn't have to try so hard, but it wasn't his place to say so. And he definitely didn't want to do anything more to upset her. Not if he wanted to keep his head attached to his body. "Take a walk with me?"

She nodded, her arms folded across her waist.

Maybe a different direction in the conversation would lessen the tension. "So what else do you do besides plan weddings, paint pictures, and be a mama?"

"Well, earlier today I let Coot railroad me into organizing the Chamber of Commerce banquet." Sarcasm leaked from her words, and she looked off in the distance, her face as stony as the creek bed. "Sounds like a pretty puny resume, but I guess it counts." They took a few more steps, and Trish sighed. "You think it's wrong for me to want to take care of myself and Bo?"

Andy shook his head. "It's actually a very noble goal."

"But?" Her troubled gaze skipped across his face.

He steeled himself with a quick breath. "But you can't question people's motives or shut them out just because they want to help. Mind if I ask a personal question?"

She raked her bottom lip against her teeth. "Okay."

It really wasn't any of his business, but he wanted to know. "Did your husband have life insurance?"

Her expression flat-lined, and she didn't speak for a long minute. "Yeah, but I accidentally let it lapse while he was in the hospital." Her words ended in a whisper.

Andy released a silent breath between his lips, fairly certain she'd entrusted him with information her family didn't know. He sensed her eyes on him, so he sent a reassuring smile.

"Please don't say anything to Dani or Steve. I don't want them to know." Her plea was tinged with panic.

Why was she hiding the news from her family? He longed to ask, but judging by the concern on her face, she'd most likely reached her quota on sharing personal info.

They strolled in silence for a few more steps, the spring day smelling of sunshine and blossoms. Trish stopped in her tracks. "Now it's my turn to ask a question."

Not what he expected. There were some things he refused to share with anyone. No matter how pretty she was. "Okay."

Doe-like eyes latched onto his. "Did you really want to buy my art, or—?"

"Yes."

"Why?"

"Isn't it obvious?" He searched her face. It *wasn't* obvious—at least not to her. "Your painting is one of the most beautiful pieces of art I've ever seen, and I'm not just feeding you a line because I feel sorry for you or want to help. I really want to buy a painting."

Trish resumed walking, but said nothing, her forehead puckered.

Andy stuck his hands in his jean pockets, his fingers scraping against the car keys. "You gonna make me beg?"

"No." She clipped the word short.

His exasperation climbed, taking his pulse along for the ride. "Excuse me for being an obtuse guy, but I don't get it. You need money to support your son. You have an undeniable gift. Doesn't take a rocket scientist to figure out what you should do."

Her face reddened. "I can't paint anymore, all right? I've tried, but nothing comes out." She choked out words, and tears pooled in her eyes. "I'd love to paint again, but when Doc died he took that part of me with him, and no matter how hard I try, I can't get it back." She bolted for the red brick church building like a frightened deer, her sandals clicking against the pavement.

5

Heart heavy, Trish plopped down on the steps in the sanctuary and cupped her face with her hands. After her most recent round of emotional backwash, it wouldn't surprise her one bit if Andy steered clear during the rest of the festivities.

Of all the times for her fickle feelings to dump themselves in the streets of Miller's Creek for public display. Why this weekend? And why Andy?

The afternoon sunlight streamed through the stained glass windows and washed the room with a cacophony of color. A boatload of flowers costing a yacht-full of cash had been delivered earlier, and she'd spent the morning adding floral touches throughout the room. Now stargazer lilies, white and pink baby roses, and lily-of-the-valley graced the archway and ends of the pews, spilling their fragrance into the air.

Mom would have been so pleased with the decorations.

She hugged her knees to her chest and released a slow breath in an attempt to steady her nerves. Why, oh why, had she told Andy about the life insurance? While it felt good to share her burden with someone besides Delaine, it also rattled her bones with fear. Could she trust him not to tell Dani?

The side door opened, and Andy entered the room, concern stamped on his features. "If you don't want me here, just say so."

Trish shook her head. "No, I want you to stay."

He trudged closer and sank to the floor beside her. "I'm really sorry, Trish. I had no way of knowing about your painting. I didn't mean to say anything to hurt you. It's a miracle I can talk at all, considering I keep inserting both feet in my mouth."

"It's not your fault. You didn't know." The AC groaned and rattled, a sudden draft of cold air blasting from the nearby floor vent. She rubbed her bare arms against the surfacing chill bumps.

"Don't give up on your painting. You're too good. Give it time. It'll come back." The intensity in his emerald green eyes made his words almost believable. Then his left cheek dimpled in a lop-sided grin. "But when that time comes, I'd better be your first client."

Trish attempted a feeble smile, but couldn't muster a comeback. A holy hush descended. *Oh, God, don't let this moment of peace end.* How tranquil to sit surrounded by the soft scent of flowers in quiet companionship. How rare and precious.

No, sacred.

Andy's sonorous baritone broke the silence. "I love these kinds of moments when God surprises me with . . ."

". . . with beauty?"

His soft gaze quickened her pulse. "Yeah." He bent forward to rest his elbows on his knees. "Those times when you feel like you're drowning in grace."

"I know exactly what you mean." Though it had been an eternity since she'd felt it—until today. She leaned back on one arm to view him better. Knowing that he knew God gave her hope that he'd keep her secret. "So how long have you been a Christian?"

He wagged a finger. "Wrong question. You should've asked how long I've been a committed Christian."

"Okay. How long?"

His well-shaped lips pressed together, and he laced his fingers. "I gave my life to Christ when I was young and pretty much lived it during my growing up years. Then in college I wandered away."

"What brought you back?"

Andy gave her a teasing, sideways glance. "You always so nosy?"

"It's my turn."

"Touché." He grinned, then continued. "Actually, the situation with my fiancée brought me back. The whole experience served as wake-up call." His tone was firm and to the point, and his eyes widened in sincerity. "I realized how close I'd come to marrying an unbeliever. I knew I needed to get right with God before I messed up a bunch of people's lives, including my own."

Trish stared at him a few seconds, impressed with his wisdom and at home in the honesty between them. Surely he was trustworthy. Besides, he lived in Dallas, not exactly a prime location for sharing her life-altering goof with people in Miller's Creek. Except for Dani. "So what's next for the great Andy Tyler?"

"Well, Andy's waiting on God to show him. Quite honestly, being back in Miller's Creek has kinda made me long for my small-town roots. I've been thinking about a move."

Her stomach sank while her eyebrows rose. Surely not to Miller's Creek. "You . . . uh . . . grew up in a small town?"

"Yep. Berringer."

Berringer wasn't that far away. "Really?"

He turned a quizzical look her way. "That so hard to believe?"

Trish was at a loss for words. "I—I guess not. You just seemed so cultured, and I thought—"

"Me, cultured?" He gave a curt laugh. "I'm not the one with all the artistic talent."

The hall door swung open, and Mama Beth bustled into the room, her carefully coiffed gray curls indicating a recent visit to Jolene at Country Cutz and Curlz. "There you are! Do you two have any idea what time it is?"

Trish checked her watch. Already 5:00? Mama Beth continued to click her tongue and scold, then exited through the same door she entered.

Andy chuckled, rose to his feet, and held out a hand to help her stand. "Guess we'd better get ready before the boss lady gets even more perturbed." He stretched his neck upward and scratched the area under his chin. "But I was sure hoping to wait until the last minute to put on that tux."

Trish would've never guessed the entire population of Miller's Creek could scrunch into every last square inch of the sanctuary. She stood at the back of the church, with only a few precious minutes to spare. Shoulder to shoulder the townspeople sat, dressed in their finest, a vivid reminder of why she loved this town.

A spark of hope ignited her insides, and she prayed that somewhere in the midst of this congregation was at least one person who needed her services. Then, as an afterthought, she added, *And please help me keep my unpredictable emotions under control.*

Chubby fingers tugged on her hand, and she glanced down into the liquid brown eyes of her son. Trish swished the silken hem of her pale pink bridesmaid dress out of the way and knelt to give him a hug. "Hi, sweetie. Did you have a good time with Uncle Steve and Papaw?"

"Yeah." His voice was breathy with excitement, and his face took on that glow of wonder only found on the face of a child. "And Andy helped me with my catching. I think I can do it now."

"Andy helped you?" When had he had the time?

A stocky pair of man legs with pants cropped much too short stepped beside them, patent black shoes a-gleam below black-socked ankles. She pulled herself to a standing position.

"See? Helping someone is supposed to be a good thing." His tone held a challenge. The slow glance he took at her attire sent quick heat scurrying to her cheeks. "And please don't think I'm feeling sorry for you or anything, but you look stunning."

His comment sent pleasure rippling through her, but she had no intention of letting him know, especially since he'd already witnessed her earlier emotional meltdown. Instead of a comeback, she smiled her thanks and made sure everyone was in place. A few minutes later, she stepped up beside Andy and sniffed.

"What?" His brow puckered.

"I smell peppermint."

He peeled back his lips to reveal a piece of chewed gum balanced between his teeth.

She shook her head and held a hand beneath his chin. "Oh no, you don't. Spit it out. Absolutely no gum on stage. The last thing Dani and Steve want in their wedding video is a cud-chewing groomsman."

"Make that a cud-chewing groomsman in a penguin suit," he said, his teeth still clenched.

Trish waited for him to begrudgingly release the gum, then moved to a nearby trash can. She arrived back in position just as the string quartet began to play Pachelbel's *Canon in D*. She hooked her arm in Andy's, and they stepped toward the light-encrusted arch of white tree branches.

Trish leaned her head toward his. "By the way, please don't think I'm feeling sorry for you or anything, but I absolutely adore those knickers you're wearing."

He turned his head toward her, his jaw agape. Camera flashes exploded from every angle as they stepped under the branches and laughed their way down the aisle.

Trish glimpsed Steve at the front of the church and immediately sobered.

He shot a quick wink, and then rocked back and forth on his heels, his gaze raised in hopeful anticipation.

Her heart swelled with joy. After years, he'd finally found the woman he'd waited for his entire life. The thought somehow brought comfort. The intensity of the pain she'd experienced over the past several months wouldn't last forever. There was a brighter tomorrow. Right?

Once on stage, she turned to face the audience. The sight of Little Bo marching down the aisle made her insides cringe. Why did he suddenly seem so small? What *was* she thinking? Her baby was much too young for this. She blinked, and an image of him fifteen to twenty years down the road flashed to mind, only now he was a groom. A day she didn't want to face alone.

Trish shook off the troubling thought and watched her son proceed between the pews, the flower girl's tiny, gloved hand in his. He took his place beside his Uncle Steve, setting off a wave of motherly pride.

The Wedding March fanfare sounded, and the congregation rose to a flurry of flashes as Dani glided between the light-clad trees, her beaded lace dress rippling as she floated down the aisle. Her happy smile was focused entirely on her groom.

A sudden stab of jealousy forced Trish to lower her head. But when she finally fought off the feelings and lifted her chin, she made the costly mistake of looking at Andy. His gaze was trained on her, and it set off a powerful thump in her chest. Though it took every last ounce of the puny strength she had left, she forced her attention to the wedding and attempted to ignore the sight of Andy in her peripheral vision.

Try as she might, her thoughts were plagued by his presence. Good gravy, why were her emotions bouncing around like a yo-yo? The wedding—that had to be it. Weddings were a celebration of true love, something every female heart craved. Well, she already had a true love. He'd just gone home ahead of her.

The dam she'd built around her heart to contain the ever-constant threat of tears wobbled, and a slight crack formed. *No!* She wouldn't cry and ruin this wedding. Trish sucked in a deep breath. Her resolve clung with razor-edged claws to the soft flesh of her heart, and bit by bloody bit, the unwelcomed emotions oozed away.

A few minutes later, Dani and Steve locked hands and gazes as Brother Mac read from his Bible. *"Trust in the LORD with all your heart, and lean not on your own understanding; in all your ways acknowledge Him, and He shall direct your paths."*

A jolt shivered down her back. She felt it again—a sacred moment of God's presence. What words had Andy used? She closed her eyes. Drowning in grace. The verse she'd known since childhood exhorted her not to lean on her own understanding, but to trust.

Easy to say. But actually doing it?

She lifted a silent prayer heavenward. Never had she had to lean on Him—to trust Him—like now. And oh, how she yearned for Him to direct her path. Especially when the path seemed plunged beneath impenetrable darkness.

In a blur the ceremony ended, and after photographs, everyone moved to the fellowship hall for the reception. Gasps of awe and delight fell from the open mouths of guests when they saw how Trish had infused the plain room with an atmosphere of elegance.

Dark paper covered the ceiling, and below it tulle and twinkle lights gave the effect of a starlit night. A huge fountain of wedding punch gurgled and flowed next to the multi-tiered wedding cake on a table near the back. Interspersed among the small trees, greenery, and scrolled iron benches lining the perimeter of the room, hidden up-lights cast soft shadows on the walls.

Andy came up behind her, his voice low in her ear. "You never cease to amaze me. This is by far the coolest thing I've ever seen."

Trish rubbed her damp palms together. Why did she suddenly feel like a shy schoolgirl talking to the captain of the football team? "Thanks. Excuse me, I need something to drink."

Before she had a chance to escape, he handed her a cup of punch. "Already gotcha covered."

She took the cup of sparkling grape juice and downed it. How did he anticipate her needs like that? And more importantly, why?

"You're doing it again." Andy took a sip from his own cup.

"Doing what?"

"Questioning my motives. Just let me be nice to you, okay? And while you're at it, you might also let your family know you need their help."

Red-hot anger surged through her system and spilled out before she could gain control. "And you might try minding your own business!"

6

Andy hung the too-tight tuxedo back on the hanger, finished off his Dr. Pepper, and gazed around the choir room. It looked—and smelled—like a bunch of guys lived here. Piles of clothing, half-eaten sandwiches, and empty Styrofoam cups trashed the place. All they needed to complete the man-cave was a big screen TV and a couple of recliners.

Trish might stop him from helping elsewhere, but he could at least help out in the background. What made her so adamant about doing everything on her own? In a few minutes he had all the tuxedos hung, trash thrown away, and leftovers packed into grocery sacks. Then he straightened the chairs.

When he finished, he gathered his belongings and made his way to the car. One more night in Miller's Creek and then he'd return to Dallas. The thought left him with an odd mixture of relief and regret, but he was too tired to figure out why. Instead, his mind fluctuated between the verse reminding him to trust God and a picture of Trish's angry face.

Andy peered out over the darkened parking lot. Only a few cars remained. Now what? He couldn't really return to Mama Beth's house. She was still busy with the after-wedding clean-up. While he didn't mind helping, the last thing he wanted was another run-in with Trish.

He mulled over the situation as he took in the starry sky, but the longer he thought about it the madder he got. So what if she got upset? Not everything was about her. Andy marched to the church in a purposeful stride, swung open the door, and headed to the fellowship hall. Let Trish fend for herself. He'd help Mama Beth instead.

It only took one glance around the kitchen to realize he was in a testosterone-free zone. Women doused with way too much perfume zipped past in a frenzy. They slammed cabinet doors and chattered like magpies, and no matter where he moved, he was in someone's way.

Mama Beth, hands in the sink, smiled when she saw him. "Hey, Andy. Trish was just here looking for you. I think she's in the sanctuary now."

Looking for him? Could it be that Little Miss "Don't-Help-Me" needed his help after all? He strode down the hall and entered the sanctuary just as she gave her father a hug. "Thanks for taking care of Little Bo for me again tonight, Dad. I promise not to make this a habit."

He patted her back. "You know I don't mind, sweetheart. We have a great time together. I just wish your Mom could've known her grandson."

It was easy to see the older man adored his daughter.

Little Bo spotted him first. "Andy!" He shouted, ran toward him full force, and launched into Andy's arms.

"Hey, buddy. You did an amazing job during the wedding."

"Really?" Little Bo's face blossomed with a big grin.

"Oh, yeah. By far the best ring bearer I've ever seen." Andy glanced up to see a surly look on Trish's face, and his muscles tensed. He swung Little Bo to the floor and made his way to the two adults.

The older gentleman shook Andy's hand. "I'm Trish's dad, Bo Miller. Glad you're here. Trish is gonna need some strong arms to get all this stuff loaded. I'm taking the young 'un back to the ranch to get him to bed." Little Bo clamped both arms around his grandfather's leg.

Trish frowned. "I'm perfectly capable of doing this myself. I'm sure Andy has other things to do."

"Nonsense." Mr. Miller's voice was gruff and paternal. "There's nothing wrong with admitting when you need help. You'll be up here all night if you try to do this by yourself."

Her face darkened, but she made no reply. Instead, she stamped to the stage and began to take down decorations.

The older man sighed in frustration. "She really does need your help, no matter what she says." He lowered his voice. "Don't let her push you away. She can be a little stubborn sometimes."

"I heard that." Trish hollered over her shoulder.

A *little* stubborn? Compared to what? A balking burro? "I'll do what I can, sir."

"You're in my prayers," the older Bo whispered, his bushy gray eyebrows crawling up his forehead.

"I heard that, too."

The older man slapped Andy's shoulder, grabbed his grandson's hand, and meandered to the door. "See y'all in the morning at church."

Trish kept her back turned as she yanked flowers and greenery from the wedding arch. She dropped flowers in a pile at her feet while the greenery went into a box. Instead of risking her ire, Andy moved to one of the branch-tree thingies and removed Christmas lights.

The silence lasted for several minutes, until finally Trish spoke. "Well, aren't you going to say something?" she snarled.

Andy raised his eyebrows. "And risk losing my head? No thanks." He turned back to his work. Several more silent minutes ticked by. Once he'd removed all the lights from the trees, he headed to work on the pew decorations, following the same steps he'd seen Trish complete on the arch. Behind him came a loud crash.

He whirled about to see the arch on the floor and Trish clutching one arm. Andy hurried to her side. "You okay?"

She nodded, but a red trickle from beneath her fingers told him otherwise.

"Let me see." Andy peeled back her fingers to reveal blood snaking down her bare arm. "That's quite a scrape you've got there, but I think you'll survive." He escorted her down the steps and seated her on the front pew, then knelt and snatched a few tissues from a box. "Wanna tell me what happened?"

"No." Her voice was thin and tight.

"Why?"

"Cause you'll rub my nose in it." Her bottom lip protruded, reminding him of a cranky child in need of a nap.

"Will not."

"Will, too."

He sent a teasing smile and pressed a wad of tissues to the wound. "Okay, then I'll tell you. You were trying to do something yourself without asking for help, and it backfired. I'm right, aren't I?"

One corner of her lips twitched, quickly replaced by a dark frown. "Told you you'd rub my nose in it."

"Only 'cause you deserve it." He looked into her tawny eyes and waited.

She shifted and let out a huff. "Oh, all right, I admit it. Sorry I've been so—so—"

"Cranky and stubborn."

Trish nodded. "It's only because I'm—"

"Exhausted and overwhelmed."

"And sick of people making me feel—"

"Incapable."

Trish became perfectly quiet and still, her eyes searching his.

Andy's heartbeat thundered in his ears, and he teetered on the verge of losing himself in her scent and the soft poutiness of her lips.

She blinked slowly, her voice throaty and warm. "How is it that you know me so well?"

He inhaled a heavy breath and stood. "I think the bleeding's stopped now. We'd better get back to work."

Trish slumped in the family pew Sunday morning and pretended to smooth imaginary wrinkles from her pink-flowered crepe skirt. Anything to be invisible. What she wouldn't give to hole up in her house, crawl between the covers, and disappear for at least a week.

Over and over, she replayed the scene from last night until she wanted to scream. What had come over her? She moved a hand to the Big Bird bandage on her arm, remembering Andy's gentle touch and teasing eyes, an image quickly replaced by his clenched jaw and detached aloofness. Clearly, she'd crossed some unseen boundary.

Andy entered the sanctuary through the hall door, his broad chest and shoulders pronounced by the baby blue polo he wore.

She slouched lower in the seat, a gamut of emotions roaring through her veins. Doc had been gone less than a year. She still loved him. Loved him with all her being and always would. *God, what's going on here? I need Your help.*

Trust Me.

"May I sit with you?"

Andy's smooth voice raised her head, and she forced a smile. "Of course. How are you?" Even before the question left her lips, she knew the answer from the shadowy bags rimming his eyes. Exhausted.

"Fine." His tone served as evidence to the contrary.

How many times had she used the same word when she was anything *but* fine?

Mama Beth slid into the pew on the other side of her. "Lands alive, but I'm tuckered." She yawned and looked at Trish. "What time did y'all get through last night? I didn't even hear Andy come home."

Trish yawned in return, the power of suggestion too strong to resist. "Around midnight. It would've been an all-nighter if Andy hadn't been there to help."

Mama Beth peered around her to Andy. "We sure do appreciate all you did."

Trish cringed inwardly. Had she even remembered to say thank you? "Yeah, thanks." Okay, that sounded distinctly less than heartfelt.

A pained expression flickered across his face. "Glad to help."

Trish snatched her bulletin from her Bible and pretended to read, more confused than ever. Why had she been so snarky toward him, not just once, but the entire weekend?

Little Bo bounced into the room with his Papaw in tow. "Look, Mom!" Wide-eyed excitement lit his face. He scooted around Mama Beth and handed her the drawing he'd done in Sunday School.

She pointed to the scraggly lettering at the bottom of the page. "What does this say?"

"Jesus went about doing good." He trailed the words with one finger as he pretended to read, his voice halting. "The picture shows people doing good like Jesus."

Trish studied the stick figures and pointed to one. "And who is this?"

"That's you doing the decorations for the wedding, and that's Andy doing good by helping you."

His words slapped her between the eyes. *Okay, Lord, I get it.* She owed Andy an apology and a huge debt of gratitude. He'd done so much to help, and there was no way she could return the favor. The least she could do was apologize after church.

An hour later the service ended, and Mama Beth latched onto Andy's arm as they moved into the crowded aisle and exited the sanctuary. "We usually congregate at my house for Sunday lunch. Hope you can join us before you head back to Dallas."

Andy sent Trish a questioning glance.

Had she made him feel so unwelcome that he needed her permission? She offered an apologetic smile. "We'd love for you to stay."

His lips curved ever so slightly, a sad smile that didn't reach his eyes. "Sounds great. I'd sure hate to miss out on more of Mama Beth's cooking."

A few minutes later they arrived at the century-old farmhouse, complete with rose arbors, white picket fence, and fragrant spring blossoms. Trish climbed the steps to the wraparound porch and entered through the squeaky screen door, nostalgia settling over her like a handmade quilt. The tantalizing aroma of pot roast with wafted from the kitchen.

"Ooh-wee, that smells good." Dad slapped a hand on Andy's shoulder. "Beth cooks the best pot roast in the county." Little Bo raced to the kitchen, Dad and Mama Beth following at a slower pace.

This was an opportune moment to do what had to be done. Instead, her hands—and stomach—twisted and writhed. "Andy, I—I . . ." The words refused to budge from their hiding place behind her teeth.

"If you have something to say, it usually works best if you just say it." Andy's dimples didn't show.

"I want to apologize again for the way I acted this weekend. I'm sorry I was so ungrateful. I guess it was just nerves and fatigue. I'm not usually so—" She blabbered words like a monkey in the zoo, until Andy stopped her by shaking his head, his blond curls a-dance.

"I enjoyed spending time with you, Trish. I'd have been lost without something to do or someone to talk to."

Her heart softened. He was far too easy on her. "I was afraid I'd been horrid."

"Nah . . . well, except for the tux." His left dimple made an appearance. "Oh, and the thing about not wanting people to help you. And I almost forgot, the—"

"I get the picture." She held up a hand, her tone almost as dry as her mouth.

Now his grin appeared with both dimples, her pulse on a rapid climb. Then, just as suddenly as it appeared, the smile vanished, the depths of his ocean eyes murky, as if his confusion matched her own.

Trish's cheeks heated. How did she make sense of these unwanted and unexpected feelings? Was she sending out signals she didn't mean or want to send? "I think I'll go see if Mama Beth needs help with lunch."

In a few minutes the meal was ready, the farmhouse table groaning beneath the weight of food. Besides the roast and vegetables, there were hot rolls and an Italian cream cheese cake she could down in a few minutes if given the chance.

Dad asked the blessing, immediately followed by serving spoons clanking against bowls and plates. "So, Andy, how's your practice going?" Dad passed the bread, aromatic steam rising from the freshly baked rolls, then raised his eyebrows and peered at Andy over the top of his glasses.

That's how she could return the favor. Without giving thought to her words, Trish barged in. "Andy told me he's actually thinking of moving to a small town. Don't you think he'd make a great replacement for the city attorney position? He grew up in Berringer."

"Really?" Mama Beth beamed. "I have kin folk in Berringer. Next time I call 'em, I'll ask if they remember you."

Andy twisted in his seat, his gaze focused on his plate. He grabbed a roll, tore off a big chunk, and crammed it in his mouth.

Dad paused mid-bite, a food-laden fork suspended in the air. "Our city attorney recently announced his retirement. We sure could use you here."

It felt great to be in a position to help him for a change. The thought made her pause. She'd been upset with him for helping her, yet here she was doing the same thing.

"Yeah, and you could help me some more with my catching." Little Bo brought a chubby-fisted fork to his mouth and shoveled in a huge bite, jabbering away the whole time.

A look of discomfort bathed Andy's red face as he swallowed the clump of bread. "It's just an idea I've been tinkering with. As appealing as small-town life sounds, I'm not sure I should leave Dallas. I'm still praying about it."

Mama Beth patted his hand. "Good for you. God will show you what to do."

Trish scratched her head. Great. Put another red slash next to her name for embarrassing him. He'd obviously not expected her to share the comment. She sawed off a bite of the tender roast and stuffed her mouth before she blabbed something else she regretted. Cut. Chew. Swallow. *Repeat.*

The cell phone in her purse jingled from its perch on the sunlit window seat. She snatched her napkin from her lap, tossed it beside her plate, and stood. Great time to make a getaway.

She retrieved the phone and escaped to the front porch with a glance at the display screen. Delaine. In the past few weeks, her friend's calls had become less about comfort and more about pressure. What now?

"Hey, girlfriend." Delaine's voice contained the same chatty friendliness it had held during their high school days. "Hope I didn't interrupt your lunch, but I've been dying to hear how the wedding went."

Trish plopped down on the porch swing. "Except for a few minor mishaps everything went fine."

"Any business prospects?"

The question she'd hoped to avoid. "Not yet." Trish chewed the inside of her cheek. "But I did get a lot of compliments, so maybe there's still a chance."

"Well, this *is* Miller's Creek we're talking about." Delaine launched into the spiel she'd heard untold times before—small towns didn't want or need interior designers—and finished with: "You need to move to Austin."

"I've told you before. I can't do that to Bo."

Delaine sighed. "I don't get it. I thought you didn't want to depend on your family."

"I don't, but I'm okay right now. I have a little left over from what Dani and Steve paid me for the wedding." Precious little.

"And what are you going to do when that runs out?"

Good question. Trish wrapped an arm around her waist and hunched over. "I'll think of something."

"Listen, I hope you don't mind, but I told a friend who owns a design firm in downtown Austin about you."

Trish's hackles rose. Why did everyone feel inclined to interfere in her life?

"She's looking to hire a new designer within the next few months and wants to see your work. Could you send some photos and a resume?"

Trish straightened at the job prospect, then resumed her slouch. While a job in Austin would provide a chance to put her college degree to work, she couldn't yank Little Bo away from all that was familiar. Nor could she imagine leaving Miller's Creek. The designer position was nothing but a last resort. "I'll think about it." Oh yeah, she'd definitely think about it. Probably all night.

"Well, don't think too long. This opportunity won't last forever." Defensiveness now sounded in her friend's tone.

The conversation ended with terse goodbyes, and Trish trudged back to the dining room. Questioning eyes turned her way when she entered the room. She sank to the ladder-back chair, fidgeted with her napkin, and picked up her fork. "That was Delaine. She called to let me know about an interior design job in Austin."

No one said a word. Finally Little Bo looked up from his plate, his bottom lip quivering. "Mom, can I go outside? I'm not so hungry anymore."

His sad voice sliced her heart. She rubbed his back with her palm. "Sure sweetie, but stay out of Mama Beth's flower garden, okay?"

"'kay." He moved to Andy's side, his brown eyes pleading. "Wanna play catch?"

Trish reached over and tousled his baby-fine hair. "Andy has to drive back to Dallas."

Andy's eyes hardened in a non-verbal reprimand. "But Andy wants to play catch first." The words were soft, but the stiff set of his jaw held challenge. He held her gaze for a second more then smiled at Bo. "Let me finish my lunch, buddy. I'll be out in a few minutes."

Her son's expression turned to instant glee. "I'll get my glove outta the car," Bo called over his shoulder as he darted to the living room and out the front door.

Mama Beth started in on her first. "Trish, you can't move him away from his family right now. He needs stability."

Her blood chilled. Since when was it Mama Beth's call to say what she could and couldn't do? With *her* son and *her* life? "I'm well aware of what Bo needs, but I also have to make a living. I'm not sure I can do that in a town the size of Miller's Creek." She somehow managed to keep her tone above the frost zone.

Dad's fork clanked to his plate, and apprehension scuttled down her spine. She yanked her head toward him.

He cleared his throat and reached into his back pocket, his face drawn tight. "That reminds me. Dani mentioned you might be struggling a bit financially, so we all took up a little collection."

A sick feeling churned her stomach to pure acid. *No. This couldn't be happening. Not in front of Andy.* She sensed his gaze on her, but couldn't make eye contact. "That's really not necessary. I'll be fine."

Dad plunked down a wad of bills. "We love you, honey. We wanna help however we can."

Trish couldn't look up. Couldn't touch the money. It was all she could do to squeak out a feeble "thank you."

7

Miller's Creek grew tiny in Andy's rearview mirror. With the top down and the air doused with the scent of bluebonnets, he puzzled over his conflicted feelings. He had a good life in Dallas. No, make that a great life. So why did it feel like he was leaving a chunk of himself behind?

He needed to figure this thing out. Needed to decide what he wanted. What God wanted for him. Trish had opened a can of worms with her comment about him moving, and Bo Miller had jumped on it like a big-mouthed bass. He sighed and pushed the thought aside.

A Texas spring day spread out before him in the open countryside, the wildflowers blowing in the breeze—a great day to fish, go horseback riding, or play baseball. Things he wouldn't have time for in Dallas.

Thoughts of his last game of catch with Bo made his chest tighten. A boy that age needed a father. His own childhood proved it. A cold chill shivered down his back. No telling how his life would've turned out had it not been for Lester Hathcock.

On a whim, he inserted his Bluetooth and punched Lester's number.

"Mmm-yello."

Andy smiled at the familiar greeting. "Hey, old man."

A contagious chuckle sounded. "Who you calling old? Have you forgotten whose birthday it is today?"

He widened his eyes. Oh, man, he'd forgotten the party his friends were throwing for him. "Yeah, actually, I did."

"Then let me be the first to wish you Happy Birthday." A muffled voice sounded in the background. "Denise says to tell you Happy Birthday, too."

"Tell her thanks, and give her a hug from me."

"Will do. What's up?"

He swallowed a sudden rush of emotion. "Just wanted to call and say thanks for all you did for me when I was growing up."

"Mind my asking what brought that on?"

Andy imagined Lester, his dark brows knit together, sprawled out in his recliner with the television remote in one hand. "I was at a wedding in Miller's Creek this weekend." He swerved to miss a long-eared jackrabbit loping across the road. "A little boy there lost his father this past year. I played catch with him, and it reminded me of you."

"You know how I feel about that." The older man's voice took on a gravelly tone. "You and Matt are like the sons I never had. I got a lot more than I gave." He changed the subject. "Ah, anyway, does that little boy have a mama?"

"Yeah, as a matter of fact he does."

"Maybe you should visit Miller's Creek more often."

Under different circumstances maybe. "It's a little more complicated than that."

"How?"

"Her husband's only been gone a few months. She's not ready." Besides, she was way out of his league.

"Is that your opinion or God's?"

Andy frowned. "Sorry. I'm not following."

"I'm not trying to be rough on you, son. I just know how you think. You get stuck in your head, instead of allowing for the possibility that God might have a different plan."

A few minutes later Andy punched the end call button. Was Lester right? Should he return to Miller's Creek? The humiliation inscribed on Trish's face when her dad tossed out the money set off an ache in his chest he couldn't shake. For the first time, he saw how much it hurt her to take help from others, no matter how kind their intentions. As much as she needed assistance, more than anything else she needed to feel capable.

Andy pursed his lips. Had it been her pain that prompted him to ask her to design his office if he made the move to Miller's Creek? Or did his motivation go deeper? He rubbed a hand across his mouth. Only yesterday he'd been afraid of getting hurt, but he'd noticed how the offer had sparked hope in her eyes. Hope was something he very much wanted to give to both her and Bo. He blinked in surprise. Where had that come from?

His thoughts flashed to the night he'd doctored her arm. The touch of her fingers on his, the warmth in her voice, the sad, chocolate-colored eyes that melted his heart. It had taken every ounce of willpower he had to put distance between them.

He puffed out a breath and tapped the satellite radio button. A bluesy jazz flowed from the speakers. Lester was right. He *did* spend too much time in his head.

Andy tried to focus on the scenery, but to no avail. A move made no sense. Trish was perfect proof that starting a business in a small town was a huge financial risk. He'd spent the first twenty-five years of his life in poverty, and had sweated blood to enjoy the kind of life his Dallas practice afforded. Why should he give that up? Why would he want to? Besides, his first stint in Miller's Creek had turned out worse than a bad blind date.

His cell phone buzzed, and he brought a hand to his ear. "This is Andy."

"Happy Birthday, bro!"

Matt's cheery voice brought a smile. "Thanks, little brother. And thanks for not calling me old."

"Oh, man, now my next comment is ruined."

Andy's mouth curved into a smirk. "Okay, lemme have it."

"Just gonna ask how many fire trucks were summoned to put out the fire on your birthday cake."

"Ha! Very funny."

His brother laughed. "I'm sure you'll return the favor when my birthday rolls around."

"Count on it. How's school going?"

"Pretty good, I guess. Had another gig last night at a coffee shop close to campus. Everyone seemed to enjoy my music."

"Good for you." Andy waited, anticipating the next comment, understanding now how difficult it was.

"Uh, look, could you send more money? I'm running low on cash, and I need gas and food."

Again Trish's embarrassment flooded his thoughts. "Sure. I'll wire it to your bank account first thing in the morning."

"Thanks, bro, I owe you."

"No, you don't. It's not a loan, it's an investment."

Andy hung up the phone a minute later. More proof that staying in Big D was the right decision. He wasn't the only person in the equation. Matt depended on him, and trying to jumpstart a career as a musician meant he could be dependent for several more years.

He increased the radio volume and lowered the roof, the wind whooshing above him as he zipped down the road toward Dallas—his home.

Two hours later, Andy rolled to a stop in the parking lot at Papa Jack's Grill in North Dallas, not really in the mood to celebrate an event that made him more aware of his age and single status.

As he entered the building, he positioned his Ray Bans on top of his head and scanned the noisy, over-packed restaurant. The air was saturated with the smell of fresh-grilled beef. His friends called out and waved from the back, and he zigzagged his way through the tables to their booth.

"Well, it's about time the birthday boy showed up. How was the wedding?" With boredom slung across his face, his law partner, Dave, reclined with one arm curled around his new wife.

Andy lowered his head. Yet another reminder of what he didn't have. *Strike one.* "Good. Sorry I'm late. I promised a kid a game of catch before I left Miller's Creek."

No one asked about the kid or their game of catch, but Ned, their second-year law clerk, waggled his eyebrows. "Meet any babes?" His tone carried insinuation. *Strike two.*

"Nope." Instead, he'd met a beautiful and talented woman. Babes were a dime a dozen.

Andy started to pull up a chair, when Serena, one of the paralegals, flashed a too-friendly smile and patted the cushion next to her. "Here. I saved you a seat."

Strike three. "Hey, you guys order me some fajitas and a glass of tea, will you? I'll be back in a sec." Andy strode from the booth, unable to get away fast enough. Barely home and already he needed a break from these people. When had their company started to grate on his last nerve?

Trish hunched over the oak desk behind the counter at Designs By Trish, and crunched the numbers. The calculator's digital read-out glared the same red, less-than-zero numbers.

With a frustrated grunt, she fell back against the rickety desk chair and hurled a ballpoint pen across the store. It bounced off the wall in pieces and landed on the wooden floors with two distinct clacks. She glanced at the almost-empty calendar and her completely-empty checkbook, and her vision blurred. What else could she do to make this work? She had no funds for advertising, and to make matters worse, school let out in a few weeks. Summertime more than likely meant less business.

Trish trudged around the counter and picked up the pen pieces, deposited them in the trash, and slumped in her chair, face against fist. She'd scheduled a couple of storefront displays for later in the afternoon, but the two jobs combined would only net a hundred dollars. Not enough. The money her family collected had paid the car payment and bought a few groceries, but the electricity bill was long overdue, and her Suburban was on the bottom side of a quarter tank. Something needed to give, or she'd have to.

The bell above the door jangled. A customer! She hastily swiped the tears from her cheeks and rose to her feet.

Carla Clark stalked toward her, her too-tight blue jeans making a sound that reminded Trish of a grasshopper. Bright blue eye shadow hiked up both sides to Carla's one eyebrow, her wiry orange hair pulled back from her face with a net.

Trish swallowed her fear. From as far back as her high school days, Carla had intimidated her with her brusque voice, muscled arms, and sheer size. "Hi, Carla. Can I help you?"

"Yeah. My kid sister's getting married."

Another wedding. Thank You, Lord. "Congratulations." Trish assumed a smile and her best sales voice. "So you saw the decorations at Dani's wedding?"

"Yeah. I liked the arch thingy and thought we could use it for Becca's wedding."

"Okay, let me check my calendar. When is the wedding?"

"This Friday."

Alarm skittered through Trish's veins, but she controlled it with a silent gulp of air. How could she possibly be expected to decorate for a wedding with less than a week's notice? She smiled up from her calendar. "Well, you're in luck. I don't have anything scheduled for that night."

Carla snickered. "Yeah, I bet."

"Pardon me?" Her glued-on smile threatened to slip.

"I bet you don't have much scheduled on any day. Miller's Creek ain't the Ritz, you know." Carla sneered and glanced around the sparse decor of Designs By Trish, then pointed to the arch Trish had reassembled for the display window. "I just wanna borrow the arch. I'll decorate it myself."

Her hope plummeted. "Oh." She released a shaky laugh. "Silly me. I thought you wanted *me* to decorate for the wedding."

"In this economy? Most of us don't have a daddy made of money, you know."

Trish waged battle with the surge of anger threatening to spill and bit back a comment with clenched lips.

"So, can I borrow it?" Carla smacked her gum, blew a large bubble, and then blasted a hole through it, showering Trish with the sickeningly sweet smell of bubblegum.

She coughed lightly—to clear her lungs—and peered down at her calendar to buy some time. The arch wasn't paid for yet. What if it was damaged during the loan? This wasn't gonna be easy. "I'd be happy to rent it to you." She feigned a chipper tone.

Carla's eyes bulged. Then she clenched her fists, the veins in her neck expanding as she released a disbelieving snort. "Rent it?" She pivoted and waddled to the store entrance, leaving grasshopper noises in her wake. "Never mind. You uppity Millers think you own the whole town. One of these days you'll learn how the rest of us live, and I'm gonna laugh my head off." Carla hurled the words over one shoulder, then slammed the antique wood and beveled glass door.

Trish flinched at the sound and brought a hand up to massage her temple. Carla was right. An interior design business in Miller's Creek made as much sense as trying to turn a Ford Pinto into a Lamborghini. What had made her think she could pull it off?

The answer hit before the question finished sounding in her brain. Because of her parents. Her design degree had been their idea, not hers. All she'd ever wanted was to be a wife, mother, and artist, in that order. Now she was clinging to her life's dream by one tenuous thread—motherhood.

She sipped her now tepid water. Everything happened for a purpose. Maybe God had directed her path toward the design degree for a time like this. He knew she'd need something to fall back on when Doc died. But in Miller's Creek?

Her cell phone vibrated and danced across the desk top. She snagged it, as a number she didn't recognize flashed to the screen. *Lord, please let this be business.*

"Designs By Trish."

"Hey, Designs By Trish, this is Law By Andy."

A giggle burst out. "You're not as funny as you think you are."

"Well, I met my objective." His teasing tone played havoc with her already frazzled emotions.

"Oh, really? And what, may I ask, was your objective?"

"To make you laugh."

Trish's heartbeat throbbed at the base of her throat, and she raised a hand to cover it. Falling for his natural charm would be so easy, but she had Little Bo to consider, as well as Doc's memory. Best to keep things on the friend level. "What's going on?"

"Well, I called to see if you'd given any thought to my idea."

"Idea? What idea?" Was it her imagination or had her tone bordered on mild hysteria? She coughed and twirled a silky strand of hair around one finger, pretty sure she knew where the conversation was headed.

"If I move to Miller's Creek, will you design my office?"

Trish scrambled for words--and more time. "Uh, so you're actually thinking about a move to Miller's Creek?"

"Yeah, go figure." He gave a short laugh. "Let's just say I've been looking at the numbers."

Numbers. Ugh! She hated them. Her eyes returned to her own lack of a bottom line. Should she say yes to the job? *No*. She couldn't. Saying yes meant putting herself into direct contact with him, and the fiasco last Saturday night after the wedding proved she wasn't ready. "I really can't make any promises, Andy. A lot of it depends on the timing. Since the wedding I've been . . . uh . . . kind of busy."

"Good for you. Congratulations."

"Thanks." Trish squeezed her eyes tight against the ensuing stab of guilt. Man, she'd just lied to him. "Sorry to have to cut this short, Andy, but I've got a couple of clients lined up for this afternoon."

"Oh, I see. Sorry to have interrupted your work. Well, you take care." Hurt edged his voice.

"You, too. Bye." Trish sat a moment with her eyes closed and her forehead at rest on her palm, the phone still pressed to her ear. The last thing she'd wanted to do was hurt his feelings. Finally she clicked the phone shut, dropped it in her shoulder bag, and grabbed her keys. Work would help take her mind off her problems. At least temporarily.

Fifteen minutes later, she removed the last of the old decorations from the store window display at Betsy's Antique Mall when her phone rang again. Trish glanced at the screen. The school? Again? She flipped it open quickly. "Yes?"

"Trish, this is Pam at the elementary school."

"Is Bo okay?" Now her voice really *did* border on hysteria.

"He's fine, but he's crying and asking for you. We've tried to calm him down, but . . ."

"I'll be right there."

Less than five minutes later, Trish arrived at the school. She entered the door to the kindergarten wing, children's copycat artwork plastered to the walls. Suddenly, a child's fearful screams reverberated down the fluorescent-lit hallway, followed by the words: "I want my Mommy! I want my Mommy!"

Hurt ripped through her chest as she sprinted in the direction of the gut-rending cries. She rounded a doorway, where Little Bo wiggled in a chair, damp tendrils of sweaty hair plastered to his forehead, his eyes swollen and red, his cheeks flushed and damp with tears.

"It's okay, honey, Mama's here." She knelt, gathered him into her arms, and crooned in his ear. "Shh, sweetie, it's okay."

He continued to hiccup and sob softly.

Trish rose to her feet. Bo's teacher, Mrs. Walsh, looked ready to hand in her resignation and hit up the fast-food industry for a burger-flipping job. "How long has he been like this?"

"Since lunch recess."

"That was two hours ago. Why didn't someone call sooner?"

The woman stiffened. "This is a school, Mrs. James, not a daycare. We try to calm the children when they get like this. We can't call parents every time the kids get in a little snit."

"A little snit? I've never seen him this upset."

Mrs. Walsh sniffed. "You'll need to talk to Bo about what happened. He instigated a fight on the playground today, his second one this week, and will have to miss recess for the next several days. I know it's been a rough year for him, but he needs to understand how serious this matter is."

Bo slumped against her, lifeless, except for an occasional shudder that shredded her heart. She knew she needed to respond, but words wouldn't squeeze past the lump in her throat. Instead she ran from the room, her son dead weight in her arms.

8

Trish laid Little Bo on the plaid sofa in the family room of the main ranch house and watched him slumber, his thumb stuffed in his mouth. She raised both hands to her cheeks. Would he ever get past the trauma of his daddy's death? Would she? The area around his eyes puckered, and he whimpered in his sleep.

Her heart ached with words she couldn't speak, her eyes pricked by stinging needles. If only Mom were here to tell her what to do.

"Did he tell you what happened?" Dad draped an arm across her shoulder, and she inhaled the comforting scent of his familiar aftershave.

She burrowed her head in his shoulder for a moment, and then motioned her dad to the other room so they wouldn't awaken Bo. "I buckled him in and got in the car," she whispered, her voice sounding like it came from some place far away. "When I turned around to back out of the parking space, he was already asleep. Apparently, he started a fight at school today—the second one this week."

Lines furrowed Dad's baby-white forehead, an obvious tan line where his cowboy hat usually rested. "That's not like him."

A weary breath burst from between her lips. She meandered to the oversized picture window and peered out, her eyes seeing nothing. "He hasn't been himself in such a long time." Trish lingered a few seconds, then returned to the table. She sagged to one of the maple dining room chairs, and stroked the bridge of her nose. This headache had morphed into a real doozy.

"Are you okay?" His tone held worry.

Trish shook her head. "Honestly, I'm at my wit's end. I don't know what to do." Her voice cracked, and she paused to gain control. "Life would be so much easier if God gave us a detailed outline of what He wants us to do, so we could at least know if we're on the right path."

He sent a kind smile. "Tell you what. I'll go fix us a glass of tea, and then I want to show you something that's helped me through a lot of tough times."

She nodded, grieved that she and Bo were responsible for the concern etched on his face.

"I'll be right back." He tottered to the kitchen.

Trish took advantage of his absence and called Betsy. "This is Trish. Sorry I never made it back, but Bo isn't feeling well."

"Sorry to hear that. Hope he's better soon." Thank goodness her voice held no reproach.

"You know how kids are. I'm sure he'll be better in the morning. I'll come in to finish the display right after I drop him off at school, if that's okay." She rushed through the explanation, hoping the plea would work.

"Don't worry about it, Trish. I've already taken care of it."

Her heart sank. No job. No money. "Thanks for understanding." She ended the call and laid the phone on the table, her mind numb. Right now she just didn't have the strength to make the second business call. It would have to wait until later.

"Here you go." Dad shuffled back into the room, and set the tea in front of her, the ice cubes clinking against the glass. He turned an object over in his hand, his eyes tender, then gave her a hand-stitched bookmark, many years old, judging by the worn edges. *"Trust in the Lord with all your heart, and lean not on your own understanding; in all your ways acknowledge Him, and He shall direct your paths."*

Trish trailed her fingers over the bumpy stitches. The verse from Dani and Steve's wedding. Whoever made this did beautiful work. She took a sip of the sweet tea. "Where'd you get this?" She passed it back to him, but he shook his head and curled her fingers around the bookmark.

"You keep it for now. A dear friend gave it to me a very long time ago. Every time I reached a point in my life when I couldn't decide which path to take, this verse helped." Dad eased back down into a chair, his hand still covering hers, and his gray-blue eyes trained on her. "I know things are confusing right now, honey. It's hard to know what to do when life yanks the rug out from under you. The best advice I can give is to trust God. I know it sounds too simple, but I promise one day this will all be behind you."

Trish nodded and rubbed his hand, willing herself to believe. He was right. God wasn't surprised by her situation. Nor was He unable to handle it. She just needed to trust Him more.

Her phone buzzed against the oval-shaped maple table, and she flicked it open. "Hi, Delaine."

Dad lowered his head, his lips pressed together in a disapproving line. He'd made his opinion about the job in Austin well known.

Her friend's voice held concern. "Hi. You sound tired. What's going on?"

"Just been a long day." Trish rose to her feet, sent her father an apologetic glance, and moved to the oak-canopied patio, out of her father's hearing. "Can you give me a few more specifics on that design position?"

Andy's brow crinkled into a frown, as gangrenous jealousy roared inside. What in the world possessed him to come back to Miller's Creek one week after the wedding? His decision to check out the town as a possible place for a private practice was important, but ill-timed. Dani, Steve, and Mama Beth all entered Granny's Kitchen ahead of him, the first two disgustingly happy.

They entered the cafe, the aroma of burgers, fried chicken, and chicken-fried steak flooding the air. Hearty laughter and chatter rang out, with many comments directed at the others, leaving him as the odd man out.

A few minutes later, they located an empty table near the back, right next to Steve's cohorts, J.C., Coot, and the grouchy guy, Otis Thacker. Based on Otis' scowling face, he hadn't changed much in the past few months.

"Hey, Mayor. Too good to sit with us today?" bellowed Coot.

Steve appeared to take it all in stride. "Not at all, but in case you forgot, I'm a married man now."

The guys all guffawed, made comments about his being henpecked, and then guffawed some more. An elderly lady dressed in a long dress and apron, her wiry gray hair pulled back in a bun, delivered ice water and menus, while her identical twin worked the other side of the restaurant. "Be right back with your coffee, Steve."

"Thanks, Granny."

Andy warred with the instantaneous jealousy that shot through him. Must be nice to live in a place where people knew you and what you wanted before you even asked. He searched the menu. "It's been a while since I've been here. What's good?"

"Everything." Mama Beth and Dani answered in unison.

"Don't mind them," Steve intoned, taking a sip from his filled cup, "even though their talking in stereo *is* a little scary."

Dani gave a sideways hug to her mother. "Great minds . . ."

". . . think alike." The older woman finished the sentence, a broad smile splayed across her face.

Steve shook his head. "Something tells me I'm in a lot of trouble. Just think, Andy, I used to be like you—happy, living the simple bachelor life."

Dani punched her husband's arm. "Watch it, mister, or you'll be sleeping on the couch."

Andy laughed along with the rest of them, but it was a laugh he didn't feel. The Granny lady returned to their table, stationed herself next to him, and asked for his order. "I'd like the catfish, cole slaw, and fries. And a cup of coffee, please."

"You shoulda said something when I was here earlier with the coffee pot." She muttered and glowered.

"Sorry."

The woman huffed and scribbled down the other orders, then came back a few minutes later with a cup and coffee pot. She clunked down the cup and sloshed coffee into it, obviously still agitated he'd neglected to follow some unspoken small town café protocol.

After she left, Dani laid a hand on his arm. "Don't mind her. Once she gets to know you, she can be really sweet."

Steve crossed his arms, rested them on the table, and looked Andy in the eye. "Dad tells me you're thinking of moving to Miller's Creek."

Andy swallowed a swig of the fresh, hot brew. "Not exactly. I'm thinking about setting up a private practice in a small town. Miller's Creek might or might not be that place."

"Well, of course, you should move here." Dani looked at her husband pointedly. "Don't you think so, honey?"

Steve frowned and shifted in his seat.

"I'd do a lot of praying first." Mama Beth stated the words matter-of-factly. "Just ask Dani. The adjustment to small town life isn't easy."

Andy nodded. "I think I pretty much understand how small towns operate."

"Yeah, Dad mentioned you grew up in a small town." Steve's eyes narrowed, an unyielding expression that always made him feel like he was under interrogation. "Berringer, right?"

"Yep. Born and raised there."

"C'mon, you two. You're gonna scare him off." Dani glared at Steve and Mama Beth, then returned her attention to him. "It *is* an adjustment, but you lived here long enough last year to know the challenges."

Andy's heart rate quadrupled just thinking about the nightmare of the entire town's suspicions and assumptions laid on his shoulders. He still found it hard to believe they suspected him of trying to torch downtown Miller's Creek.

Dani continued. "It's difficult, but not impossible."

Her comment didn't instill a lot of confidence. The food arrived, and Andy concentrated on his meal to allow him time to think. He took a bite of the mouth-watering catfish and glanced at Steve's friends—what did he call them?—the old codgers? No, the old geezers. They all leaned forward and spoke in conspiratorial whispers. Why did he get the distinct impression he was already a rotten grape on the town grapevine? Or was his imagination making too much out of it?

After lunch, Andy spent the afternoon driving around Miller's Creek and settling into his room at Mama Beth's, then drove to the Miller's ranch as the sun lowered in the western sky.

He stepped out of his car and peered up at the Colonial-styled house. Surrounded by giant oaks, the brick two-story seemed better suited to the Deep South—with antebellum plantations and trees dripping Spanish moss—instead of the rolling hills of central Texas. He wandered up the massive steps and rang the doorbell, still puzzled over why Steve had invited him for supper.

The lanky cowboy answered the door, hand extended. "Hey, Andy, come on in."

Andy shook his hand and entered, his eyes immediately drawn to the enormous chandelier.

"My mother was from Atlanta, Georgia." Steve spoke the words like an excuse for the house and motioned for Andy to follow him across the marble floors. "Dad lives here alone now, so Dani and I are living with him while our house is built on the old homestead."

They stepped through the kitchen and onto the back terrace, an expanse of flagstone shaded by ancient oaks. The patio overlooked a large metal barn and wood-fenced horse paddock, and the entire family gathered around a large rectangular table.

"Andy!" An apron around her waist and surprise in her voice, Trish jumped to her feet at the far end, her eyes wide and her smile even wider. Then, just as suddenly, her mouth clamped shut, and she plopped into her seat, as if his presence made no difference at all. "I didn't know you were coming." A glare directed at Steve accompanied her accusatory tone.

"Sorry, Sis, I forgot to mention we needed to set another place for dinner. I'll get it."

With the characteristic long strides of a man always in a rush, Steve entered the house, while Trish's dad motioned for Andy to take a seat between him and his daughter. After he settled into the wooden chair, he sent a grin and a wink across the table to Little Bo. "Hey, buddy. Wanna play catch later?"

Instead of the spunky response he expected, the boy slouched lower and jerked his head away without a word, refusing eye contact.

Andy wrinkled his forehead, unease churning in his gut. He shifted his gaze to Trish. "Is he okay?"

Her dark eyes contained sorrow. "He had a bad week."

Throughout the meal Andy kept an eye on Little Bo. Trish tried to coax him to eat, but he merely picked at the food, his expression empty and void. He stared blankly, his mouth pinched and drawn, almost as if he were there in body only. Like the rest of him had moved on to a very dark place. What had happened in a week's time to bring about such change?

The roasted chicken was delicious, but impossible to fully enjoy because of his concern. When he finished his plate, he scooted his chair away from the table. "My compliments to the chef."

"Thanks." Trish sent him a faint smile, her face still carved with sadness. She'd eaten very little herself, her thoughts obviously preoccupied with her son.

Andy reached for his glass, wet with condensation, and swigged his iced tea. "You cooked all this?"

She smirked. "Don't sound so surprised."

"I'm not." And he meant it. She was the most capable and accomplished woman he'd ever met. If only she could see it, too.

Steve made a sound in his throat. "Andy, I talked to Bill Braddock, our city attorney, this afternoon. His last day is at the end of the month." His voice all business, Steve leaned his chair back and steepled his fingers. "I told him you might be interested. Is it all right for me to have him contact you?"

"Sure." Andy reached for his wallet and procured a business card. "I'll be here all weekend if he'd like to talk." It wouldn't hurt to at least look into the situation. After all, that's why he'd come—to see if Miller's Creek was where God wanted him.

Trish rose to her feet. "Guess I'd better get this mess cleaned up."

"Let me help." Andy bounded to his feet without thinking, then caught his mistake and grinned apologetically.

To his relief, she smiled in return. "Thanks. I appreciate it."

He gathered dishes and followed Trish into the house. "So you and Bo live here, too?"

She shook her head, turned on the spigot, and rinsed the plates, then deposited them in the stainless steel dishwasher. "No, I live a little way down the road. My house is hard to see from here because of the oaks. I'll show it to you later if you'd like to take a walk."

"A walk would be great, especially after the delicious meal."

The work completed, Andy and Trish strolled down a well-worn path to her house, the area blanketed with oak trees and prairie grass and sprinkled with bluebonnets and Indian paintbrush. Her house soon came into view. Made of Texas limestone, the rustic cedar posts and a metal roof completed the look of a Texas ranch house.

They strolled around back to a large deck, which overlooked a grassy meadow. A cottage stood in a grove of trees to the right. "Who lives there?"

"That's my art studio." Her voice turned solemn. "Right after were married, Doc built it for me."

"I'd love to take a look at more of your artwork."

Trish pressed her lips together, tucked a strand of hair behind her ear, and peered off in the distance. Finally, she released a heavy sigh. "Sure."

They made their way across an overgrown pathway, bypassing an equally unkempt flower garden. Trish looked the other direction and stopped short of the door. With a deep breath, she inched forward and twisted the doorknob, the door creaking out a groan that mirrored her face.

The one-room cottage, decorated with cobwebs, smelled of musty disuse. A small kitchenette sat to the left, and an overstuffed chair to the right. Along the rear wall, natural light flooded in through a bank of windows, and dust danced in the beams.

A variety of canvases leaned against the window frames. He drifted toward them, drawn by a combination of curiosity and fascination. One at a time, he examined them, more awed and impressed than ever. The artwork was every bit as spectacular as he'd imagined.

Trish anchored herself near the doorway, like a frightened cotton-tail rabbit, torn between freezing and bolting. She clutched one elbow, her face pale.

"Your work is beyond beautiful, Trish. Words can't do it justice."

She made no reply.

"You wanna leave?"

Trish nodded and escaped out the door.

As he exited the room, Andy gave one last look around. This room *was* Trish. From the decorations to the paintings . . . even the dust and cobwebs. Maybe one day the hurt and confusion could be cleared from her life, and she'd be able to return to the art she once enjoyed.

Without speaking, she glided toward the beckoning pasture, now back-dropped by a gorgeous Texas sunset, apparently not ready for the stroll to end. Andy followed and allowed the beauty of the early May evening to wash over him.

Trish finally broke the silence. "It was tough to open that door and go in. I haven't been there since before Doc died."

Andy took time to think through his response. The last thing he wanted was to hurt her further. She seemed so vulnerable. So fragile. "I could tell it was difficult, Trish, but it was a major step in the right direction. I'm proud of you."

Her eyes swam with instant tears. "It used to be such a happy place. Now it seems . . . ruined." Her words ended in a murmur.

Andy seized her hand and halted, purposely not speaking until she looked him in the eye. “Not ruined, just in need of some TLC. One step at a time.”

She withdrew her hand and continued the walk. They approached a wooded area, where a narrow path disappeared in dark shadows.

Andy eyed the dense grove, old fears clawing his insides, his neck hairs bristling. He choked on the desert dryness that puckered his mouth and battled his desire to run. “We’re going in there?”

Trish came to a standstill a few steps down the shaded path, her eyes full of questions. “It’s okay, Hansel. I brought bread crumbs, and I’ll make sure we’re not baked into gingerbread by a wicked witch.”

He didn’t return her smile. “I’d rather not, if you don’t mind.” He hated that his voice quaked.

“Okay.” She turned back, and they moved toward the house. “Wanna tell me why?”

“No reason. Just need to get back. So tell me, what’s up with Little Bo?”

Trish filled him in. She lowered her head and voice. “He hasn’t been back to school. I just don’t have the heart to make him go.”

Anger swept over him at the callousness of Bo’s teacher. “He has to, Trish.”

“I know. It’s just so hard to see my son . . . check out.” A muffled groan escaped her, and immediate tears spilled down her cheeks and dripped from her chin.

Her knees started to give way, but before she crumpled to the ground, he pulled her into his arms while sobs shook her body. The scent of her shampoo drifted past his nose, her hair soft and silky against his cheek.

God, please take away her hurt and pain. Show me how I can help her and Bo without making her feel inadequate. He stroked her back to offer comfort, overwhelmed by the tender feelings surging through him.

Eventually she pulled away and swiped her wet cheeks, her lashes spiked with tears. "I'm so sorry."

"Don't apologize for your feelings." He clutched both her hands and forced her to look at him. "Allow yourself time to grieve. Not just your husband's death, but its impact on Bo. Holding it in will only create more problems down the road."

Trish nodded. "You're right, bu—" Her cell phone jangled, and she retrieved it from her pocket. "Sorry, Andy, but I need to take this call."

She traipsed a few feet away and rested against the rough bark of an oak, her shoulders stooped and one arm curled around her waist. An overpowering urge to step in, fix her problems, and shelter her from life's storms ballooned inside him. But how could he help when she wanted nothing more than to help herself?

Her words wafted toward him on the breeze and sent a chill down his spine. "Thanks, Delaine. I'll compile a resume and send it to her right away."

9

Andy parked his car in the popular West End district of Dallas and hurried to an upscale bistro to catch an early lunch. The past weekend had given him more questions than answers, and he was still no closer to a decision on moving to Miller's Creek. On top of everything, he hadn't been able to get Trish and Bo out of his mind. Like a Texas-sized mosquito, it constantly buzzed in his thoughts.

He entered the restaurant and allowed his eyes to adjust to the dark interior, while enjoying the delectable aroma. Then a familiar voice caught his attention—one he hadn't heard since the night before he was supposed to get married.

Sheila.

He turned his back and prayed she wouldn't see him. Hoped she'd think he was just another person waiting for a table at the packed-to-capacity restaurant.

"Andy?" The syrupy voice he'd once found adorable now curdled his stomach.

He attached a smile to his face and pivoted to deal with her head-on. "Sheila. Sure didn't expect to see you here."

The perceptive look that crossed her face let him know that his clumsy attempt to act surprised hadn't worked. Sheila smirked. "Come on, Andy, we can be big people. There's no way we're going to avoid running into each other from time to time."

A predatory glint appeared in her eyes, and she stretched her red claws toward him.

Andy shook her hand in a gesture of friendship then wiped his hand on his pants. Her grasp always had a clammy feel that freaked him out.

"Andy, I'd like you to meet my friend, Chase." She offered no further explanation.

Not that he needed one. The way she had her arm possessively linked in his pretty much said it all. "Nice to meet you, Chase. Let me guess, you in banking?"

"Close. Personal finance. How'd you know?"

"Lucky guess." Educated guess based on Sheila's expensive tastes.

Chase, the all-American-guy type, grinned to reveal a toothpaste-commercial smile. "How do you two know each other?"

Sheila leaned back and shook her head, eyes wide.

Andy chuckled. "Let me tell him, Sheila. It's such an interesting story, don't you think?" A look of horror washed over her face, but he continued. "Sheila and I were engaged. In fact, the night before our wedding I caught her kissing her old boyfriend."

Chase's toothpaste grin faded. Andy patted his shoulder. "Nice to meet you, Chase. Keep an eye out for those old boyfriends of hers. She collects 'em like Barbie dolls." Andy whirled around and stomped out the door, the delicious food smells stalking him.

He let out a frustrated breath as he pulled out of the parking space into typical Dallas traffic. Sheila was right. They ran in the same circles, and he couldn't avoid her. She'd serve as a constant reminder of his bachelorhood. On the bright side, she'd also be a reminder of the out-of-control fast ball he'd dodged.

Though the confrontation with Sheila left a queasy feeling in his gut, his hunger pangs were stronger. He pulled into a fast-food drive-through and ordered a burger to-go, then headed back to the office.

Andy entered through the back door and hurried to his suite. A boring shade of beige greeted him. Beige walls, beige carpet. A different kind of prison, but a prison none-the-less.

He'd just plopped down in his leather desk chair when Debbie, the firm's receptionist, buzzed him. "Mr. Wayne on line one."

"Thanks, Deb." He pressed the button. "Mr. Wayne, this is Andy Tyler. How can I help you?"

"As much dough as I'm shelling out, you'd think you could get my son's case moving along a little faster." Mr. Wayne, his voice razor-edged, was obviously used to getting what he wanted when he wanted it.

Andy pressed a hand to his stomach, which felt more unsettled with each tick of the clock. When would these wealthy dads realize he had no control over the speed of the justice system? Better yet, when would they start showering their kids with time instead of money? Then they wouldn't need his services. "Mr. Wayne, the judge sets the date of the hearing, not me. I promise as soon as I know more, I'll be in contact."

The man didn't express a 'thank you' or a 'good-bye,' but slammed the phone with so much force Andy's ear continued to ring long after he laid down the receiver.

He peeled back the paper wrapper on his burger to take a bite, his mouth salivating, but the buzzer sounded again.

"Yes?" He pelted the word in frustration.

"Mr. Robert Simms on line one."

As soon as he said hello, Andy regretted taking the call.

"Mr. Tyler, I'm in debt collection, and our records show your father has neglected six months of payment on his overdue account. We thought you might like the opportunity to help him before we take legal action." He spoke the words in a matter-of-fact monotone.

Andy ran a hand down his neck. "How much this time?"

"Two thousand plus."

"Send me an itemized bill." He gave the man his fax number, then banged the phone to the receiver, his insides pure acid. He'd had all he could take, and it was only noon. He buzzed Debbie.

"Yes, sir?"

"Hold all calls until further notice." He slouched in his chair and scarfed down his now cold burger. The constant phone calls and meetings were part of his job, but everything else was his choice. And a choice meant he could determine what to do next. He could stay in Dallas with a life he now hated, or he could move to Miller's Creek.

His thoughts turned to Trish and Little Bo. Under the tragic circumstances, there would be challenging days ahead, but he yearned to do for Little Bo what Lester had done for him—to make a difference.

He'd already crunched numbers and met with the Miller's Creek city attorney. It'd be tough at first, but between the job for the city and picking up private clients on the side, it should work.

Andy drafted a quick e-mail to his partner to request a conference, then called Steve to confirm his decision to take the job. A few minutes later, he hung up the phone, his plan taking on new dimension. He tilted the chair back and laced his fingers behind his head, his confidence skyrocketing. Why hadn't he decided to make a fresh start a long time ago?

Next order of business . . . to call Trish.

Trish's legs thrashed. The anger in Dad's eyes sent waves of shame crashing over her. "I told you no, and you did it anyway! Your disobedience put you and your brother in danger!"

She bolted to an upright position, her heart pounding against her ribs, and peered groggily around the room, the bed sheet twisted around her ankles. Just a nightmare. She brought a hand to her face and breathed out her relief. It'd been years since she'd remembered the time she deliberately went for a horse ride against her father's orders. Along a gravelly butte, her horse had slipped and hurled them both into a ravine. Steve had risked his life to rescue her.

Trish flopped back against her pillow. Funny how a childhood memory could still haunt you. She was in the ravine again, and the blame lay squarely on her shoulders. Letting the insurance lapse had been an accident, but it was still her fault. Would Steve and Dad have to rescue her once again?

The alarm clock usually glared red numbers, but this morning it was blank. From behind the mini-blinds the sky glowed brightly. Trish hustled out of bed and snatched her cell phone, gasping when she saw the readout. Almost eleven? They'd overslept, and on the day she planned to take Bo back to school. She ran to the kitchen. The microwave clock was blank, too. The electric company must have grown tired of waiting for payment and turned off her power.

She scrambled to wake Little Bo and get him ready, grabbed the last granola bar for him to eat in the car, and dashed to school. Within thirty minutes they stood outside the brick and stone building. "But I don't wanna go to school, Mommy. Please don't make me."

Trish knelt in front of him in the gravel parking lot. He thrust out his bottom lip and cocked his head to one side. Puppy dog eyes—she hated when he used his puppy dog eyes. "Sweetie, you have to. Mommy has to go to work so she can pay your baseball fees. And someone I know has a birthday coming up." She smiled and tickled his belly.

He pulled away. "I don't wanna play baseball." He hung his head and stuck his thumb in his mouth.

Why did this have to be so hard? She rose to her feet, grabbed his hand, and started for the building. "I'm sorry, Bo, but you have to go to school."

Her son whimpered and drug his feet.

Trish gulped in air, yanked open the steel door, and sidestepped a group of teachers who stood in the hall. She ignored their stares and whispers and continued on to his classroom. Good timing. The class had just returned from lunch and was pulling out their nap mats under the supervision of Mrs. Walsh.

Disregarding the woman's stare, Trish ushered Bo to his cubby to put his backpack away. Carla Clark's son stood nearby with a group of boys. "Look, the thumb-sucker's back." He pointed at Bo and laughed. The other kids followed his lead.

Trish sent them a hard stare, then guided Bo to a table where children were working puzzles. "Look, Bo, you love puzzles." She pulled out a chair, and he sat with reluctance.

With a deep breath, she marched to Mrs. Walsh's desk. The woman seemed a little more approachable today. "Mrs. Walsh, Bo told me the Clark boy has been calling him names on the playground. That's why he started the fight." The teacher opened her mouth, but Trish continued. If she didn't get the words out, she'd lose her nerve. "I've had a talk with Bo about his behavior, and he's promised not to let it happen again. Could you please see that the other boy is kept away from my son?"

"Mrs. James, I can't do that. I will have a talk with Brody, but Bo has to learn to get along with the other children. He's already a loner. It's not good for him to be isolated."

Tears threatened, but she blinked to hold them at bay. "I know, but right now he's fragile. If you could just try to help him through until the end of the school year, I'd appreciate it."

"I'll do what I can," she said, a begrudging tint to her voice.

"Thank you." Trish hurried to where Bo sat, his eyes pinned on her. She bent down to give him a hug. "I have to go."

He frowned, his dark eyes moist. "Mommy, please."

Her stomach churned. This was for his own good. "After school I'll take you for ice cream and a trip to the park." Trish ran from the room before he caused a scene.

Behind her Little Bo started to sob. Not only was she a horrible businesswoman, she was a horrible mother. She pushed through a line of children and out the door, shaking and crying. Only when she reached the privacy of her car did she give in to her tumultuous emotions. She cried all the way to the store.

As she unlocked the door to Designs By Trish, her stomach grumbled. She set down her things in the musty-smelling building, grabbed a package of saltines, and gulped down three or four to appease her growling belly. Okay, she could do this. She had to for Bo's sake. Trish opened her desk drawer and retrieved the phone book.

A while later she clicked her phone shut. The last call had been made, and no one needed their store fronts decorated. Now what? Call people to see if they wanted their living rooms redone? She rested her forehead against the heel of her palm. *God, I don't know what to do. I'm trying to trust You, but when the checking account is overdrawn and we need groceries, it's kind of hard. Help me.*

Trish checked the time. Already two o'clock. She nibbled at another cracker until it was half-gone, then stared at the other half in disgust. She was tired of crackers. Tired of being hungry. Her cell phone buzzed as she placed the uneaten half back in the waxy paper. "Hello."

"Hi, Trish. It's Andy."

She slumped in her chair. "Hi."

"Bad day?"

"No worse than any other, I guess."

The line grew quiet. "You okay?"

"Peachy."

"Uh, I wanted to let you know I've decided to make the move."

Great. Just what she needed—someone else who felt compelled to rescue her. She had nothing. No words to say. Nothing to encourage him the way he'd encouraged her.

"I'm going to set up a temporary office in City Hall while I build my living quarters and office across from the train depot." He sounded excited about his plans. "I need your help."

Trish snorted. "Are you asking or telling?"

"Neither. I'm begging. I have to stay in Dallas this week to tie up loose ends, but I'd like my temporary office ready when I arrive Friday evening." He let out an audible sigh. "Look, Trish, I know this is short notice and I know you're busy, but I really need your help."

She sat up straighter. Why not take the job? Her main concern had been to keep distance between her and Andy, but he wouldn't even be here. "I'll need money for purchases."

"Set up an account, and I'll wire whatever you need." He shuffled papers in the background, and she imagined him cradling the phone between his shoulder and sandy curls. "I'll also send you half of whatever price you set up front, and pay you the second half this weekend."

A burden the size of Texas rolled off her chest. "You've got yourself a deal, Mr. Tyler."

After they straightened out the details, Trish clicked her phone shut, her mood suddenly buoyant. Her first real client. And not a wedding, but an actual office space. Maybe other businesses would see the benefit of her services. Sure it was only one job, but at least it would help pay the bills and give her portfolio a boost.

Amazing how life could turn around in a heartbeat. She grabbed her purse and keys and headed for the door with a jauntiness in her step she hadn't experienced in ages. First she'd set up Andy's expense account. Then she'd treat herself to a nice lunch.

Later that afternoon when she picked up Little Bo from school, she felt like a different woman than the frantic mother who had dropped him off. And to her delight, Bo looked better, too.

He bolted out the classroom door, his face bright with an excited smile. "Guess what, Mom? I learned to tie my shoes today." He knelt in the crowded hall and proceeded to untie his shoe. "Watch. First I make two bunny ears then I cross 'em. Next I have to tuck one under the other." Bo fumbled the last step, and his mouth turned down at the corners.

"Here, honey, let me help." Trish bent down.

He pushed her hand out of the way. "No, Mom. I can do it myself." He started the process again, his expression a combination of concentration and determination. His words rang in her ears. *I can do it myself.* He finished with a lopsided bow, and then sent a triumphant grin.

Suddenly, the path ahead came into focus for the first time in months, so clear she could see a fork in the road. One road led to dependence on her family. The second road would be rough, and one she'd have to travel on her own. It might even mean leaving Miller's Creek, but it was better than feeling inept. She stood, her spine ramrod straight, her shoulders squared.

Yes, she could do it herself. And she would.

10

Trish stared at her father, unsure how to respond. "We're doing okay."

Dad pinned her with his eagle-eyes, making her feel like a twelve-year-old who'd been caught smoking behind the barn. "You're hiding something."

She faced the pine cabinets and sink and scraped food into the garbage disposal, the grating noise adding to her shredded spirit. Would he ever treat her like an adult? After she loaded the breakfast dishes in the dishwasher, she slammed the door and twisted the knob. The motor whirred, and water trickled.

"Look, you're over here all the time cooking my meals and cleaning the house. At least let me pay you for your time." His throaty words held barely-contained emotion.

It was true. She cooked his breakfast and supper, cleaned his house, and washed his clothes. Even if he could pay her enough to meet the mortgage each month it would help. *No!* She refused to take the easy way out. These things she did for him because she loved him, not for a handout. It wasn't like it was any big deal, especially since her house was a quick walk away. "It's a little tough right now, Dad, but we're going to be okay. Andy's already paid me half of what he owes me. I should get the rest today."

"And then what? Have any more jobs lined up?"

She turned toward him, lips pressed, and shook her head. "Only the possible position in Austin."

The news apparently cut into him, because his forehead furrowed, and he flinched. "Are you actually considering that move?"

She steeled her resolve with a quick breath. "I might not have a choice."

Dad lumbered from his seat and placed his large hands on her shoulders. "You can't do that to Little Bo."

"I'm not doing it *to* him. I'm doing it *for* him. There's a huge difference."

"You know all of us are willing to help."

"Of course." She pulled away from his grasp and wiped crumbs from the counter and deposited them in the trash. "But I also know I'm a big girl and can do it myself." Okay, now she was regressing. A minute ago she felt like a twelve-year-old, now she sounded like she was five.

"That's nothing but stubborn pride talking, Patricia Diane!"

His angry words slapped her in the face. It had been years since he'd used her full name.

A weary sigh escaped him. "Remember the verse I showed you the other day?"

"The one about trusting the Lord?"

Dad nodded. "Don't depend on your own strength when you can depend on God."

"I *am* depending on God." Her anger spiraled upward, increasing the volume of her words. "I just don't want to depend on your charity." The words came out more forceful than she'd intended, and her father grew stone quiet.

Finally he broke the tense silence. "How do you know that God doesn't mean to provide for you through us?"

Trish arranged the dish towel to where it hung perfectly from the oven handle, ignoring his question. "I have to go. I'm meeting Andy to put the finishing touches on his temporary office."

"On a Saturday?"

"Yes. See you later." She hurried out the French doors at the back of the house before he reduced her to a screaming two-year-old.

The spring morning already held warmth, the air dry and dusty. Little Bo lounged beneath a small grove of oaks and petted Steve's golden lab.

"Come on, honey. We have to go into town. Mama has work to do."

"I want to stay here with Papaw."

"No." Her son was her responsibility, and no one else's. "You need to come with me."

"Why?" His chin held a defiant tilt.

"Because I said so." How she'd hated those words as a child, and had even sworn she'd never use them. "Come on."

"Please, Mom, it's Saturday." His voice took on a whine. "There won't be anything to do."

"You can take some books and puzzles. Now let's go." She checked her watch. The last thing she needed was to be late to a meeting with her only client. "Bo, now." She struggled to keep her anger in check. "We don't want to keep Andy waiting."

"Andy?" His head shot up, his eyes hopeful. "Andy will be there?"

"Yes."

He sprinted toward their house, only a few steps away, but concealed by live oaks. "Gotta get my glove and ball."

Trish stared at his retreating back and frowned. She should be glad he'd agreed to come with her so easily. Instead it left an uneasy feeling in the pit of her stomach.

She followed after her son, entered the kitchen from the garage, and moved to the sink to rinse out the coffee pot. At least the house was clean. Another sleepless night had provided plenty of time for the housework.

The sound of Little Bo digging through his toy box echoed down the hallway. She flipped the handle on the faucet. It clattered into the sink, and a spray of water shot into the air, drenching her clothes and leaving puddles on the counter and tile floor. Her cry of surprise brought Bo hustling into the room.

"Whoa, a gusher! What happened?"

Trish licked water from her lips and put a hand over the fountain, but only managed to spray herself more. Tears formed and slid down her cheeks. At least they weren't visible with all the water on her face.

Bo dissolved into giggles. It had been so long since he'd laughed full out with nothing to hold him back. On a whim, she allowed the water to shoot between her fingers and sprayed him. He squealed and laughed even harder.

Her clothes dripped as she hurried to the linen closet down the hall and grabbed a stack of towels. She placed one on top of the geyser. In a matter of seconds it turned from dusty gray to slate. As she moved to grab another towel, the microwave clock glared the time. Andy.

With one hand on the soaked towels, she reached for her cell phone and dialed his number.

"Hey, where are you?" His voice held an exasperated edge.

"I'm sorry I'm late, but we've had a minor crisis."

"What's wrong?" His tone took on immediate concern.

Trish grabbed another towel and plopped it on top. "The kitchen faucet broke and is shooting water everywhere. I'm going to have to call a plumber." The thought subdued her. How much would *that* cost?

"Don't call yet. I'm on my way. Look under the sink. There should be water shut-off valves."

She opened the cabinet doors and peered under. Two eye-shaped valves stared back. "Yeah, I see them."

"Turn them both off and stay put. I'll be there ASAP." The phone clicked, and the line went dead.

Trish followed his instructions, and miraculously, the geyser stopped. She turned to survey the damage. Water everywhere. "Here, Bo." She threw a dry towel his way. "Use this to dry yourself off, then start mopping up the water."

They'd just about finished when Andy tapped on the door leading in from the garage. Trish motioned him in. Bo dashed to him and latched onto one leg.

"Hey, buddy." Andy hoisted him into the air, then sat him on his feet with a pat on the back.

Bo smiled and took off toward his room.

Dressed in cargo shorts, a University of Texas t-shirt, and flip-flops, Andy smelled of soap, and his eyes held a devilish glint that teased her. "Do you always take a shower fully clothed?"

"Very funny." She closed the door against the escalating outside heat. "Tell me again why you're here."

"Just call me Mr. Fix-It." He dangled a plastic bag from B & B Hardware on two fingers.

Once again, Andy—or Mr. Fix-It, as he'd put it—to the rescue.

A half hour later he reached under the sink to turn on the valves. "That should do it." He lifted the faucet handle and water streamed from the spout. A dimpled grin appeared on his face.

"Thanks." Unexplainable annoyance flashed through her. "How'd you know what to do?"

He shrugged. "It's just a guy thing."

From nowhere, a memory scuttled to the forefront of her thoughts. She'd had a flat tire and called Doc for help. He'd left his clinic to come change the flat. Without warning, tears escaped down her cheek. She swiveled to hide them.

Behind her, Andy cleared his throat. "Actually, a guy I worked for in high school was a building contractor and a jack-of-all-trades. He taught me." His soft tone of voice told her that he'd seen her tears. "You okay?"

Trish wiped the tears and turned to face him. "Yeah. I just never know when something will set me off. Little things, you know, like walking into the living room and seeing his favorite chair empty, or hearing a car drive up and wondering if its him." She shook off the pain, leaned against the granite counter, and crossed her arms, suddenly feeling inept. "Is there anything you're not good at?"

Andy's eyebrows rose. "Of course." He dried his hands on a towel.

"Such as?"

"Such as carrying heavy boxes full of candles and glass globes." He winked and launched the soppy hand towel her direction. "Now it's your turn to help me, but you might wanna change first."

Trish eyed her soaked jeans and t-shirt. No telling what her face and hair looked like. "Gee, you think?"

Little Bo entered the room and stood quietly, his baseball glove in one hand and a ball in the other.

Andy's lips once more curled into a smile. "Why don't you change while Bo and I have a quick game of catch?"

"Yippee!" Bo scooted for the door, but Andy captured him and swung him up on one shoulder, much to her son's delight. Laughter gurgled from him.

She grinned as the two exited, then immediately sobered. Andy's first day in Miller's Creek, and Little Bo was already attached. Thank goodness, she wasn't.

Andy looked on as Trish wrestled the silk ficus tree into place, its leaves rustling. The grayish white tree trunk contrasted with the slate gray wall she'd painted during the week. His gaze traveled around the office to the wrought iron lamps with the Texas lone star, then on to the brown leather sofa, antique oak desk, credenza, and barrister shelves.

She'd done a remarkable job in a short period of time, and now he'd be ready to open up shop on Monday. A quick glance at the clock made his shoulders sag. He wasn't ready for the time with Bo and Trish to end. How could he prolong their time together? All morning long, Trish had maintained a cool distance that gnawed at him like a fish nibbling bait. She had erected a wall, and the sooner he climbed over it the better.

"Is something wrong?" A frown sent wavy lines scurrying across her forehead.

"Not at all. I just can't believe what all you've accomplished in one week's time."

Her lips curved in a pleased smile. "Thanks. I'm glad you like it. The color of this focal wall is dark, but I knew it would work with all the natural light."

"It's perfect." Exactly what he would've picked had he chosen it himself. His mind returned to the interior of her house. It had been perfect, too, everything neat and orderly. In fact, too neat, especially compared to her dusty studio and overgrown flower garden.

"I didn't have time to purchase artwork. I'll do that next week."

The weathered gray of the fence post in the painting he'd seen at church would look great on the empty wall. He started to mention it, but thought better of it. Things were going well enough at the moment, and he didn't dare say anything to ruin the tentative peace.

With his baseball and glove, Little Bo slouched on the couch, his cap pulled low on his head, but not low enough to conceal his boredom.

Andy reached over and tugged the cap sideways. Bo giggled and turned it back to its place.

"Bo, you know better than to wear that cap indoors." Trish's voice snapped.

The boy didn't look up, but in slow motion removed the cap from his head, which sagged to his chest. He let his arm fall onto the couch, where it squeaked as it landed against the leather.

"Aw, c'mon." Andy teased. "Give the kid a break. It's Saturday. The cap doesn't bother me."

Trish's stormy look gusted across him. "He's my son, not yours."

He raised his eyebrows and pursed his lips. She was right. He had to be careful not to overstep the boundaries.

"Mom, I'm hungry." Bo whined his words.

It *was* past noon. Maybe he could treat them to lunch. Would she go for it?

Trish eyed the bronze clock on the wall. "I think we're almost finished here then we can go home and fix you a grilled cheese sandwich."

Bo released an exasperated breath between protruding lips. "I'm tired of grilled cheese sandwiches all the time."

"How 'bout lunch on me?" Andy stuck his hands in his pockets and jangled his car keys. "I noticed a new Mexican food place in town. Thought we might check it out."

Little Bo brightened. "Can we, Mom?"

She turned her head to one side, lips skewed, her features crossed with doubt. "I'm not sure it's a good idea. You have homework to do before the baseball meeting this afternoon."

Bo folded his arms and harrumphed. "We never have any fun."

Andy grinned at Trish, not above doing a little pleading and pouting himself. "Please. I don't want to eat alone my first day in town, and I'm really hungry for fajitas."

She studied him with cautious eyes.

"You'd be doing a starving man a big favor."

"Oh, all right." She grinned and threw both hands in the air in defeat.

Little Bo bounded from the couch and encircled Andy's legs with a bear hug. "Thanks, Andy!"

"Whoa, whoa, whoa. Aren't you forgetting who you really need to thank?" Andy tousled his silky brown hair.

Bo turned and scuttled from the room. "Oh yeah, thanks, Mom."

A few minutes later they arrived at the house now converted into a restaurant. For a Saturday, the dirt parking lot at Soldano's was packed. All eyes in the place latched on them as they entered the room decorated to look like a hacienda. No telling what kind of rumors would spread.

The unmistakable smell of Tex-Mex cuisine floated in the air, and Andy's stomach growled. A beautiful Hispanic girl dressed in a traditional Mexican blouse and skirt led them to their table, her dark hair rivering down her back.

"Good to see you, Gracie." Trish hugged her, then scooted into the booth beside Little Bo. "Have your classes already ended?"

"No, I'm just home for the weekend to help Papa and my brothers." She handed them each a menu. "I have finals next week."

"So how does it feel to have your freshman year of college almost behind you?" Trish opened the plastic-encased menu, but kept her eyes trained on the beaming young lady.

"Actually because of dual credit classes, I'll be a junior when the semester ends."

Andy's eyes widened. Impressive. "What're you studying?"

"Political Science, but eventually I plan on getting a law degree."

"My kinda girl." He extended a hand. "I'm the new city attorney, Andy Tyler."

"Nice to meet you, Mr. Tyler." Gracie gushed as she shook his hand a little over-enthusiastically. "Mr. Braddock said you'd be coming to town, but I didn't expect you so soon. Will you need a clerk or receptionist for the summer?"

Man, this girl moved fast. "Well, I might. Depends on how much work I'm able to scrounge up."

"Here's my phone number." She jotted it on the back of an order ticket, ripped it off, and handed it to him. "Please give me a call if you need some help. I'm a very hard worker."

"I can tell."

"What can I get you to drink?"

They gave their orders, and as the girl whisked away from the table, Andy popped a chip loaded with spicy salsa in his mouth. "So tell me more about Gracie. I take it her last name is Soldano?"

"Yes. Her mother died when she was twelve. She has four older brothers. A sweet girl with high expectations and a strong work ethic."

"Sounds like the right person for the job."

"You couldn't do any better."

A few minutes later, their food arrived. The fajitas turned out to be some of the best he'd eaten, tender and juicy, with just a hint of lime and cilantro, and the tortillas were hot, fresh, and homemade.

Across the table, Trish scarfed down her food. A frown furrowed his face. Maybe she was just a healthy eater. She devoured another enchilada in four bites. Then again, maybe she was starving to death.

He attempted to draw her into conversation, but with no luck. She maintained her cool façade, almost as if she were determined to keep distance between them.

When they left the restaurant a while later, Trish checked her watch. "Well, Bo, it looks like we're going to the park. Your baseball meeting is only forty minutes away. By the time we got to the ranch it'd be time to turn around and come back. Might as well stay in town."

"All right!" Bo bounced up and down while Trish admonished him to be a little quieter.

Now was his chance. He had a million things to do, but he wasn't about to miss the opportunity to spend more time with them. "Mind if I tag along?"

Her eyes rounded. "Uh, no, I don't guess." She twisted her lips to one side and gazed at the ground.

"I don't have to if you don't want me. Just sounded like fun."

She raised a hand. "No, please, you're more than welcome to join us." Her answer came a little too quickly to ring true.

Bo positioned himself in front of Andy, his head tilted. "Maybe me and you can play some more catch. I need lots and lots of practice."

"Sounds like a plan, little man."

Bo chortled and raced ahead of them.

A few minutes later, they pulled into Creekside Park, two blocks from Andy's office and apartment on the top floor of City Hall. The creek, bordered by gnarly-barked oaks, bubbled its song into the spring day. Nearby a cardinal joined in.

Bo made a bee-line for the fort-like structure in the center of the park.

Andy turned to face Trish. Good, time alone to get to know her better.

Trish patted her stomach. "If I ate like that everyday I'd weigh two tons. And by the way, thanks for lunch."

"You're welcome, and you don't have to worry about the two-ton thing. If anything, you could stand to eat more. You look a little scrawny to me."

She yanked her head toward him, a frown darkening her face.

Man, it didn't take much to set her off. He sent a teasing wink and smile.

Trish emitted a forced laugh. "Let's walk to the creek. There's a boulder near the water's edge where I can sit and keep an eye on Bo." They'd only taken a few steps before she spoke again. "So tell me about your family."

Andy tensed. He hadn't planned on this line of conversation. "Just me and my younger brother. He's going to school at the University of Texas."

Trish gave a soft laugh. "Don't tell my Aggie brother. And what about your parents?"

"No longer in the picture." He tried to keep his tone light. As they passed an oak tree, he snapped off a twig and broke it into two pieces, tossing them both to the ground.

"Sorry to hear that. Sounds rough." Her questioning eyes softened.

"Yep." Enough of this. "How's your work going?"

Her chin rose, and she inhaled sharply. "Fine. I have a pretty good job prospect."

His heart skipped a beat. Was she still considering the Austin job? If so, what if he'd relocated to Miller's Creek just as she and Little Bo moved somewhere else?

11

Andy crammed the last bite of ice cream cone he'd bought at the new drugstore into his mouth, then crunched and swallowed. He swung open the glass door for Trish to enter Miller's Creek Community Center, which sat on the opposite side of the square from City Hall. A group of guys, deep in a heated discussion, sported t-shirts, jeans, and baseball caps and congregated at the front of the dark room near a long folding table plastered with papers. The room was full of dads and their excited boys, the noise level and sweaty body smells escalating by the second.

The strained look on Trish's face revealed her discomfort. Only two other women were in the room. This had to be difficult. Was she thinking about her husband again?

Little Bo didn't look much better as he craned his neck toward his mother. "Mom, please don't make me do this. I don't wanna play T-ball." His subdued words trembled.

She wrapped an arm around his shoulders. "But you love baseball. Remember how much fun you had last year?"

Little Bo didn't answer. Instead, he viewed the other boys sitting with their dads, and his eyes took on sorrow.

Trish turned to Andy, her eyes pleading.

He knelt beside Bo. "Why don't we just stick around long enough to see what they have to say? Then you can make your decision. How's that sound?"

Bo nodded. Trish sent an appreciative smile, then made her way to three folding chairs on the back row. The chairs squeaked and rattled as they sat.

The guy wearing a John Deere cap placed a thumb and finger at the corners of his mouth and gave a shrill whistle. "Okay, y'all settle down. I know you're excited about the new season, so let's get started. We'll begin with T-ball."

A few groans sounded from the audience. Andy couldn't tell if it was the older boys or their dads.

The John Deere man continued. "We have enough boys signed up for four teams, but only three coaches. Any of you willing to take on a team of energetic five- and six-year-olds?"

A few guffaws and negative comments sounded, but no one volunteered. The man waited, his eyes scanning the room.

Coaching a team would definitely help him get involved in the community, but would he have time with a new practice? Andy glanced at Little Bo, his thoughts on Lester and the older man's impact on his life. This was his chance to make a difference in the life of a young boy who needed him. He stood. "I'll do it."

Faces turned toward him, some not so friendly. The man's eyes narrowed. "Sorry, sir, don't believe I know you."

"Andy Tyler, the new city attorney." The words echoed in the now eerily quiet room.

"Nice to meet you. Welcome." The words didn't match the man's unsmiling face. "You have any coaching experience?"

"No, sir, but I played ball all through college."

The man let out a short laugh. "Playing college ball is a lot different than handling a bunch of rowdy boys. You sure you're up for the challenge?" Masculine laughter reverberated from the brick walls.

Heat crept up his neck. "I'm game."

The man waited a long minute. "Any objections?" Whispered discussions took place across the room, but no one spoke up. Another long minute passed. "Okay. You're hired. Before you leave we'll need you to fill out the paperwork authorizing a criminal background check."

His heartbeat thundering in his ears, Andy took his seat, an immediate wave of doubt flooding over him. What had he just gotten himself into?

Little Bo came to stand beside him, his eyes full of admiration. Andy held up a fist, and Bo bumped it with his, releasing a contagious giggle. His lips turned up in a grin that melted Andy's heart. He'd made the right call.

An inscrutable expression covered Trish's face. What was in those troubled brown eyes of hers? Apprehension? Appreciation? A mixture of both?

Half an hour later, Andy clutched the team roster and followed Trish and Little Bo outside.

"Let me see." Trish snatched the paper from his hand and scanned the list. Her eyebrows rose.

"What?"

"Congratulations, you have some of the biggest troublemakers in town on your team." She practically crowed the words, then handed the list back to him, the May breeze trying to tug it from his grasp.

"Ah, c'mon, they can't be that bad. They're little kids."

She turned and made her way down the sidewalk. "Take my word for it." She kept walking, but called back over her shoulder. "And if you think they're bad, wait until you meet their parents."

The following Monday afternoon, Trish attempted to corral a squirming mass of wild boys. The little guys' laughter and excited chatter ricocheted off the concrete floor, sweat already pouring from them in the afternoon heat. She waved a hand in front of her face to stir up a slight breeze in the midst of writhing boy bodies and blew out a breath that fluttered her bangs. Why had she volunteered to help with the team?

Andy entered the dugout, his hair curling up around the edge of his Texas Rangers baseball cap. "Hey, guys, pipe down!" His firm, but kind tone caught their attention, and they quieted, except one.

The Clark boy—the one responsible for Bo's trouble at school—continued to prattle away. Trish pressed her lips together and made a move toward the kid to silence him.

"Hey, young man, what's your name?" Andy's voice rang out behind her, and she shifted so she could view them both.

The kid wore a cocky smirk. "Brody. Why?"

"'Cause I asked you to get quiet, and you didn't." Andy pinned the boy with a dominating gaze, and the silence in the dugout grew more oppressive than the humid heat. Finally, he turned his focus back to the group. "That's more like it. Everyone have a seat and listen up." He squatted in front of them, rotating his head as he spoke, looking each boy in the eyes. "Guys, the main thing we're here to do is have a good time, but I also want to teach you a few things about baseball. We're gonna work hard on hitting and catching and running."

"Running? Man, I hate running." Brody Clark's tone dripped disdain.

To his credit, Andy ignored the comment, as if it weren't worth his time to respond. "First, I'm gonna hit a few balls to you, and I want you to field them and throw them in." He demonstrated how to hold the tip of their gloves to the ground, then turned them loose, their hoots and hollers sounding like Indian braves on the war path.

Trish looped her fingers through the chain-link fence in the dugout and relished the southerly breeze blowing through her sweat-dampened hair.

Andy tapped balls toward the boys like he'd coached his entire life, his easygoing gait and attitude the perfect line-up for a team-full of rowdies. In a matter of minutes he'd won them over, and judging by the smiling faces of the parents in the old wooden bleachers, they were also pleased.

Bo focused on every word Andy spoke, his face jubilant as Andy hit him another grounder. *Lord, let this help him get past the accident and move on with his life.*

"Great job, Bo!" Andy cupped his mouth to yell the words then gave him a thumbs' up.

The joy on her son's face merged with unadulterated admiration, and Trish's breath clung to the inside of her throat. What if he got too attached? The anxious thoughts curdled her empty stomach. Good grief, didn't she already have enough to fret over? Why add more? The unsettled feeling continued to nag.

Next Andy had the boys take turns at bat. "Line the bat up with the top of the T, then pull back and hit the ball, keeping your arms and the bat straight."

Trish's heart ached as Joey Peterson—a child with a terrible home life, as evidenced by his ragged clothing and unkempt hair—tentatively tiptoed to the batter's box. With his bony, bird-like frame, she doubted he could even lift a bat, much less swing it. After listening to Andy's instruction, Joey nodded, hoisted the bat to his shoulder, and swung, but only managed to smack the rubber part of the T. The ball landed in the dirt with a thud.

"Way to swing that bat, buddy. I can tell you're gonna be a real slugger." Andy patted his shoulder, then scooped up the ball and repositioned it. "Now you just have to make contact. Don't take your eye off the ball when you swing, and let your arms come all the way around." Andy pretended to hold a bat to demonstrate.

Joey tried again. Crack! The bat made contact, and the ball sailed in between first and second base. "I hit it!" Hollering at the top of his lungs, Joey bounced like a pogo stick, while the rest of the team scrambled to recover the ball.

"Atta boy, Joey!" Andy resembled a kid himself, his face crinkled in a broad grin. "Gimme five, dude."

They slapped hands, and Joey, a new-found confidence in his step, swaggered to the field to let another boy have a turn. When Andy faced her, she quickly erased the admiration from her eyes and replaced it with cool disinterest. He already had several fans, and she had no plans to join the club.

Practice ended a half hour later. Andy huddled the team together to remind them of the next practice, then sent them on a run. "Three times around the bases before you go home."

All the boys dashed off as fast as their pint-sized legs would carry them, except Brody, who headed for the dugout.

"Brody," Andy called after him. "Where you going?"

"I don't wanna run." He turned his back and resumed his leisurely trek.

Andy broke into a lope and beat him to the entrance by a couple of steps. He bent forward, hands on his knees, to make eye contact. "Sorry, bud, but if you're on this team, you do what I say."

The fence rattled. "It's time for me to get Brody home for supper." Carla's deep voice sounded behind her.

Trish turned.

Carla's expression mirrored the same disrespect as Brody's. "Surprised to see you here, Trish."

"Why?" She tried to maintain a calm, even tone.

Carla glanced slyly toward Andy, then shifted her electric-blue eyelids to Trish. "Already in the market for a new man, huh?"

Trish's flesh flushed ice-cold, and her fingers furled into fists.

Andy stepped up between them. "Hi, I'm Andy Tyler. You Brody's mom?"

"Yeah."

"Nice to meet you." He cleared his throat and crossed his arms. "I'm sure you realize how important it is for Brody to follow the same rules as the rest of the team."

Carla didn't bat an eye, just chomped her bubble gum. "Sure, but not tonight. I already told you. I gotta get him home."

Andy held her gaze a minute more. "Okay, but if he's not able to run the bases by the first game, he'll sit on the bench."

A string of cuss words missiled out of Carla's thickset lips as she gripped Brody's hand and yanked him toward the parking lot.

Andy stood for a long moment, his long-lashed eyes narrowed and lips protruded. Then he clamped his mouth in a firm line and turned to face her. "She always like that?"

"Mmm-hmm. She used to cause trouble when we were in school together, and now her son has taken her place." She swallowed her discomfort. This had to be said. "Sorry you overheard her comment about us. I assure you that's not the case."

Andy grabbed the metal bats and slung them into an army-green duffel bag where they clanged against each other. "Don't worry about it. I know her type."

"Be careful. She can stir up quite a hornet's nest when provoked."

He returned his focus to the parking lot as Carla spun out in her old Ford pickup and sent gravel spewing. "Thanks for the warning."

"You did a great job with the kids." Trish blurted the words then hesitated, unsure how to continue. How could she express her gratitude without playing into Carla's insinuation? "I'm not sure Bo would've played this year if not for you."

Andy grinned, causing her heart to pound faster. "Thanks. I'm not sure I would've coached if not for him."

One by one, the kids completed their laps and trotted out the gate to waiting parents. Trish checked her watch. Good. She had just enough time to get to Dad's, fix them all some supper, then get Bo home for homework, a bath, and bed. After that, she'd work on locating the building plans Andy had requested. Little Bo galloped up, his face flushed with sweat and excitement. "That was so much fun."

Before she could respond her cell phone buzzed. She flipped it open and moved it to her ear. "Hi, Dad."

"Hey, honey. Listen, don't worry about fixing supper for me tonight. I'm eating in Morganville."

Morganville? Trish furrowed her eyebrows. What was he doing in Morganville? He ended the call before she had a chance to ask, and left her staring at the phone, puzzled.

"Something wrong?" Andy stood nearby, in his usual hands-on-hips pose.

"No, just a little weird. Bo and I usually eat with Dad, but he just called to say he's eating in Morganville tonight." What would they eat? More crackers and grilled cheese sandwiches?

"Well, I know a poor starving bachelor that would love to have you cook for him. I've had a hankering for steak all day."

Her eyebrows twitched with a brief frown.

He must have noticed it, because his smile was quickly replaced with a questioning look. Did he already regret the offer?

She pressed her lips together. “Sorry, but I’m fresh out of steak.”

“Well, I can remedy that.” Without allowing her time to protest, he sauntered to the parking lot, bat bags in tow, Little Bo on his heels like a lovesick puppy following his master.

But Bo was *her* puppy. A sigh ripped from her throat, and she trudged after them. How was she supposed to deal with this?

Later Trish forked the meaty rib-eyes from the pot-bellied grill, the heat from the charcoal blasting her face. The aroma of fire-licked beef wafted from the plate, her salivary glands quick to respond. Not surprising considering she hadn’t eaten since breakfast.

Andy peered up from his perch in the breakfast nook when she entered, his arm at rest on the chair behind her son. Bo slumped over an assortment of papers. The scene twisted her insides into a knot—a knot she’d never untangle. At least homework would be done, and one less thing for her to do later. But with Bo so content and agreeable when Andy was around, how would he ever recover if and when Andy was no longer there? No matter how hard she tried to ignore it, the troubling thought niggled at her.

Bo shoved a paper under Andy’s nose.

His blue-green eyes awash in merriment, Andy snatched it away and held it up to examine it. “This is the best handwriting I’ve ever seen.”

Her son chuckled, his face a-glow. “Nuh-uh. You’re just saying that.”

Andy leaned down close. “If I had writing like this when I was in kindergarten, they probably would’ve moved me to second grade.”

Trish set the barn-red plates on the table. “Y’all ready for supper?”

"I thought you'd never ask." Andy jumped up to help. "That smell is driving me crazy."

Bo cleared away the stack of papers. When she pushed a plate of food his way, he raised both fists in the air. "Yay! No grilled cheese sandwich!" He stabbed a bite-sized piece of steak she'd carved for him and stuffed it in his mouth.

Trish's cheeks heated, and Andy winked. "Well now, I happen to love grilled cheese sandwiches. In fact, that's what I'm going to ask for next time."

Her heart lurched. Next time? Could she take any more? Already her heart could burst under the pressure. Somehow she had to let Andy know this would *not* be a regular occurrence.

Bo shook his head, still chewing with chubby chipmunk cheeks. "You wouldn't like 'em if you had to eat 'em all the time."

Andy must've read the embarrassment on her face, because he rapidly changed the subject. "We ready to bless the food?"

Trish nodded. "Would you mind saying the blessing?"

They all joined hands—*joined hands!*—as if it was the most natural thing in the world. As if they were a family.

When the prayer ended, Andy gave her fingers a squeeze, and her pulse catapulted into overdrive. Okay, after Bo was in bed, she had to make sure he knew where she stood. That is, if she could figure it out.

As the meal wore on, her shoulder muscles unknotted, and she enjoyed the time more than she'd first thought possible. The tender steak melted in her mouth and left her rejuvenated. Conversation flowed with frequent rounds of laughter. They finished the meal, and Trish turned to Bo, battle-ready. "Time for a bath, and then bed."

"Oh, Mom, do I have to?"

Andy gave him a look of mock surprise. "Of course you have to. Anyone who plays on my team has to be clean and asleep by nine o'clock."

Bo grinned, and in a surprise move, rose from his chair and headed to the bathroom without a fuss.

Trish forced her mouth shut. "How'd you do that, and how much would you charge to do it every night?"

Andy shrugged, a cocky, lopsided grin sprawled across his handsome face. "You just gotta have the magic touch."

"Well, you have it all right." But was that a good thing? She stood to clear the table.

He joined in without a word, humming a cheery tune as he scraped dishes, loaded the dishwasher, and wiped down the table and counters.

A flurry of unease skidded along her spine. What if this—whatever *this* was—was only setting all of them up for major disappointment and heartbreak?

They'd just finished cleaning up when Bo plodded in wearing his Veggie Tales pajamas, Larry the Cucumber prominently displayed on his chest, and a book tucked under one arm.

Just like before Doc died. A painful lump lodged in her throat and brought a blinding sting to her eyes.

Andy's humming halted in mid-stream, his widened eyes perusing her face. "You okay?"

Trish faced away, palms plastered to the counter. "H-he brought a book to read. He hasn't done that since . . ."

"How do you want me to handle it?" His voice held the calm of a glassy mountain lake.

She peered over her shoulder at Bo's expectant face. "Would you mind reading to him? He's had trouble sleeping recently, and it might help."

"Okay." He sauntered over to Bo and placed a hand on his shoulder. "Hey, bud, want me to read that book to you?"

Bo grinned wide, his eyes almost disappearing, then latched onto Andy's hand and tugged him toward the sofa. Andy sank to the cushions and propped a pillow behind his back while Bo wiggled onto his lap.

"What reading material do we have here?"

"It's my horse book."

Her stomach landed at her feet. *His favorite book.* Would it be too much for him to handle?

Warm and relaxing, Andy's voice soothed her soul like a gentle summer rain. A few minutes later he grew quiet and rotated his head toward her. "He's out. Want me to carry him to bed?"

He couldn't possibly be asleep. Trish hurried to the sofa. The sight of her son sleeping peacefully in Andy's arms brought quick tears that flashed both hot and cold. She moved her lips to speak, but no words sounded. Instead she pointed the way and followed.

Andy laid Bo in his bed and gently covered him with a blanket, his jaw pulsing. He stood, with his gaze locked on Bo for a moment, then glanced at her, an inscrutable expression on his face. "We need to talk." His eyes bored into hers, exposing every inch of her soul.

"Let me turn on the lamp for Bo first."

"I'll wait in the family room." He pivoted and strode away.

Trish closed her eyes. *God, help me know what to do and what to say. I don't understand what's happening, and I'm scared.*

A verse she'd memorized as a child flooded her thoughts. *What time I am afraid, I will trust in Thee.* Yes, trust. That's what she needed to do, but why did she constantly require a reminder?

12

Andy escaped to the safe and comfortable confines of the family room and rubbed a hand across his mouth, the evening stubble on his chin making a scratchy sound. He wandered to the back window that. The meadow, now dark and fathomless like beckoning deep water, appeared both cool and menacing. Too late. He was already in way over his head.

It would be far too easy to get used to this routine of home and family. But was it the right thing to do? He raked a hand through his hair and down the back of his neck. Why had he dared to test troubled waters? The undertow tugged at him now, drowning him in "what-ifs." *God, give me wisdom.*

Trish's footsteps sounded on the hard-wood floor behind him, and he turned. She didn't smile. "Would you like a Dr. Pepper?"

"Yes, please."

A study in casual elegance, she glided to the kitchen, sans shoes. Ballerina-like, with long limbs and a slender neck, she reminded him of a graceful swan afloat on a sea of trouble. Her hands trembled as she removed two glasses from the well-organized cabinet, filled them with ice, and opened a two-liter. The fizzy liquid hissed, then sizzled and popped as she poured it over frozen cubes.

He took the glass she offered, then trailed behind her to the mossy-green sofa. He sank down on the opposite end and searched for a way to start the conversation.

Trish perched on the edge of the cushion, as if allowing herself the option of a fast getaway. "This is awkward, Andy, but it needs to be said." She ran a hand up one arm. "Bo is getting attached to you, and it scares me." The murky depths of her dark eyes swam with worry.

"I'm scared, too." Did he dare reveal his fear of giving them his heart, only to have it crushed?

"I can't take the chance of you backing out of his life."

He looked her square in the eye, a nerve rippling in his jaw. "I wouldn't do that to him."

Her scouring gaze softened. "No. I don't believe you would." The softly-spoken words carried a wellspring of sadness. She sipped from her glass, then returned it to the wooden coaster. "In all fairness to you, I should tell you our days in Miller's Creek are most likely numbered."

Andy's heart plunged, and he lolled his head back against the couch to stare at the rough-hewn cedar beams. Why worry about things beyond his control? He'd sought God's guidance on this move and had to trust that things would work out according to His plan. "You mentioned earlier that Bo's has problems sleeping. Anything else?" He turned to look at her.

She closed her eyes momentarily, her face awash with pain. "Nightmares, sucking his thumb, barely letting me out of his sight, trouble at school . . ." Her voice ebbed away.

Andy's chest tightened. "Does he ever talk about the accident?"

"No." Her head drooped, her thick brown hair curtaining her expression like a waterfall over a dark cave.

He resisted the urge to shove the curtain away. "Is he seeing a counselor?"

Trish nodded, hugged herself, and rocked back and forth. She continued to slump, her shoulder blades protruding from her back in bony angles. "He's been diagnosed with post-traumatic stress disorder."

Post-traumatic stress, the same stuff soldiers endured after a battle. Shell-shocked—the perfect description for the hurting little boy. "How is he around horses?"

Trish visibly stiffened and raised her head, a frown hovering above muddy-watered eyes. "I don't allow him around the horses anymore." Her words were liquid steel.

He shifted in his seat, propped his right ankle on the opposite knee, and laid an arm along the back of the couch. "Did he enjoy horse riding before?"

At first she didn't answer. Instead she peered down at her hands. "He loved it. In fact, he'd just gotten his first horse earlier in the year." She blinked slowly, her expression blank, an icy mask frozen by haunting memories.

How far could he push without sending her over the edge? It didn't matter. He needed to know. More importantly, she needed to know. "Has he expressed an interest in riding again?"

Her shoulders rose and then shimmied down with her ragged exhale. "I've seen him looking at the horses, but he hasn't said anything. Why all the questions?"

"Because I think it would be good for him to ride again. He feels disconnected right now, like nothing will ever be the same."

"His father died. Nothing *will* be the same."

"So you want him to go on being like this?" His words sounded harsh, but she had to face the facts. He pressed his lips together and sent an unvoiced prayer to heaven. "Look, Trish, I know this is hard, but you basically have two choices. You can either find a way to help him back from the dark place he runs away to, or you can encourage it in a roundabout way by pretending everything's okay. If we don't help him, he might run away and never come back."

Her mouth opened, then clamped shut, her eyes afloat with angry tears. "We? What 'we?' I appreciate what you're trying to do, but he's my responsibility. Not yours." The pain-filled words were strangled with emotion. "You can't just fix people and situations like you fix a broken faucet."

Andy started to answer, but then shook his head. "I don't want to fight, Trish. I only want to help." He brought a hand up to tuck a loose strand of hair behind her ear. At the same exact time she leaned toward him, and they were suddenly nose to nose. His gaze lowered to her lips, his heart pounding like a jackhammer.

Suddenly the air was pierced by a terror-filled scream.

Trish's head whipped around. She bounded to her feet and raced to Little Bo's room.

Andy followed and flipped on the light. The room reeked of urine.

Bo's hair clung to his forehead in damp, sweaty tendrils, and the sheets tentacled his feet. He writhed about, as if pursued and captured by submerged monsters.

Trish's face paled, and tears rivered down her cheeks as the ocean-blue sheets beneath her son's body darkened. "He wet the bed. He hasn't done that since he was two." Her voice was an agonized whisper, and her knees buckled.

Andy positioned an arm around her shoulder to steady her. "It's okay, Trish. Let me help."

She shrugged off his arm. "I don't need your help!" Trish sank to her knees at the side of the bed, her attention centered on her son, her long fingers stroking his arms and face. "Hey, sweetie, it's okay. You just had a bad dream."

Little Bo jerked awake and bolted upright, his mouth hinging open as he sucked in great gulps of air. With eyes like deep, dark pools, he satisfied his cavernous mouth with his thumb.

Trish gathered her son to her chest, the fear and despair on her face slicing through Andy. If only she'd let him in.

He bent down close. "Hey, buddy, I have bad dreams sometimes, too. Wanna talk about it?"

Bo shook his head and stared blankly at the soaked sheets, streams sliding silently down his chubby cheeks.

All Andy could do was place a hand on each of their shoulders, on his heart a prayer, and on his lips salt-water tears.

Later that week, Trish swung open the heavy wooden door to City Hall and clopped across the well-worn oak floors to where Wanda Cates, the city secretary, typed away at an old Remington. Her half-lens reading glasses, complete with a dangling beaded chain, perched on the end of her long nose.

Wanda continued pecking away, her mouth set in an unyielding line, until she reached the end of whatever-it-was she was doing and glanced up. "Why, Trish, I didn't know it was you. Why didn't you say something?" The words were spoken in her typical nasal twang. "How ya' doin', girl?" She scampered from behind the metal desk and engulfed Trish in a hug.

"Fine."

"Well, my goodness, don't you look all business-like?" Wanda stepped back to take in her attire, her gaze halting at Trish's hair. Her lips twitched. "Don't think I've ever seen you wear your hair up like that."

Obviously not intended as a compliment.

The older woman moved back to her chair and plopped down. "Steve's not in right now. He's at Granny's having coffee with the old geezers."

"That's okay. I'm actually here to see Andy Tyler."

Wanda's dark eyebrows waggled up her forehead. "Oh, I see." Her tone matched her facial expression, both of which screamed busybody. "You know, when I first met Andy, I didn't much care for him, but he's a really nice guy. Not that you're looking, but if you ask me, he'd make great husband material."

Alrighty, then. "Well, I'd better go. Don't want to be late. For my business meeting." She over-emphasized the last words, then waved and headed up the stairs.

Trish hesitated outside Andy's office, tugged on the front of her gabardine jacket, and checked her pulled-back hair with trembling fingers. A bobby pin had loosened its grip in the May wind, so she secured it, then with a cleansing breath, assumed her business persona and opened the 50's-movie-detective-style door to Andy's temporary office. Just here to do her job and then leave.

The room still smelled of fresh paint, and gorgeous natural light spilled in from the tall windows lining the outer wall of the room. What an awesome place to paint. The thought took her by surprise, and she pushed it away. *No.* Painting was something the old Trish enjoyed. The new Trish didn't have time. Instead, she'd become father, mother, and sole bread-winner for a very troubled little boy. That was all that mattered.

Andy swiveled in his chair, the phone to his ear. He grinned and held up one finger. "Yes, Mr. Thacker, I can meet with you later this afternoon. Will three work for you?"

Otis Thacker? Why would he need Andy's services? She glanced around the office that overlooked the city square and chomped down on her bottom lip. The focal wall, a bullet gray, contrasted nicely against the exposed brick of the outer wall.

"My retainer fee is five hundred dol—" Andy's eyebrows shot up suddenly. "Yes sir, I know that sounds like a lot, but if you compare it to the amount other attorneys charge, it's quite reasonable."

A loud, irate voice exploded through the phone, and Andy yanked it away from his ear, grimacing. When the blast ended, he scowled and brought the receiver back to his face. "Yes, sir. Thank you for your . . . er . . . insightful comments. We'll discuss it this afternoon. I look forward to our meeting." The distaste on his face contradicted his calm voice.

Andy hung up the phone, released a puff of air, and gave his head a rapid shake as if trying to dislodge the burning words. "Sorry about that." He checked his wrist, then grinned up at her, a devilish glint in his eyes and dimples. "Right on time. I like that."

An unauthorized smile sprang to her lips, but she squelched it immediately. "I've managed to find several house plans that match what we discussed." Her business voice held a tremor, but maintained the icy coolness she'd hoped for. *Come on, Trish, you can do this.* She reached into her briefcase and secured the only file folder that actually contained anything.

Both his smile and the light in his eyes faded, and he motioned toward the conference table next to the bank of windows. "Okay. Let's have a look."

Trish stepped to the table, her business heels tapping against the wooden floors. She lowered herself to the padded, metal-frame chair and opened the folder of house plans she'd found online, avoiding eye contact and holding herself ramrod straight. "I believe we discussed a reception room, conference room, and office space, with living quarters in the back?"

"And a basement." His eyes bored through her with unyielding scrutiny.

She angled her head away. "I found plans that offer a few different options. In this one, the parking would be located on the side—"

"What's going on?"

Trish looked at him. Big mistake. She lowered her gaze. "I-I don't know what you mean. I'm here to discuss the plans for your new office. In this one, you could—"

He pounded his palm over the papers in front of her, blocking them from view. "Is this the way it's going to be between us now?"

"What do you mean?"

"Little chilly in here, don't you think?"

She hoisted her chin and looked him square in the eye. "I think it's for the best for us to keep a certain professional distance."

"Why?" His sea-green eyes and thrust-out jaw challenged her. "Is this about what happened the other night?"

Trish glanced down at her twisting hands. Would he have kissed her had it not been for the incident with Bo? "Yes."

"Look at me."

She repositioned her business mask, swallowed, and faced him.

His gaze searched every square inch of her face, then came to a standstill at her eyes, holding them until she was forced to look away.

"I see." Andy bolted to his feet, muttering something about impossible women, while he raked a hand through his wheat-colored curls. Then he strode to a window and stared out, one hand on his hip, the opposite elbow propped against the rusty brick wall. After a moment, he released a heavy sigh and lowered his head. "I don't understand." His voice softened, and he trudged back to his chair and sat, elbows on knees, facing her. "We never got to finish our conversation the other night. I'm not trying to stick my nose where it doesn't belong. I only want to help."

"We've been through this before."

"Yes, but it's a little more serious this time, don't you think?"

"My point exactly." She took a deep breath, her stomach churning. Best to just lay it out in the open. "I appreciate all you've done for Bo. He adores you."

"But?"

"But I don't think it's wise to have any more episodes like the other night."

"Episodes? What does that mean?" His face hardened. "I thought we had a lovely evening in spite of how it ended. I enjoyed spending time with both of you."

Trish pushed her chair away from the table with a scraping sound and stood, crossing her arms. From this vantage point she could see the pecan and oak trees encircling the town square gazebo.

Andy eased over to her, and rested a shoulder against the brick wall. "You're afraid. I understand that. It's scary for me, too."

She faced him, her anger on the rise. "So what if I'm afraid? I have a right to be. I have a little boy to protect."

His eyes registered shock. And then hurt. "You actually believe I'd do anything to harm him?"

"Not intentionally." Trish forced herself to calm down. Getting emotional wouldn't solve anything. "You saw how he was with you the other night, before . . ." She couldn't make her mouth form the words. "He hasn't been like that with anyone, not even Steve, since Doc died. Somehow you're replacing his daddy."

Andy pursed his lips, his eyes soft with concern. "Trish, I'm not trying to take your husband's place. I'm trying to help Bo cope with his loss."

"Why?"

He looked down quickly. A little too quickly. "Because someone made a big difference in my life when I was his age." The words hinted at past pain.

"Is that why you were asking all those questions about Bo and horses?"

"I grew up around horses. There's a connection with them that's hard to explain or duplicate. It's like they can sense what humans are going through."

The trees across the street billowed in the stiff spring wind. She understood exactly what he meant. "I know. I grew up with them, too." She inhaled slowly, then released the breath. "But since the accident, I can't . . ." Memories of the day attacked with fresh intensity.

Andy put a hand on her arm. "You okay?"

She nodded. Another lie. Would there ever come a time when the horrific scenes from the accident didn't haunt her? When she no longer saw the horse's hooves connect with Doc's skull, or her husband crumple to the ground, his face covered with blood? Her bottom lip quivered.

With one hand on her back, Andy guided her to the table and pulled out a chair for her. He continued to stand and leaned against the conference table with his legs and arms crossed. "When I lived in Dallas, I volunteered at a horse farm that specialized in equine therapy for troubled kids. I saw firsthand what it did for them, and I believe it might be just the thing to help Bo. I'd like your permission to take him horseback riding."

Had he not heard a word she'd said? She folded her arms across her waist and watched a lone gray cloud float across an otherwise blue sky.

"I'll take things slow at first, just having him around me while I look at the horses. Then I'll have him help me groom a horse, and—"

Enough. She'd heard enough. Her palms hit the table, and she pushed her chair away. "It still comes down to the same thing, Andy. He's going to get more and more attached to you."

"What's wrong with that?"

"I'm his mother."

"I know. I'm not trying to take him away from you." He yanked out a chair and sat, his eyes scouring her face, as if he'd stumbled across new information or had a sudden flash of clarity. "This isn't about him, is it? It's about us."

Her heartbeat thudded in her ears. He couldn't be right. Was she afraid of letting him get too close? *Oh.*

The left side of his mouth curved upward and created a one-sided, winking dimple. "I'm right, aren't I?" His tone held wonder.

Trish swallowed the cotton in her mouth. No more beating about the bush. It was time to set the matter straight once and for all. "You've been wonderful to us, Andy, and I appreciate it more than you'll ever know. But I love my husband. Still. With all that I am." She paused to allow her brain to catch up with her mouth. "You heard Carla's comment about us the other night. I'm sure other people in town are thinking the same thing. It's way too soon for me to even think about life with a different man, especially with my son to consider."

Andy hung his head, his fingers laced in front of him.

She sensed his hurt. "Please say something."

"What am I supposed to say? I understand where you're coming from. I really do. But I want to get to know you better and to spend time with you."

Trish turned toward the table, straightened the mussed papers, and closed the folder of building plans. "I work for you, Andy. You're my son's T-ball coach. That's it." She hated that her words sounded so cold and uncaring, but she didn't know how to put it any other way.

"So you're saying no to the horse therapy idea?"

"Yes." She handed him the folder, grabbed her briefcase, and stood. "You can look through these on your own. If none of them work, let me know, and I'll keep searching." She strode to the door.

Just as she reached it, he spoke. "Let me ask you something before you go."

She pivoted, the look on his face causing her stomach to cinch. "What?"

"Have you prayed about this? Or is this a move you're making on your own?"

Fair question, but one she had no intention of answering.

13

Andy gulped down the rest of his Dr. Pepper, then crumpled the aluminum can one-handed, his gaze trained on Trish's receding back. From the baseball field behind him rang out the laughter and chatter of happy-go-lucky boys anticipating the advent of summer.

But not Bo.

Alone in the dugout, thumb in his mouth, he hunched over, a little old man in a five-year-old's body.

Pain knifed Andy's heart. How much longer was Trish going to avoid him? Couldn't she see Bo was worse? He let out an exasperated breath and strode to the dugout. The last thing he wanted to do was pressure her, but they were losing precious time.

"How's it going, slugger?" He tugged at the bill of Bo's baseball cap and plopped down on the bench beside him.

Bo gave no acknowledgement. He stared blankly at the field, a wall the size of Fenway Park between them.

"You ready to field some balls?"

Again he said nothing.

Andy scratched his neck, his frustration building. The second night this week Bo refused to talk to him. Refused to talk to anyone. Refused to take part in practice. They were losing him, and it was Trish's fault. Her and her stupid pride.

A crunch of metal sounded behind him, and Andy jerked his head in the direction of the crash. Trish! He bolted to his feet and sprinted to the parking lot.

By the time he reached her, she'd already climbed from her Suburban to survey the damage. She hurried over to Carla Clark. "I'm so sorry. I didn't even see you."

"It helps if you check your rearview mirror. Just look what you've done to my pickup!" Her face livid red, Carla muttered a profanity, kicked at the dirt, and sent a shower of gravel thudding into the grass.

The 1980's model GMC pickup, its bed rusted out, now boasted a caved-in passenger side door, while Trish's back bumper looked none the worse for wear. But considering the age and appearance of the pickup, Carla's fury seemed unwarranted. Besides, the pickup's dent coordinated so well with the crumpled tailgate held in place with a bungee cord.

A keening wail sounded behind him, and Bo dashed past him and latched onto Trish's legs with a death grip.

She freed herself from his grasp, knelt, and engulfed him in a hug. "Shh, honey. I'm okay."

Carla muscled her way over, her hands clenched into fists. "Hope you have insurance."

"I'll see that your pickup is repaired." Trish managed a calm façade, but she blinked hard several times, and her voice wavered.

A minute later, Carla's pickup tore from the parking lot, exhaust fumes in its wake, the lack of a muffler roaring her rage.

Trish ushered Little Bo to the backseat of the Suburban and buckled his seatbelt. "I'm taking Bo home." She refused eye contact as she spoke, then shut the door and moved to the driver's side.

Oh no, she wasn't getting away that easy. He scooted in front of the Suburban and rested a hand on the door handle. "You've gotta do something about this, Trish. He's getting worse."

"We have a doctor's appointment tomorrow."

Andy lowered his hand and moved out of the way. Good. At least she was taking a step in the right direction. "Let me come and ask about the horses."

"No."

"Why not?"

Trish didn't answer or even look at him. Just climbed into the front seat and slammed the door behind her, then started the engine and drove away.

The Thursday night practice ran slower than molasses in wintertime, and Andy struggled to keep his focus. His team needed his attention, but neither his mind nor his heart would cooperate. Every part of him longed to run after Trish and shake some sense into her. How could she not see how desperate the situation was?

Finally, practice ended. His stomach grumbled from lack of food, but there was only one thing on his mind. This had to be settled. Now.

Fifteen minutes later, he pulled into her driveway. *God give me the words to say. Help me get through to her.* He strode to the front door and rang the door bell, then pounded. She'd have to answer eventually.

Trish cracked the door a minute later, her eyes swollen and red, and her cheeks damp.

His heart crumpled. He yanked open the storm door and pulled her into his arms where she clung to him and cried.

When her tears were spent, she pulled away. "I'm sorry. I have no right to—to—"

"To cry in my arms?"

She nodded feebly, then lowered her head.

He grabbed her hand, led her to the family room, and eased onto the sofa next to her. "Where's Bo?"

Trish pressed her lips together, her eyes round and sad. "In bed."

Alarm skittered down his backbone. "Already? It's only seven. Did he eat?"

She shook her head. "I tried. He wouldn't eat anything." Her eyes closed slowly, the tears returning. "What am I gonna do?"

He stretched out a hand, lifted her chin, and stared into tear-filled eyes. "You're gonna get through this. Both of you. But you've got to stop being so stubborn. Please let me help."

Her face contorted, and she struggled to maintain control, but said nothing.

"What time is your doctor's appointment?"

"Three. In Morganville." Trish snatched a tissue from a nearby box and wiped her face and nose, then hunched over, her arms wrapped tightly around her waist. "I usually pick him up from school a few minutes early."

"Let me drive you and talk to the doctor."

Doubt waged war on her features. After a long minute, she gave her head a defeated nod and released a breath, her face so full of sorrow it shredded his heart.

Thank You, Lord. He raised a finger and brushed away a stray tear that wandered down her cheek.

As they entered Dr. Wyse's office, Trish tucked Little Bo's hand in hers and gave it a gentle squeeze. The room was designed with kids in mind, with toys, books, kid-sized tables, and bean bags, but well-organized and lit with sunshine. Soft, soothing music and a vanilla-scented candle made it a womb-like place, safe and comforting.

The kind-faced woman met them at the door. "Hi, Trish." She knelt in front of Bo, her eyes instantly concerned. "He's worse?"

Guilt punched Trish in the gut. Maybe she should've called to let her know he'd had a setback. She stepped aside to allow Andy in the room. "Dr. Wyse, this is a friend of ours, Andy Tyler."

The doctor stood and stretched out a hand. "Nice to meet you, Mr. Tyler. Why don't we all have a seat?"

"Andy is Bo's T-ball coach, and he has a few questions." Trish rushed through her carefully-rehearsed spiel as they made their way to the leather office chairs.

"Okay. First let's see if we can find a special toy for Bo to play with, and then you can fire away."

The woman, clad in a flowing dress that depicted Noah's Ark, laid a gentle hand on Bo's back and guided him to the toys. She offered several alternatives, but he refused each one, until she handed him . . . *a stuffed horse*. He tucked it under his arm and plopped down on a beanbag.

Trish shifted in the chair and shot a quick glance at Andy. His eyes didn't hold the I-told-you-so look she'd expected.

Dr. Wyse made her way back. "Okay, now for your questions."

He cleared his throat. "I'd like to introduce Bo to equine therapy. I used to volunteer at the Sunnyvale Ranch near Dallas."

"I've heard of that ministry. They do great work." She edged forward and crossed her arms on the desk. "What is your relationship to Bo?"

"Just a friend."

Trish shook her head. "No. He's more than a friend. Bo looks up to him like a father figure. Which leads to my next question. Is Bo's attachment to Andy healthy?"

"It's actually healthier to have a father figure than to not have one."

Not what she wanted to hear. She brought a hand up to brush back her hair. How was she supposed to encourage Bo to have a relationship with someone without losing herself? "Really?"

Dr. Wyse stared at her a long moment then flicked her attention to Andy. "Do you have a family of your own, Mr. Tyler?"

"No, ma'am, but I'm concerned about Bo." He stopped and looked at Trish, his eyes sincere. "And Trish. I want to help."

"I see." Dr. Wyse peered her way again then lowered her gaze, an understanding smile on her lips. "I think that's very noble of you, Mr. Tyler. Of course, if Trish has problems with it, then maybe it's not for the best."

Andy's mouth opened halfway. "I don't understand." His tone held hurt.

"Bo is very tuned-in to Trish's emotions right now. If he senses any doubt toward a person in her, he picks up on it." She tapped her nails against the desk then addressed Trish. "But you also need to consider the positive impact a father figure and the horse therapy might have on Bo's life."

Her body went numb and her thoughts tangled—a long lasso looped with knots. She'd do anything—*anything*—to help her son. Even if it meant losing her heart. "So you think horse riding would help?"

Dr. Wyse gazed at Little Bo, who stared out the window, the furry pony on his lap. "I don't know if you've noticed, but he's chosen the horse the last few times. Have you noticed any other attachment to horses?"

Trish's skin tingled. *The book*. Andy's soft green eyes focused on her. "Y-yes. He has a horse book his father used to read to him at night. He chose that book for Andy to read to him not long ago."

A crinkle appeared between the woman's eyes. "It could be he's subconsciously trying to tell us something. Children can't always verbalize what they're feeling, so they find other ways to tell us." Dr. Wyse pursed her lips for a moment, one hand on her mouth, seemingly deep in thought. "Does Bo like to draw?"

"Yes."

"I'd like to try something new today." Dr. Wyse stood and moved to the child-sized table near Bo, motioning for Andy and Trish to follow. She eased into a seat and patted the chair next to her. "Bo, why don't you join us? We're going to draw."

He plodded to the chair, the plush horse still squeezed under one arm. The doctor passed out blank paper to all of them, the pages whispering against the bright yellow tabletop. "Today I want us to draw a picture of something we'd really like, even if it's something that makes us afraid."

An array of colored pencils and crayons lay in baskets in the center of the table. Bo grabbed a green crayon and started drawing, the only sounds the background music and his crayon scratching against the surface of the paper and table.

Andy snatched up two pencils. Their eyes met as he held one toward Trish, and an unexplainable force tugged at her heart. She took the pencil and lowered her gaze to the blank sheet of paper, her throat like a vise. What if nothing came out? What if she couldn't do this anymore?

Within a few seconds, the blank paper sucked her in the way an empty canvas had once lured and beckoned. She abandoned herself to the joyful urge and drew without thinking, only stopping long enough to pick up other colored pencils, her ears tuned to the conversation between Dr. Wyse and Bo.

"Tell me what you're drawing, Bo." The woman's voice was soothing and calm, like the musical trickle of the creek after a spring rain.

"It's my horse, Domino."

Trish's heart pounded faster, but she forced her eyes to her paper, afraid she'd shatter the tenuous moment.

"You have your own horse?"

"Yep. Daddy and Mommy bought him last year for my birthday." His voice took on an excitement and eagerness—almost a hunger—Trish hadn't heard in such a long time.

"I bet you like to ride Domino, don't you?"

He didn't answer right away. "I love to ride him, but I haven't ridden in a long, long, long, long time." Now his voice was sad.

Trish swallowed the tears lodged in her throat, and glanced up at Bo's pallid face. Andy had his gaze trained on her son, too, his eyes oozing love and compassion.

"Does riding Domino again make you afraid?" Dr. Wyse's voice was non-threatening, and she continued to sketch.

Bo didn't answer with words, but nodded, his brow furrowed with wavy wrinkles.

"Are you afraid he'll kick you?"

Thick heavy lines now crossed his paper, his agitation stabbing so hard Trish's left fist clenched in her lap, her fingernails scooping into soft flesh. She opened her mouth to speak, but Andy laid his hand on her arm and shook his head.

Dr. Wyse repeated the question, a little softer.

The chubby crayon fell from Bo's hand, clattering to the table. He slumped in his chair, shoulders sagging. "I'm afraid it'll make Mommy more sadder."

Immediate tears spilled down Trish's cheeks. Andy encircled her shoulders with a strong arm.

"Bo," Dr. Wyse knelt in front of her son, forcing eye contact. "Would you like it if Andy took you riding?"

Bo looked at Trish, his dark eyes holding an odd mixture of sorrow and hope. "Only if it's okay with Mom."

"Of course, it's okay, sweetie." Trish reached across the table to caress his cheek. "I know how much you love Domino."

Bo nodded, a small smile on his lips. "Yep, but not more than I love you."

Tears flowing freely, Trish leapt from her chair and engulfed him in a hug. She snuggled into his warmth, her lips against his baby-shampoo-scented hair. "I love you, too, sweetie, and I'm glad you and Andy are going to ride horses together. Domino misses you."

Bo pulled away, his chocolate eyes searching hers. "You'll come with us, won't you Mom? Can we go when we get home?"

Trish didn't know how to answer. She had no desire to ride again. *Ever.*

Andy came to her rescue. "We'll talk about it on the ride home."

"Thanks for drawing such a beautiful picture and telling us how much you love horses." Dr. Wyse patted Bo's back. "Would you mind going out to the waiting room with Andy? I think Miss Judy probably has a treat for you. I'd like to talk to your Mom alone for a few minutes."

"'kay." He hopped from the chair, clutched Andy's hand and tugged him toward the door, his expression bright. A complete turnaround in such a short time. If only she could bounce back like that.

Trish used fingertips to wipe away tears and followed Dr. Wyse to the leather chairs.

The woman scooted a box of tissues across the desk. "That was a major breakthrough for Bo. I feel certain the horse-riding will be good for him. There's a lot of truth to the adage about dusting yourself off and getting back on the horse."

"I agree."

Dr. Wyse eyed her knowingly. "Now I want to talk about you."

"Me?" Trish's eyes widened, and she rubbed her bare arms. "Okay."

"Don't feel guilty that Bo's reason for not wanting to ride horses had to do with you. It just shows how much he loves you."

Trish nodded, blinking back more tears that flooded the never-ending reservoir flowing beneath the surface.

"Do you trust Andy with your son?"

"Yes."

"Do you think he's a good role model and a good person?"

"Without a doubt." Where was she going with this line of questions?

"Then what are you afraid of?" The woman pushed a paper across the desk—the drawing she'd done while she listened to Bo and Dr. Wyse.

Her pulse pounded and she blinked. Hard. She'd meant to draw someone else. How could this have happened? She studied the picture. Bo. Herself. Both with smiles on their faces. But the part that bothered her was the third person in the sketch.

A man.

Not a man with a cowboy hat and handlebar moustache, but a man with sea-green eyes and sandy curls. She knit her eyebrows together.

"Trish, what about this picture makes you afraid?"

"I-I didn't mean to draw that. It doesn't mean anything."

Dr. Wyse didn't respond immediately, a silence that seemed to stretch with insinuation. Then the woman's head cocked to one side and her face took on kindness. "You don't have to experience guilt if you have feelings for this man. It's normal to care about someone who cares for you and your child."

"B-but Doc's only been dead a few months."

"The fact that it's only been a few months doesn't make it any less final. Your husband's not coming back."

In a daze, Trish slowly rose to her feet and turned her back, one arm encircling her waist, one shaky hand on her lips. "It just seems so wrong."

"It's not wrong to have feelings of love for another person. Wrong comes with how we express it." She hesitated briefly. "Or fail to express it."

Love? Was she falling in love with Andy, or was it only admiration and gratitude? She swallowed and forced the question from her mind. "But what if . . .?"

"What if it doesn't work out?" Dr. Wyse drifted from behind the desk with a smile, and placed a hand on Trish's shoulder. "That's a chance we take in our interactions with others every day. The real question is what if you allowed your guilt and fear to keep you from a relationship that has the potential to be wonderful? Not only for you, but for your son?"

Andy's paper still rested on the sunshine yellow table. One glance and her heart sank.

Blank.

14

"Don't you think a paying job is a prerequisite to a marriage proposal?" Andy intentionally huffed out the words. How could Matt ask for more money in one breath and casually mention asking his girlfriend to marry him the next?

"Chill, bro. I didn't say I was gonna ask her tomorrow." A defensive hurt resonated in Matt's tone.

The bat bag slammed against the concrete floor of the dugout, the metallic clink of the chain link fence rattling in reply. Matt's news wasn't what bothered him and he knew it.

"Are *you* doing okay?"

Andy had to grin at Matt's turnaround question. He ran a hand down the back of his neck. "Yeah, I'm okay. Just busy and tired." He had nothing to complain about. Business was better than expected, but loneliness had loomed over him all week. What good was a successful practice if he had no one to share it with?

Matt continued. "You haven't sounded this cranky in like forever, dude. Maybe I should come for a visit."

Andy chuckled. "Sounds good, but you might wanna wait 'til I have a place for you to sleep. My little apartment barely holds me."

"And how long will that be?"

His brother's words immediately sobered him. Good question. "The contractor was supposed to break ground today, but we've had a lot of rain this week." So much rain that he still hadn't taken Bo riding, and ball practice had to be canceled. He'd missed Bo and Trish something awful, but knew better than to push. Trish needed her space, and he didn't need to butt in on their private family time. "The ground-breaking has been postponed 'til next week, provided everything dries out."

The wooden bleachers groaned beneath the burgeoning crowd, and jabbering little boys threatened to climb the chain link fence around the dugout. "Hate to cut this short, Matt, but the game's about to start. Do me a favor. Don't propose 'til I've at least had a chance to meet the girl."

Matt laughed, short and forced. "Got it, bro. Hope y'all win. Talk to you later."

Andy hit the end call button on his cell phone just as Brody Clark swaggered into the dugout. It took every ounce of willpower he had to be civil to the kid. He'd missed more practices than the rest of the kids combined. Figured that he'd show up for the first game. *Lord, give me patience and wisdom.*

Trish rounded the gate of the dugout lugging a tall cooler. Her sleek pony tail poked through the back of her purple Legal Eagles baseball cap.

Something about her seemed . . . mended. "Here. Let me get that." He grabbed the heavy cooler and set it on the end of the bench. Something sloshed. "What's in it?"

"Water for the kids." She flashed a brilliant smile.

Of course. Why hadn't he thought of it? As the summer heat and humidity escalated, he'd need to bring drinks to practice as well. "Have any cups?"

"No, but I'll head to the concession stand to see if they have some we can borrow."

Andy reached for his wallet and handed her a five. "If not, maybe they'll let us buy some."

She took the money and pivoted, looking back over her shoulder with a grin. "Yeah, leave me to do all the grunt work."

He laughed, his heart suddenly light.

Bo perched on the bench away from Brody. "Hey, buddy, how was school today?"

Bo glanced at Brody with wary eyes. "Fine."

Yeah, right. Knowing Brody, he was probably still causing playground problems. "Sorry we didn't get to go horse-back riding earlier this week."

"It's okay. You can't help it when it rains."

Andy grinned and pushed the bill of Bo's hat down to his nose. "True. How 'bout tomorrow?"

Bo giggled. "You'll have to ask Mom. If I ask, she'll say no." He craned his head way back to view Andy from underneath his cap.

"Mmm, good point." Andy scratched his chin. "She'll probably tell me no, too, come to think of it. We'll have to put our heads together to figure that one out."

"Figure what out?" Trish tapped him on the shoulder.

He rotated, and she deposited the change in his hands, a sleeve of cups under one arm. "I . . . I mean we, well, uh . . . Bo and I want to go horseback riding tomorrow. Wanna come?"

Her eyes lost a bit of spark. She pressed her lips together, and her shoulders rose as she inhaled a deep breath. "Okay, but only . . ." Trish stared at Bo with mock sternness. ". . . only if he finishes his homework."

"Aw, Mom."

"Hey, bud, she's right. Homework comes first."

"Yeah, but it's hard. It's gonna take me fifty one-hundred million years."

Laughter exploded from him. "Sounds like we need to work on your numbers." Andy squatted in front of him. "Tell you what.

In the morning I'll bring donuts. We'll do your homework, then go for a ride. How's that sound?"

Bo brightened. His whole body shook like a puppy with his tail a-wag. "All right! Homework help, donuts, *and* horseback riding!"

Trish sent Andy a smile that warmed him from the inside out. Did she have any idea how gorgeous she was? *Stop it, Andy.* He repositioned his cap. She still loved her husband. The sketch she'd drawn at Dr. Wyse's office—a man with an arm wrapped protectively around her and Bo—proved it. He had no right to intrude on the memories of her dead husband. She needed time. Time to grieve. Time to heal.

He rubbed a hand across his mouth. Why did it always come down to more waiting?

The kids' excitement was contagious, and Andy soon forgot his earlier bad mood. He sauntered to the field, hands on hips, and took it all in. Nothing like a baseball game, especially opening night—a pleasant spring night, the tantalizing aroma of buttered popcorn, happy laughter.

Families.

The ache in his heart intensified. How long before he had a family? He heaved a heavy sigh. Better just face facts. It might never happen.

Finally the game got underway, with the Legal Eagles up to bat. Joey sent a line drive up the middle, right to the pitcher, who ducked. Somehow the kid managed to knock the ball down with his glove, then bobbled it a couple of times. That gave Joey the chance he needed to make it to first.

Little Bo, second in the lineup, hit a grounder to third. He raced to first base as fast as his little legs would carry him, his face a picture of unswerving determination. Trish cheered him on from the dugout.

As Bo's foot hit the base, pride swelled in Andy's heart. "Atta boy, Bo!"

Bo punched a fist into the air, his face plastered with a giant grin.

The Pirate's third baseman overthrew the ball and it rolled to the fence near the dugout. Joey had stopped on second, but instead of watching the game, now waved and chatted to his friends in the outfield. Bo stepped off first, but waited for Andy to tell him what to do.

"Joey, take third!" Andy cupped his hands around his mouth and yelled. Joey raised both arms in question. "Take it to third base!"

The boy peered down at the rubber mat base, scratched his head, then yanked up the base and sprinted toward third.

Heat climbed up Andy's chest and onto his neck and face, the crowd roaring with laughter.

Then, as if things weren't bad enough, the Pirate's first baseman trotted back with the ball and tagged Bo, whose foot was still off the base. *Off the base!*

"You're out!" hollered the ump. He yanked a thumb over his shoulder. The crowd hooted even louder.

The Pirate's first baseman taunted Bo, then laughed about it with the right fielder.

Bo's little face grew red with anger. He stomped a foot and pushed the kid to the ground.

The crowd "ooh"-ed, then immediately grew quiet.

The umpire stomped down the first base line, his lips clamped. Andy fell in line behind him, his frustration mounting. The ump stopped short of Little Bo. "We won't put up with that kind of behavior!" He pivoted and lumbered back to home plate.

Andy crossed his arms and glared at Bo. "We're *not* gonna have that on this team! You're on the bench for two innings."

Bo gaped at him, tears flooding his eyes. "But . . ."

His heart crumpled, but he had no choice. "Sorry, Bo. We'll talk about this later. Take the bench."

Crying, Bo stumbled past him to the dugout, where Trish met him with open arms. "It's okay, honey, don't cry." She fired Andy a mother-bear glare.

Brody started in on Bo. "Quit 'cher cryin', you little baby."

"Brody!" Andy's voice sounded sharper than he intended. "You're up."

The beefiest kid on the team, Brody grabbed a long bat and sauntered to the tee. He made solid contact on the first swing, the air splitting with the crack. The ball sailed into the outfield.

Much to the crowd's delight and amusement, the center fielder for the Pirates bent to scoop up the ball and lost his cap. Instead of throwing in the ball, he removed his glove, picked up the cap and dusted it off, then put it on his head, his coach about to bust a gut near third base.

Brody easily made it around the bases, and Carla's hoots and hollers sounded from beyond the chain link fence.

Andy gave him a high five as he passed. "Way to go, Brody! That's how to do it." As he turned to pat Brody on the back, a searing ache pierced his heart. Little Bo hunched over at the end of the bench, tears dripping from his chin. Trish was nowhere to be seen.

Two seconds earlier Trish had been happy. Happy that her life—that Little Bo's life—had made a turn for the better.

Now this.

Trish stood under the rickety bleachers, empty popcorn boxes and drink cups at her feet, and swiped at angry tears. The sounds of the game—of people having fun—boomed above. Why had Andy yanked Bo from the game? Yes, Bo had shoved the kid and shouldn't have, but Andy had come down on him way too hard. Crushed him.

Carla's immediate hurtful words, now on auto-rewind, replayed in her mind. "If you'd quit babying him, maybe he'd stop sucking his thumb."

A fresh round of pain sliced through her. *Enough.* Trish wiped tear-dampened hands on her blue jean shorts and marched to the bathroom to wash her face. She'd sit out the rest of the game in the stands.

When she returned to the bleachers ten minutes later, the scoreboard revealed a three-run lead for the Eagles, with the Pirates now at bat. Little Bo hunkered down in the dugout, arms across his chest, his bottom lip poked out in a pout. Andy knelt in front of him, his voice so low she couldn't make out the words. She resisted the urge to scramble down the bleachers and give him a piece of her mind. Instead, she gulped in a deep breath and released it through her nose.

The Eagles kept the Pirates from scoring during the first two innings, further proof that Andy knew how to coach. Bo's next turn at bat rolled around and her stomach lurched. Two outs and the bases loaded.

Bo trotted to the batter's box. He carefully lined up the bat with the ball the way Andy had showed him and swung as hard as he could. The bat hit rubber and sent the ball spiraling to the dirt.

"That's okay, sweetie!" Trish clapped her hands. "You'll get it next time!"

On the second swing, the bat sliced through nothing but air.

"C'mon! My grandpa can swing better than that!" Carla's voice sounded from near the dugout.

Trish's blood boiled as Bo's shoulders slumped. People seated nearby craned their necks toward her, but she kept her mask in place, retreating behind the safety of her sunshades.

"Take your time, Bo!" Andy called from the dugout. "You can do it, buddy!"

On the third swing, Bo made contact, and the ball tumbled down the first base line, Bo right behind it. The pitcher for the other team scooped up the ball and tagged Bo. *With a little too much force!*

"Yeah, he got 'em. That's three!" The ump yanked a thumb over his shoulder.

Bo fell to the ground, and the other boy towered over him, his curled lips in an inaudible taunt.

She jumped to her feet and held her breath. *Don't do it, Bo.*

To her relief, he stood, dusted himself off, and hurried to pick up the bat.

Trish plopped to the wooden seat, brought her hands to her face, and released a grateful sigh as Bo's teammates scattered from the dugout to their various positions. Well, all of them except Bo.

Like a weary hunter returning empty-handed, he drug the bat in the dirt as he trudged to the dugout. Andy rushed to him. Whatever he said lit a spark in her son, and he disappeared into the dugout. A few seconds later he appeared, cap slightly askew, and hustled to first base. He slapped his glove as the first batter for the other team approached the tee, and began to chant: "Hey, batter, batter, batter, batter."

Carla Clark's grating voice floated to her ears from nearby, where she stood with a group of her friends. "The only reason Bo is playing first base is 'cause Trish is Coach's girlfriend. He's only using her son to get to her."

Rage crawled from the pit of her stomach, clawing its way to the surface. Was it true? Did Andy have ulterior motives?

After the comment, focusing on the game proved impossible, her gaze continually vacillating between Andy and her son. In spite of the earlier incident, Bo still thought the world of Andy, evidenced by the way he jumped through hoops to please him. Dr. Wyse had mentioned that a father figure would be good for him, but couldn't Dad or Steve fill that role instead?

Trish shook her head. Her father's health prevented him from doing many things little boys needed to do, and Steve was a newlywed. His responsibility was to Dani, not her. For whatever reason, Bo had chosen Andy. But how was she supposed to deal with the fact?

Familiar voices sounded from the bottom of the bleachers. Steve and Dani, with Dad and Mama Beth in tow, ascended the steps. They took up the empty seats beside her, Steve scooted close, his long legs folded at an odd angle to fit in the cramped space. "Sorry we're late, Sis. We went out to eat and got held up at the restaurant."

Out to eat? Why hadn't they invited her and Bo? Her mood morphed from sour to surly. Funny how her family always had time for Mama Beth, but not her. And it was happening more and more often. Almost as if the woman had taken her place. "Mama Beth went?"

Steve nodded, his eyes shaded by his cowboy hat. "Yeah. Something wrong?"

She bit back a retort and looked back to the field.

"So how's Bo doing?" Her brother glanced to first base, where Bo stood, hands on knees.

A snort escaped before she could contain it. "All right, if you don't count Andy yanking him out of the game."

Steve's dark brows shot up his forehead. "What happened?"

"Bo barely touched the Pirate's first baseman earlier and Andy sat him on the bench."

"Good."

Trish whirled her head around. "What?"

"Sis, Andy had no choice. If he let Bo get by with it, the other boys would follow suit. Not to mention what everyone would be saying about you and Andy."

She let the words sink in and heaved a sigh. He was right. Andy did have to correct Bo, but he didn't have to do it in anger. There would still be an after-game discussion.

Trish tried to force the incident from her mind, but thoughts and images kept wiggling their way in and sucked the enjoyment from the rest of the game. The other four, on the other hand, enjoyed themselves immensely with continued conversation and laughter. So much so, that by the time the game ended, Trish was relieved she didn't have to be around them anymore.

She descended the steps with them and said goodbye, then watched as they ambled to the overflowing parking lot. A frown puckered her eyebrows. Was something going on between Dad and Mama Beth? Surely not. Mom had only been gone nine months. A sour taste deposited itself on her tongue.

Trish swallowed against it and made her way to the dugout to get Little Bo. He met her at the gate. "We won our first game!" Tendrils of sweaty hair framed his lit-from-within face.

"I know. Good for you!" She gave him a hug, his smell worse than a wet puppy. "Don't forget you get a free snow cone."

"First I have to help Andy clean the dugout."

Trish stiffened. "Why do you have to clean it?"

"'Cause I shoved a boy."

She forcefully straightened her fingers to keep them from curling into fists. "I see."

Andy glanced up at her terse words. "Something wrong?"

"We'll discuss it when Bo goes for his snow cone." *And then some.*

Bo attacked the trash strewn around the dugout, and two minutes later the area sparkled.

Andy patted his back and smiled. "Thanks, buddy. You did a great job. Better hustle after that snow cone." He faced Trish with crossed arms, his expression grim. "Ready for that discussion?"

Trish waited until Little Bo moved out of ear shot. "You had no right to jump on him earlier. What he did was wrong, but you responded in anger. He trusted you, and you hurt his feelings."

"I wasn't angry. I was frustrated and probably came across a little harsher than I intended. I already apologized."

Like an apology was enough. "And then you made him sit the bench *and* clean the dugout?"

He nodded, his jaw muscle pulsing.

"Overkill, don't you think?"

"No, I don't think." Andy hesitated, then released a sigh. "Look, I can't let the guys get away with that kind of behavior. I didn't want to come down on him, but I had no choice. I would've done the same with any of them, and I couldn't show Bo any favoritism."

Trish shifted her weight to her right leg. "In case you've forgotten, a few months ago he lost his father. And you, of all people, should know how fragile he is right now. Don't you think you could've given him a little bit of a break?"

"Not when it comes to his behavior." He picked up the bat bag and swung it over his shoulder. "Don't make excuses for him, Trish. You're not doing him any favors."

"I'm not making excuses for him. You have no idea what it's like not to have a father."

His expression grew stone cold, and he moved close. Too close. In his eyes a storm brewed. "You know nothin' about me, lady. Nothin'."

The chill in his words pierced like icicles.

He stepped around her and stalked off toward his car.

15

Trish padded from her bedroom the next morning, bleary-eyed. That settled it. No more evening arguments with Andy. Had she slept at all? She raised a hand to rub her forehead while she traveled down the hall toward the sound of way-too-cheery-for-this-early-in-the-morning music. Curled up with his blanket, Bo lay on the couch entranced by a kid video. She lifted his shoulders and eased down on the sofa, cradling his head on her lap. His eyes never left the TV.

His sleepy-little-boy look, complete with rosy cheeks and mussed hair, roused motherly warmth inside her. If only she could keep him from growing up so fast.

"Did you sleep okay, sweetie?"

"Uh-huh." He droned the words.

She could've asked if he'd climbed Mount Everest and his answer would've been the same. Trish picked up the remote and paused the DVD. "Good."

Bo frowned up at her, now fully alert. "What'd you do that for?" he groused.

Trish tweaked his button nose. "'Cause we need to talk. I'll turn it back on later."

"'kay." He flopped on his back and peered up at her with trusting eyes.

"You know you shouldn't have pushed the first-baseman from the other team, right?"

"Yeah." His expression held remorse. "Andy told me that, too. I was just so mad."

"Why?"

He shrugged. "I just get sad and mad a lot."

Her throat cinched. "A lot?"

Bo nodded. "But I don't mean to feel mad."

Trish understood the anger and had felt it in herself more than she wanted to consider. "I get angry, too, Bo. We all do. But we have to learn to control it."

"Were you angry at Brody's mom last night when we left the game?"

"What do you mean?" Trish thought back to the night before. She *had* been angry with Carla over her mean-spirited comments. Obviously, Bo had sensed it.

"She smiled at you, and you just walked right past. Were you mad?"

Trish sighed. Nothing like having to admit your shortcomings to a five-year-old, especially when you were calling *his* behavior into question. "Yes, I was mad, but I was wrong to act that way." She gazed into the dark eyes that reminded her so much of her own. "Tell you what. From now on, let's both remember to count to ten before we act in ways we shouldn't. We'll count when we start feeling angry."

"'kay." He smiled, an impish grin that skewered her heart.

She tousled his silky hair. "Want some cereal for breakfast?"

"Nope, I'm waiting for donuts."

Andy. She'd forgotten his promise to bring donuts. Would he still come after their disagreement? "Mmm, sweetie, I don't know if Andy will come or not."

"Why?"

Trish searched for words—words that would most likely ruin his day. "I was a little angry with Andy last night, too."

Bo bolted upright and glared at her. "Did you forget to count to ten?"

She tried to hide a smile by pressing her lips together. "Yes, but I'll call him later to apologize."

He flopped back against her lap, his face sullen. "Great. No donuts, homework help, *or* horses."

Pangs of guilt swept over her as she clicked the DVD back to play mode. Why did everything have to be so complicated? She eased up from her position, lowered Bo's head to the cushion, and wandered to the front room where she'd set up her easel to take advantage of the morning light. An unfinished canvas adorned the easel, one she'd started after the last visit to Dr. Wyse—the visit where her desire to paint had experienced rebirth.

She strode to the canvas, a sudden and strong longing to reconnect with Doc. Already the arms and chest in the painting were complete. She closed her eyes to recapture the feel of her face pressed to his chest, his arms holding her tight.

Nothing.

Trish opened her eyes, the canvas in full view. His face. She needed to paint Doc's face. Needed to see him again. Needed to remember his loving gaze.

She prepped her palette and fingered a brush, immediately lost in the joy of painting. Why had she given this up? Hastily, she shaped the face and dabbed color for his eyes. Blue. His eyes were blue. So why did they carry a greenish tint? She added more paint to her brush and tried again.

Standing back to view her work, she gasped. The face staring back wasn't Doc at all, but Andy. Fury spread throughout her body, faster than a Texas wildfire. An anguished sob escaped. She grasped her largest brush, immersed it in paint, and attacked the canvas. Angry red and black slashes appeared, then blurred as tears formed in her eyes. Her shoulders shook and the paintbrush clattered to the hardwood floor. She sank to her knees, grateful the TV volume overpowered her sobs.

How long she sat there she didn't know, tears streaming while she stared at the canvas, now a study in rage. The ringing doorbell catapulted her to her feet. She hastily wiped her face and smoothed her hair, then hurried to answer the door.

"I brought donuts!" The fresh-baked smell hit at the same time Andy's cheery voice rang out. He searched her face and frowned, his eyes troubled.

"Donuts!" Little Bo sprinted past and latched onto Andy's legs. "I knew you'd come. Mom said you might not 'cause she forgot to count to ten, but I knew you'd come!"

Andy chuckled and swung him up onto one shoulder. "When Andy says he'll bring donuts, he'll bring donuts, even if Mom did forget to count to ten, whatever that means." He winked at Trish, his dimpled grin cutting through the gloom. His eyes moved past her to the painting. When his gaze returned to her face, it held soft understanding.

"Yay for donuts!" yelled Bo as he punched a fist into the air.

"Yay for donuts *and* homework!" Andy stepped to the dining room and plopped Bo into a chair.

"Not yay for homework." A disgusted look replaced Bo's smile. Uh-oh. Hopefully, Andy was ready for a less-than-pleasant side of Bo—the side he showed when he didn't get his way.

Andy squatted beside Bo, elbows on his knees. "Donuts first, then homework."

Surprisingly, her son grinned back. "'kay. Then horses."

"Horses it is." Andy patted his shoulder and rose. His smile disappeared as he addressed her. "Can I speak to you alone?"

Her pulse ca-thumped in her throat. Oh, how she dreaded this. "S-sure." She traipsed to the family room out of Bo's earshot, Andy right behind her. Trish faced him. "I want to apologize for the way I acted last night."

"No, I'm the one who should apologize. Sorry if I came down too hard." His tone and expression were bathed in humility.

She shook her head. "You didn't. I over-reacted."

"Friends?" He held out a hand and also sent another award-winning grin.

Her heart lightened. Even Attila the Hun couldn't resist that smile. She took his hand. "Friends."

"Want some donuts?"

Trish giggled. "If there are any left. Bo loves donuts."

Andy poked out his belly and patted it. "A man after my own heart."

More laughter rumbled from her throat. "The last I heard, that's not where your heart is."

His smile waned and his eyes flickered. "So true."

Andy's jaw unhinged. Trish moseyed to the table where he and Bo worked on homework. In jeans, t-shirt, boots, and hat in hand, her country girl roots showed through stronger than ever. Seeing her like this made his head spin—a far cry from her usual attire. He rose to his feet. "Looks like you're ready to ride." Why did his mouth cotton like he'd spent all morning in Death Valley heat?

"Yes." She glanced over to where Bo painstakingly finished his handwriting assignment. "Thanks for helping him with his homework. He responds to you so much better than he does me."

"Probably just a guy thing."

Bo hopped from his seat. "I gotta change clothes. I can't ride Domino in my pj's." He sped past them to his room.

Trish faced him, her smile bright against her olive complexion. "I know the horse riding will be good for him, even if I was a bit bullheaded."

"Bullheaded? You?" He sent a teasing grin. "You have an old quilt we could take with us?"

"Yeah, why?" The area between her eyes wrinkled.

"I, er, took the liberty of picking up a few things for lunch, just in case. Thought we could enjoy a picnic while we're out, if that's okay."

Trish's eyes lit. "What a great idea. I'll be right back."

While she hurried after the quilt, Andy headed out to get the food he'd brought for lunch. Good thing he'd thought of the picnic idea, since it gave him another chance to spend time with Trish and get to know her better. To prove he really did care about Bo *and* her. As he sauntered past the front room, the easel and painting stopped him in his tracks.

At least she'd tried to paint again, but from the looks of it, things hadn't gone well. He took in the black and red slashes. *Anger*. Little Bo wasn't the only one dealing with it.

Lord, show me how to help them.

A few minutes later they all strolled toward the horse barn behind the main ranch house, picnic essentials in hand, and Bo chattering happily.

Andy caught Trish's attention and hoisted his eyebrows. "Does he always talk this much?"

"Only when he's excited." The happy lilt to her voice was accompanied by a smile. "I haven't seen him like this in forever. I have you to thank."

"Yeah well, if he keeps this racket up, you may change your mind about thanking me."

The barn smelled of fresh hay and instantly transported Andy to childhood—long summer days at his grandparents' farm—with plenty of hard work, great food, and priceless memories. After they'd saddled the horses, Bo tugged on Andy's hand, his eyes full of fear. "I changed my mind. I don't wanna ride anymore."

Just what he'd expected. Somehow he had to convince him to try, but without pressure. Andy knelt beside him. "I know you're afraid, Bo, but why don't you at least go up to Domino and hold out your hand?"

Bo cowered behind Trish, anything but convinced. "Why?"

"So y'all can get used to each other again. My guess is Domino missed you as much you've missed him."

Bo chewed his lip for a moment, then tentatively approached Domino, his hand outstretched.

Trish inhaled sharply, and Andy rested a hand in the small of her back to calm her doubts. Hopefully, she wouldn't say anything to ruin this chance for Bo to heal.

The paint horse snorted, edged closer to Bo, and nuzzled his shoulder. "Hey, Domino, you missed me?" Her son beamed as he stroked the horse's velvet nose. "Mom, he missed me!"

"I can see that." Her words warbled.

Bo hugged Domino's lowered head and grabbed the reins. "Let's walk first, Domino." Amazing. The kid knew instinctively what to do. He led the horse around the barn, then back to where Trish and Andy waited. "I think I'm ready now."

Andy patted his shoulder, his heart about to burst out of his chest. "Yeah, I think you are, too." He helped him mount and then adjusted the stirrups. "You okay?"

Bo smiled down, a calm confidence exuding from his face. "Yes, sir." He turned a troubled gaze to his mother before heading the horse outdoors.

Trish faced the Palomino mare she called Sandy, her expression wavering.

Bo wasn't the only one walking wounded. Andy moved to her side. "You ready to give this a try?" He tried to keep his tone calm and casual.

She let out a shaky breath. "My head knows its okay, but it's so much harder than I expected."

"Just take it slow and easy like Bo did. You'll be all right."

A few minutes later, she inhaled deeply, released it, and mounted.

A grin spread from his heart to his face. "You look like a rodeo queen."

"That was a very long time ago, maybe even a different lifetime." Her eyes glazed a bit before she peered back down at him. "Just a fair word of warning, city slicker. You'd better saddle up quick, or Bo and I'll leave you in the dust." Trish tugged the reins, nudged the horse with her heels, and trotted out into open sunshine.

Andy didn't hesitate, but mounted and trotted after them. This had the makings of a great day.

An easy-going camaraderie blanketed their time together, Bo happier and more connected than ever as they galloped across open pasture. The change in his demeanor affected Trish as well. She laughed and teased and smiled, the lines normally furrowing her forehead erased.

Trish led her horse into a ravine, Bo on her heels. Immediately the terrain turned from grassy to rocky, and instead of dull thuds, the horses' hooves clip-clopped, stirring ups clouds of dust that infiltrated his nose and mouth. A smoky-blue mesa loomed in the distance.

The family-type outing made his chest tighten and ache. The last thing he wanted was more heartbreak, but for today—for this brief, joy-filled day—he'd allow himself the possibility of how life with them at his side might play out.

At lunchtime they located a grove of trees for their picnic. While Bo chased baby frogs near the creek, Trish spread out the blanket, and Andy retrieved the food from the knapsack. He lowered himself to the heavy quilt and pulled items from the bag. "Chips, soda pop, chicken, and my personal favorite, chocolate chip cookies."

Trish sat beside him. "Looks like you've thought of everything." She spoke softly, a hint of a smile hovering on her lips.

"It's not much."

She laid a hand on his arm and drew his gaze. Her eyes held sincerity. "It's everything. Do you know what you've done for us? I don't know an adequate way to express—"

"Happy to help." Andy patted the hand which still rested on his arm. "In fact, seeing you both so relaxed makes me glad." No, more than glad. *Overjoyed.*

Trish pulled her hand away. "You know what I think?"

He raised his eyebrows in response.

"I think God brought you into our lives."

How many times had he thought the same thing? "The same is true in reverse. I'm not sure my move to Miller's Creek would have been as successful without you and Bo. Further proof that God directs our paths when we trust Him."

She nodded and gazed into the distance. "I used to think I had a lot of trust, but since Doc died I'm not so sure."

He opened a can of pop, the fizzy liquid tickling his nose and quenching his thirst. "Not sure if you trust yourself or God?"

"Both. I think I know what I'm supposed to do, but nothing seems to be working out the way I thought it would. Did I hear Him wrong?" The words grew husky.

"I can't answer for you, but I'll say this. In my own life, there've been times when I followed my own way only to reach a dead end."

She removed her hat and leaned against the gnarly bark of an oak. "I'm *not* following my own way. At least I don't think I am." Her eyes grew dark. "What do you think?"

His neck hair bristled. Red alert. Danger zone. How was he supposed to answer her question without landing himself in a heap of trouble? He sent a quick prayer for help. "From my perspective, you seem mighty determined to exert your independence."

Her frown morphed to a scowl. "There's nothing wrong with being independent. I think God expects us to do our part."

"I agree, but independence can be a real hindrance to trust. I mean, if we can handle it ourselves, then why do we need God?"

Trish ducked her head, obviously a million miles away. When she looked up, it wasn't at him. "Bo, come eat some lunch."

Bo grabbed a handful of food, then headed back to the creek. Trish's eyes followed him, a contented smile at play on her lips. "He's like a different kid today. The way he used to be."

"I notice a change in you, too." He grabbed a chicken leg from the baggie and nibbled on it.

"Me?" She sounded surprised.

He picked up a nearby acorn and flicked it at her. It hit her arm and bounced to the blanket. "Yes, you. It's good to see you smile. And I think your enjoyment of the day means more to Bo than you realize."

"How so?"

He licked his mouth and tossed the chicken bone toward the creek for the critters to enjoy. "For a while there, I was afraid you might let your work take precedence over Bo."

"I have to support my son."

How could he warn her of the danger without revealing too much? "I know, but he's already lost his father. He doesn't need to lose you, too."

Trish grew pensive. After several tense moments, she finally spoke. "You have no idea how hard it is to be mother, father, and sole breadwinner."

"You're right. I don't." He met her direct gaze. "But trust me when I say I know how Little Bo feels." He'd lived through it, and still had the scars to prove it. The two situations might look different from the outside, but the results were the same. A very confused little boy.

Again she was silent, but her eyes perused his face until the scrutiny unnerved him and made him glance away. She pelted him with an acorn to garner his attention, a teasing smile at play on her lips. "Payback. Tell me about your childhood."

Andy scooped up the acorn she'd thrown, but this time hurled it toward the creek. "Not much to tell."

"Well, you had one, didn't you?"

"I guess." Why was she pushing him?

"Tell me about your family."

"Maybe some other time."

Her expression took on hurt. She frowned, then rose to her feet and meandered to the creek.

He pressed his lips together. There was no way to explain his background. She came from a good family—well-respected members of the community—the same kind of people who looked down on people like him. Telling her would only lead to trouble.

Andy stood, picked up the lunch leftovers, and sauntered back to his horse. His cell phone vibrated in his pocket. "Hey, Matt."

"Hi, bro. You might wanna sit down."

His heart thudded. "Why?"

"I just got word that Lester Hathcock passed away from a massive heart attack."

16

Trish gasped at the time displayed on the Morganville National Bank marquis. She'd never make it home in time. Scurrying to her parked Suburban, she pitched her portfolio, day-planner, and purse into the passenger seat. Though it was only early June, the inside of the car was an oven. She sniffed. Something in the backseat was definitely cooked. Eew! With sweat beading on her forehead, she zipped out of the parking space and headed to the highway. So much for her resolution to prove to Andy she could be a mom *and* a businesswoman.

Their conversation on Saturday had left her feeling more inadequate than ever, but she was determined to prove him wrong. She *could* have a career without sacrificing her son. A car honked and cut her off. Her hands gripped the steering wheel. "Crazy driver!" She muttered the words and tapped her brakes.

There'd been nothing from Andy all week—no phone calls, no ball practice, no visits. After the picnic, they'd practically galloped all the way back to the barn, and he'd left in a hurry with a quiet mention to Trish that a friend had died.

She flipped on her blinker and edged into a turn lane. What was there about his past that he felt compelled to hide? The annoyance and hurt she'd felt on Saturday returned. He knew more about her current situation than her family, but clammed up after one question about his.

As she topped the hill, a long snake of cars came into view. Just great. Her frustration mounted, then she remembered her promise to Bo to count to ten when she felt angry. She took a deep breath. *One. Two. Three.* Where was her cell phone? She rummaged through her purse contents with her free hand, alternately searching for the phone and keeping an eye on the traffic. Her fingers curled around something rectangular. She pulled out a container of breath mints, popped one in her mouth, and continued to dig. Found it! She hit speed-dial.

"Dad, sorry I'm late. I'm running behind, but I'm on my way." Traffic crept to a standstill, and her air conditioner now spewed the rancid odor of car exhaust. *Four. Five.*

"I was supposed to be somewhere ten minutes ago." He sounded grumpy.

Maybe her good news would put him in a better mood. "I lined up two clients in Morganville."

"Hmph."

So much for that idea. *Six. Seven.* "I'm stuck in traffic, but it's starting to move." If five miles an hour was considered moving.

"You're in Morganville? Still?"

She grimaced. "I'm sorry. Listen, Bo needs to be at the ball field at 5:30. Could you get him dressed? That way when I get there I can take him straight to town for his game." She, on the other hand, would be in a business skirt, heels, and pantyhose. Not fun in ninety-degree heat.

"I'll get him dressed, but we'll be at Beth's. Bye."

The phone clicked. Mama Beth's again? Like a cluster of spiders, uneasiness tickled her spine, but she forced it away and scratched her neck. Oh well, it would make Bo less late if she didn't have to drive to the ranch to pick him up. Relentless questions continued to circle and gave no rest. Over the past few weeks her family had all but deserted her. She saw them at church and Sunday lunch, but that was about it. Perhaps a move to Austin *would* be best.

Traffic crawled as minutes ticked by. *Eight. Nine.* Finally, she reached a passing lane and zoomed around the other cars.

Trish's cell phone buzzed. She grabbed it and pressed the talk button. "Hello?"

"Hey, girl!" Her best friend's standard greeting, spoken in typical exuberance.

"Delaine, guess what? I just lined up two design jobs."

"Good. Tell me more."

Trish quickly outlined the two jobs. "It's not much, but at least it's a start."

"Well, it's something, I guess." Delaine didn't sound convinced, and Trish pictured her doing her nails on the other end, completely bored by Trish's small-town life. "Do you have any plans for this weekend?"

"No. Bo's t-ball game is tonight, so the weekend is free. Why?"

"I miss you. Why don't you bring Little Bo down for the weekend so we can have some girlfriend time?"

Trish thought about the pressure she'd been under. Self-imposed, to be sure, but still it would feel good to get away for a mini-vacation. Maybe Delaine could help her sort through some of her confused feelings about Andy. "Sounds heavenly."

"Great!"

Realization dawned. Where would she get money for gas and food? She could ask Dad just this once, and when Andy's new office was finished she'd pay him back. "Tomorrow's the last day of school, so Bo gets out early. We'll leave right after I pick him up."

The conversation ended, and Trish chunked the cell phone onto the passenger seat, sneaking a quick glance at the time. The traffic jam had thrown her even further behind. She pressed the accelerator. Not two minutes later, a siren sounded, and in her rearview mirror red and blue lights flashed.

Her heart sank. *Ten.*

Andy gazed at the packed parking lot, hands on his hips. Families migrated toward him. Excited boys outfitted in baseball uniforms scurried to their respective dugouts while moms and dads wrestled younger children from their car seats and chatted about their day and what they'd have for supper. He, on the other hand, stood alone, a deserted island in the midst of an ocean.

Where were Trish and Bo? Only a few minutes remained before the game started, and he'd hoped to have time to ask them to the Morganville end-of-school carnival tomorrow night.

Yesterday's funeral inundated his memory. He released a heavy sigh and studied the ground while pins pricked his eyes. Lester had been more than a friend—more like the father he'd never had—his life a shining example of all that Andy longed to be. And it all started with helping Bo.

Life was brief. Too brief. Lester's unexpected death proved it. There was no time to squander. He wanted a family, and not just any family. No one would do except a sad-eyed mother with a gorgeous smile, and a pint-sized bundle of father-starved boy. There was no denying the truth. He cared about them both.

Andy removed a rolled-up bag of sunflower seeds from his back pocket and deposited a handful of the salt-covered kernels in his cheek, then sauntered to the dugout to prepare the kids for the game. "Everyone have their gloves and caps?"

A chorus of replies all sounded at once. Hopefully they were affirmative. "Brody, if Bo doesn't make it I want you to play first base."

Brody's typical cocky attitude took over and he swaggered toward a group standing near the dugout entrance. "Hear that? Coach moved me to first base."

"Brody!" Andy's sharpened voice pierced through the chatter. "More bragging like that will land you on the bench."

"Yes, sir."

Andy's eyebrows shot up. Maybe he was finally getting through to the kid.

A few minutes later the game got under way. During the first half of the inning, the Eagles managed to shut out the Mariners. Their three line drives to Brody at first base sent the other team to the field in a short amount of time. Trish rushed up with Little Bo just as the Eagles were about to go to bat. Bo's head hung low and his bottom lip quivered.

"Sorry we're late." With red, swollen eyes, Trish looked she'd had quite a crying jag.

"You okay?"

"Yeah, just a crazy day." She huffed a puff of air from her mouth and looked into the distance. "Anyway, I'm going to sit in the stands if you don't need me."

If only she realized how *much* he needed her. Andy watched her walk away, her skirt bouncing around her calves as she gracefully maneuvered the steps in high heels, her shoes clunking against the wooden bleachers. Little Bo slumped against the chain link fence. Poor guy. He'd obviously had a rough day. "Hey, buddy, you ready to play?"

Bo shook his head from side to side, then brought his arm up to his nose and sniffled.

Andy patted his back. "That's okay. When you're ready just let me know."

The rest of the game sped by in a blur. Andy attempted to keep his mind on the game, but it kept straying back to real life. What was going on with Trish and Bo now? Should he even bother asking about the carnival? One thought led to another, and his focus soon turned to his father, the man who'd been responsible for his existence—at least biologically.

He used his sleeve to swab sweat from his forehead. At Lester's funeral, he'd heard more than one person comment about his father's "condition," but just couldn't bring himself to go check on the man. Instead, when the graveside service ended, he'd expressed his regrets to Denise Hathcock, crawled into the Z, and headed back to Miller's Creek.

Andy crossed his arms and then pursed his lips to spit out a sunflower seed shell. His father hadn't bothered with him or Matt when they were growing up, so why should he give a hoot what happened to him?

Instant guilt rained down. God had provided all he needed. Who was he to turn his back on someone who needed God's grace? The man was his father, good or bad. He'd find the time to check on him, even if it meant a trip to Berringer.

The game ended with another big win for the Eagles. Andy congratulated the guys, and after he released them, they immediately charged toward the concession stand with cheers and shouts, leaving sweaty smells in their wake. Bo slouched in the same position he'd assumed for the entire game. Andy plopped beside him just as Trish rounded the corner of the dugout.

"How come you didn't let him play?" Barely-concealed anger edged her question.

Andy's hackles rose. "He didn't want to play. Why were you so late?"

"Work." She hoisted her chin, her eyes issuing a challenge.

He'd tried to warn her about Bo last weekend. Didn't she know her son took priority over a stinking job? Couldn't she tell his reluctance to play was her fault?

A cell phone jangled, and Trish scrounged around in the suitcase she called a purse. "Hello?"

Her gaze met Andy's and her face reddened. "Can I call you back later? I really can't talk right now." Silence descended as she listened. "Yes, sir, I know." She turned her back, and took a few steps away. "Yes, I'll put the check in the mail tomorrow." Trish clicked the cell phone shut and dropped it in her purse. Her shoulders rose then sagged before she rotated to face him. "Bo, let's go home so we can talk."

Bo stood and trudged to his mother's side, and they moved outside the fence. Trish grabbed her son's hand, then glanced at Andy briefly before they walked away.

He battled conflicting emotions, his desire to spend time with them victorious over the anger. What was the harm of asking? All she could do was say no. "Wait!"

Trish faced him, and Andy jogged from the dugout to join them. "Would you and Bo like to go to the end-of-school carnival in Morganville tomorrow night?"

Bo perked up, his face radiating light. "Just like what we used to do before Daddy . . ." His words trailed off and he lowered his head.

Trish pressed her lips together for a moment. "I'm sorry. We can't."

Her son snapped his head up, his brown eyes wide. "Why not?"

"When school's out tomorrow we're leaving for Austin." She sent her son a quick, close-mouthed smile.

Andy's heart plunged to his stomach. So she'd reached her decision.

17

"Get in the car!" The words pelted from Trish's lips propelled by fury. Would Bo's incessant whining never end?

Her son burst into tears and threw open the back car door with violent force, then climbed in and slammed it behind him.

Trish unclenched her fingers and released a deep breath, guilt seeping into her soul. Why had she lost control again? She brought a hand to her forehead in a vain attempt to rub away the lines that had become permanent fixtures on her face. It took so little to make her snap lately.

She lugged the suitcase to the back door of the Suburban and hoisted it in place, then climbed in the driver's seat. Sobs still sounded from the back seat, interspersed with sniffs.

"I'm sorry I lost my temper, Bo, but I need some time with Delaine."

Bo didn't answer, but continued to sniff and stare out window. It was gonna be a long drive.

Trish backed out of the driveway and headed toward Austin, a prayer on her heart. *Lord, help us have a good time, but more importantly, give me answers. Show me what You want me to do.*

A few miles down the road she checked the rearview mirror. Bo was already asleep. Her thoughts turned to the look on her father's face when she'd asked to borrow money for the trip.

Total shock. His words still echoed in her mind. "Are you really thinking about moving?"

She'd assured him the trip was just to visit Delaine, but she hadn't been completely truthful. This weekend was a test. A test to see how Little Bo responded to city life. A test to see if she could make a go of her design business in Austin. Trish let out a weary sigh and prayed once more for wisdom and direction.

Three hours later they pulled into the driveway of Delaine's posh two-story, Little Bo awake, but unusually quiet.

Delaine flew out the door and engulfed her in a hug. "Trish! It's so good to see you." Her friend pulled away, her face framed by a hip new haircut. "We're gonna have such a good time catching up." She knelt in front of Bo. "Hey, kiddo, remember me?"

Bo nodded, one corner of his mouth turned up in an attempted smile. At least he was trying.

"Hope you like pizza, 'cause the pizza guy just delivered a couple."

His face brightened. "I love pizza."

Delaine's musical laughter filled the air, and she grabbed his hand. "Well, c'mon, then. Let's go inside and get some. I also picked up a few video games for you."

He relinquished Trish's hand in favor of Delaine's. So far, so good. Or was it? Apprehension nibbled at her brain, but like an evasive mouse, it scurried away.

Later, the pepperoni and supreme pizzas devoured, Trish followed Delaine to the plush parlor for girl talk, suddenly feeling like a guest on *Lifestyles of the Rich and Famous*. Was Delaine even the same person who shared sleepovers and boyfriend talks? "I love your house, Delaine. You obviously don't need my services."

Delaine laughed and plopped down on the cushy couch. “Francesca, the woman who wants to see your portfolio, just redid it for me. Have a seat.”

She relaxed into the overstuffed sofa and inhaled. Everything smelled new and fresh. As much as she loved her Texas ranch house, it *would* be nice to start over with a clean canvas. To leave the bad memories behind. “You’ve done so much to make Bo feel welcome with the pizza and video games. I really appreciate it.”

“My pleasure, though I must confess I had ulterior motives. I wanted to be able to talk with you uninterrupted. If you don’t mind my saying so, kids can cramp your style.”

Trish reflected on the statement. Did Delaine have a problem with Bo or just kids in general? “So what’s been going on in your life?”

“Well, I’ve met someone.” Her friend’s eyes took on a twinkle. “He’s a plastic surgeon with a thriving practice.”

Girl talk for “He’s loaded.”

“Best of all, he doesn’t want children either.”

Trish felt her eyebrows crank up a notch. “You don’t want kids?”

“Nope. For a while I did, but I’ve seen how they change my friends’ lives, and not necessarily for the better. There are too many other things I want to do.”

Trish sipped her soda. “Such as?”

“Travel. See the world. Build my business. You know, fun stuff.”

In other words, stuff you could do when you didn’t have kids.

Delaine swung her feet up to the sofa, her back against the arm of the couch, her perfectly pedicured toenails inches away. “How are things going with you?”

Trish's ego deflated. No luxury two-story in a gated community. No plastic surgeon. Just more of the same old routine. Take Bo to school. Try to find work. Wash clothes. Feed Bo. Help him with his homework. Put him to bed. Then get up the next day and do it all over again. "Not much to tell."

"You mentioned you picked up a couple of jobs in Morganville, right?"

"They're small jobs, but every little bit helps."

Her friend's eyes narrowed. "Still having a rough time, huh?"

How tempted she was to lie. Instead she nodded.

Delaine hugged one of the velvety cushions to her chest. "You really should move to Austin."

As usual, her friend had wasted no time in applying the pressure. "I don't know, Del—"

"It would be so much easier for you here. You'd have all the work you want, plus some. Austin has great schools for Bo." She hoisted a well-sculpted eyebrow, a suggestive smile curling her lips. "I could introduce you to some of my available men friends."

Andy's dimpled grin made its way to the front of her memory. "It's still too early for that, but there is someone in Miller's Creek."

Delaine straightened, her eyes suddenly full of interest. "Really? Who?"

"The new city attorney. His name is Andy."

"The same Andy Bo talked about non-stop over supper? I got the impression he was Bo's t-ball coach."

"He is." Trish combed a strand of hair behind her ear and curled her legs beneath her. "He's taken quite an interest in Bo."

Her friend's expression changed to soft sadness. "Be careful, Trish. Just because he cares about your son doesn't mean he cares about you."

Fire burned in her veins. "I know that." The words crabbed out of her mouth. Was Andy only interested in being a father figure? She fingered her glass and stared, the dark liquid like the muddy depths of her confusion. Andy's face had been crestfallen when she'd announced their trip to Austin. He truly loved her son. Of that she had no doubt. But how did he feel about her?

Thankfully, Delaine changed the subject, and the rest of the evening was spent reliving fun high school times.

The next day at a nearby water park, Bo, his hair wet and sticking up in cute spikes, grinned at Delaine as she reclined on the chaise lounge near the kiddie pool. "Thanks for bringing us to the water park, Miss Delaine. This is lots of fun." He squinted at Trish. "We need to tell Andy about this."

Delaine peered at Trish over the top of her designer sunglasses. "Honestly, if I hear him mention that name one more time, I'm gonna scream. Are you sure it's a good idea to let Bo get attached to this man?"

"I'm not 'tached to him," protested Little Bo. "I just like him. He's a nice man who plays catch and takes me horseback riding."

Trish raised an eyebrow at her friend. "He hears everything. Even when you don't think he's listening."

"Little pitchers have big ears," whispered Delaine under her breath with a hint of exasperation.

"I'm not a pitcher. I play first base."

With that last remark ringing in their ears, Little Bo sprinted toward the water slide.

They shared a laugh, then Delaine fanned her face with both hands. "I need something to drink. It's much hotter than I expected."

Trish scanned the pool area where Bo splashed around a giant mushroom fountain. "I actually think the temps are very comfortable."

"Want something to drink?"

She thought about her dwindling cash. "No, thanks." She'd need the money for gas to get home.

"You didn't eat lunch, and now you're not thirsty? In this heat?"

"I had a long drink at the water fountain not long ago."

When Delaine returned a few minutes later, Trish tried not to ogle the tall raspberry slushy, but instead monitored Bo's movements.

Her friend slurped through the straw. "I thought after we wore the kid out, I could hire a high school girl I know to watch him tonight while you and I hit the nightspots."

A wad of discomfort landed in her stomach. "Sorry, Delaine. I don't leave Bo with people I don't know."

"But I've already made plans to meet some friends."

"Go ahead and meet them. I'll stay with Bo."

"But I invited you down for the weekend. I'd feel bad."

Trish waved a hand. "Please. I don't mind if you spend time with your friends. That would give me time to enjoy that huge jetted swimming pool you call a bathtub." And time to think about what she should do.

Bo had enjoyed the trip—a five-year-old boy's dream with pizza, video games, and a water park. Austin obviously offered more recreational activities than Miller's Creek, and the drive through the state's capitol proved its growing-metropolis status. There was new construction everywhere, and new construction meant plenty of business.

And plenty of competition.

Trish awoke Sunday morning to scrumptious smells wafting from the kitchen. She padded down the hallway.

Delaine was already dressed and made-up and buzzing around the room. "There you are, sleepyhead. I thought I got home early last night. It was only eleven o-clock and you and Bo were both sound asleep."

She raised groggy eyelids. Should she tell her they'd both gone to bed at nine? "You're sure busy this morning. What's going on?" Of course. It was Sunday. "Oh, church. I'll get Bo dressed and ready."

Delaine laughed. "No, silly. I invited some friends over for brunch. They'll be here in about an hour."

Panic snaked through her insides. Brunch? Friends? An hour!? Delaine was decked out in expensive designer Capri's and a matching jacket. All she had was her jeans and t-shirts and the threadbare hausfrau dress she'd brought for church. "I wish you'd told me you were planning this, Delaine. I didn't bring anything to wear." Her words seeped the irritation she felt.

She stopped in the middle of the kitchen, one hand on her hip as she eyed Trish up and down. "Hmm . . . you still wear size 8?"

Trish nodded.

"Relax. I have something that'll look perfect on you. An outfit I bought last summer on my trip to Morocco."

Forty-five minutes later, Trish donned the outfit which hugged her figure like a surgeon's glove. The cream color complimented her dark complexion, and the dainty beaded stiletto sandals provided the perfect finishing touch. Trish eyed her reflection and raised fingers to her cheeks. When was the last time she'd allowed herself to look so grown-up and sophisticated? Ever?

As she made her way to the kitchen she checked in on Little Bo. He was dressed and sitting in front of the TV with the video controller. "Are you going to be okay in here by yourself?"

He nodded in a game-induced trance.

The guests began arriving a few minutes later, all friendly and full of chatter. The noise level in the room instantly quadrupled. Delaine tugged Trish in front of a well-dressed woman. "This is the lady I was telling you about. Francesca Giorelli. She owns her own design business in downtown Austin. Francesca, this is Trish James."

The woman, hair chopped short and eyes made-up big, held out a jewel-bedecked hand, an oversized silver bracelet dangling from her wrist. "So glad to meet you, Trish. I'm always on the lookout for new talent to add to the firm."

Her nerves on red alert, Trish shook her hand and attempted a smile. "Then you have lots of business?"

Francesca laughed, a deep throaty sound that reminded Trish of a feline purr. "More than I can handle. I've had to be very selective about which clients I take. Nothing under fifty grand."

Trish struggled to keep her jaw from flapping open. "I see." *I see?* This woman was a prospective employer and that's all she could say?

The smile faded from the woman's face. "Excuse me, Trish. I see someone I need to speak with. Let's chat later. Nice to meet you."

"You, too."

Delaine elbowed her and waggled her eyebrows. "What did I tell you? Tons of work for you here in Austin." She edged closer. "So what do you think of my gorgeous plastic surgeon?"

Peter Huggins, Hollywood-handsome, leaned against the fireplace a few steps away like a panther about to pounce. He smirked with insolent eyes and raised his glass.

"He seems, uh, very nice."

Another woman Trish didn't know grabbed Delaine's arm. "There you are, Delaine. I want you to tell me about that lovely painting you have hanging over your fireplace."

Now alone, Trish decided to check on Bo, but Peter stepped in front of her, blocking the hallway. "Not leaving so soon, I hope?"

"Uh, no, I was just going to check on my son."

"I'm sure he's fine." His voice was razor-edged silk, and he ran his gaze down her chin. "Delaine didn't tell me you were such a classic beauty. Have you done any modeling?"

What rock had Delaine found him under? "No." Trish was just about ready to spear the man's foot with her stiletto heel, when Delaine possessively linked her arm in Peter's, her eyes glittering.

"So what are you two talking about?"

Trish gave a close-lipped smile. "I told him I was just about to check on Bo. Now if you two will excuse me."

Later that afternoon, Trish carried a very sleepy little boy to the Suburban and buckled him in, then turned to face her friend. "Thanks so much for the weekend. We both had a wonderful time."

Delaine gave her a hug. "Thanks for coming. I hope you'll give more thought to moving to Austin. I'd love to have you closer."

Trish let out a puff of air. "I'll definitely give it some thought." And then some. She pulled herself into the driver's seat, waved, and drove toward the interstate that would lead them home. With Bo asleep, she had plenty of time to rehash the events of the weekend and think things through.

No matter how painful, she had to face the facts. She wasn't making enough money to support her son and pay her bills. A move to Austin would provide a good job to meet their needs. Bo needed stability, but her family had their own lives to lead. Yes, Andy had more than made up for the deficit, but the whole situation filled her with fear. Without Bo, she would be tempted to see where the road with Andy might lead, but under the circumstances, it made no sense. Impossible decision. How was she supposed to know what to do? *God, what do You want?*

Trust and wait. The words were immediate, a still, small voice sounding in her thoughts.

Wait for what? Bankruptcy?

Was it wise to call? From his small apartment, Andy peered out over downtown Miller's Creek, the area emptied of traffic and people on this cloudy Monday evening. Everyone had gone home to their families, while he'd just returned from his nightly visit to the Morganville nursing home.

After discovering dad's dementia, he'd known he had to do something. The man was way past being able to care for himself. Guilt sliced through him. If he'd taken the time to find him earlier, would it have made a difference?

A weary sigh escaped as his thoughts returned to Trish and Bo. He'd been over the situation a thousand times in his mind. Like a hamster on a spinning wheel, he'd agonized over it all weekend while she was away. He had to convince Trish to stay in Miller's Creek, but how? It was too soon to confess his feelings. That would send her sprinting to Austin faster than anything.

He unclipped his cell phone and pushed speed-dial for Trish's house, breathing a silent prayer for direction.

Bo answered.

"Hey, bud, this is Andy."

"Hey, guess what? We went to the coolest water park."

Unease stabbed at him. Bo liking Austin was *not* a good omen. "Sounds like fun. Is your mama there?"

"Yep. I'll go get her."

Several minutes later she came on the line, breathless. "Hi, Andy."

"Hi. What took you so long?"

She laughed, a melodic sound. "Sorry about that. I was actually out in the cottage, painting." Her voice held a happy lilt, and he imagined a sparkle in those tawny eyes of hers.

"You sound happy."

"I guess I am."

Dread filled his heart. "So the weekend in Austin went well?"

"Very well." She offered no further information.

"Glad to hear it." *Okay, that was a lie.* "Glad to hear you're painting again. You know, I bet you could sell your paintings professionally."

This time her laughter held cynicism. "It's nice of you to say so, but I'm not so sure, especially in this economy."

He plopped onto the futon and took a swig of cool water, his pulse pounding. *God, give me the words to say.* "Thought maybe we should get started on the new building. You still planning on helping me out?"

"Sure. I guess. I mean, if you want me to."

"I want you to."

"Okay. What would you like me to handle?"

"Everything. Locate a building contractor, and then decorate and furnish the entire house and office space . . . except the basement." He already had another purpose for that space. That is, if everything worked according to plan.

"I assumed that would be storage space for your office." Even her tone held a frown. "I don't mind purchasing file cabine—"

"That won't be necessary." The less said the better. "Why don't I set up an account like I did for my temporary office, so you can order what you need and also pay yourself?"

"That's a lot more leeway than most clients give. Are you sure you wouldn't rather have me bill you? I don't want any special favors."

"I trust you, Trish." Why couldn't she get that through her beautiful, thick skull?

"However you want to handle it is fine with me."

Finally. "I'll set up the account tomorrow. Just let me know when you need more. Why don't we meet on Thursday to go over plans? Will that give you sufficient time?"

"It should. When and where?"

"Ten a.m. at my office." The conversation grew uncomfortably quiet. Would she go ballistic if he asked about the trip? "So tell me about Austin."

"We had a great time. I think we both needed the time away."

"Good. You, uh, still thinking about moving?"

In the silence he could almost see her will-you-let-it-rest glare. "As a matter of fact, yes. I know I could be successful with an interior design business there. In fact, I met the lady interested in my portfolio."

His heart plummeted. "And what about Bo?" He hated the accusatory edge to the question, but he couldn't help how he felt.

"*My* son would have access to some of the best schools in the state."

He yearned to tell her that Bo needed the security of the familiar. To tell her how much he cared. But he didn't dare say more.

"I haven't had the chance to ask about your friend who died. Were you very close?"

Andy's throat constricted. "Yes."

"That must have been difficult. Was he a classmate?"

"No."

She waited, as if she expected more. "Why are you so close-lipped about your past?"

The question socked him in the gut. How could you explain to someone who had no point of reference what it was like to feel judged because your father was a drunk? The drunk who no longer even recognized him. "Maybe there's nothing to tell."

"Maybe." Her tone screamed disbelief. "But it seems to me you're trying to cover it up."

White-hot heat coursed through his veins. The queen of social masks was accusing *him* of covering up?

"I don't mean to sound unkind, but if you expect me to answer your questions about my plans and past, I think it's only fair for you to reciprocate."

The white-hot heat turned to icicles. "It's not like you've been completely straightforward with me either."

"What are you referring to?"

"I know you're in financial trouble, and your family suspects it, too." As the words sloshed from his mouth, he knew he'd overstepped his bounds. Again.

18

Trish squeezed into the bright yellow sardine can of a car. After checking for oncoming traffic, she zoomed away from Hank's Used Car lot in Morganville. Already she missed the interior space of the larger vehicle, but some things couldn't be helped. The switch to a small car made financial sense. It gave her enough money to get rid of the car payment and have a little cash left over. Besides, a small car meant better gas mileage, which could only help when you were on the verge of bankruptcy.

She cracked a window to get rid of the stale smell and tucked her now windblown hair behind her ears. Otis Thacker had been on her back for three months to pay her monthly lease on the shop. It wasn't like she didn't want to pay him. The two design jobs she'd picked up in Morganville had provided food money, but little else. How could she drive around in a nice Suburban when she owed so many people?

Time to pull out all the stops. If she couldn't make a go of it in Miller's Creek, she needed to know soon. Like before summer was over. If they had to move, it needed to happen before Bo started school in the fall.

Andy's handsome face loomed in her mind, but she pushed it away. Other than work and baseball, she hadn't seen him in the two weeks since their argument. During the times she'd been around him, he'd been mentally elsewhere, his mind obviously on something more important. She slid a hand down the opposite arm to chase away goose bumps. Under the circumstances, this distance between them was a good thing. Now if she could only convince Bo of the fact.

Within a half hour she pulled up to the front of Designs By Trish. She entered the two-story brick building and looked around the space, empty except for boxes she'd packed for the move.

A sick feeling landed in her stomach, and she moved a hand to her abdomen in an effort to still the wild dance inside. She'd had such high hopes when she'd signed the lease. If only it didn't feel like she was throwing in the towel. If only she could've made this work. She clenched her teeth. Enough of the "if only's."

Trish lifted a box and trudged to the car. She wedged it in the tiny back seat. Okay, it would've been smarter to move this stuff *before* she sold the Suburban.

"What are you doing?"

She jumped at Andy's unexpected and demanding voice, and bumped her head on the car ceiling. With one hand on her head, she faced him.

He stood off to one side, hands on his hips, his eyes and forehead wrinkled.

Her mouth went dry, a sour taste on her tongue. "Clearing out the store."

His face paled. "Why?"

"It doesn't make sense to pay a lease when I can run the business from home." She stepped around him and hurried back inside the store.

He followed, his steps echoing on the wooden floors. "But the store front and sign let people know you're in business."

"Pretty expensive advertising, if you ask me." She hoisted another box with a grunt.

He grabbed one also and tagged along behind her. "Whose car?"

"Mine. I traded the Suburban for it."

Andy slid his box in the backseat and turned to face her, his lips taut. "Is there something—"

"I'm fine."

His eyes narrowed. "You sure?" His tone and expression held doubt.

"I'm fine." Trish rushed inside to get one more box for the front seat. The sooner she filled the car, the sooner she could leave. It was pretty obvious this move would take more than one trip, especially with a cracker box for a car.

Andy blocked her way. "Say 'you're fine' one more time and I won't believe you."

She peered into his green eyes. "I'm . . ."

". . . fine. Yeah, you said that already." He frowned. "Do I owe you money?"

Trish forced a smile. "No. For the number of hours I've put in, I've been sufficiently paid. Once the building is in the dry, I'll have more work to do."

"Have any other jobs besides mine?"

She heaved a sigh. "Not that it's any of your business, but no." Trish balanced the box between her body and the building, locked the door, and moved to the car, Andy on her heels. "I'm really not trying to cut you off, Andy, but I've got to get this load home and come back for the rest." Before she owed Otis another month's rent.

He hustled around her and opened the car door. "Let me know if there's anything I can do."

"I'm fine."

Andy lips curved upward, but the smile didn't reach his eyes. "Yeah, yeah, I know."

He stared as she pulled away from the curb, his expression full of concern.

The dashboard clock read 4:45. She'd told Dad she'd be home by 5:00, and she should still have time to make it. After supper, she'd borrow one of the ranch trucks and bring Bo back to town with her to get the rest of the stuff. Then she'd call Otis.

A mile out of Miller's Creek, a grinding noise sounded from beneath the front part of the car. She pressed the accelerator, but the car only moved slower. Trish steered to the side of the road. The engine continued to run, but the car wouldn't budge.

This wasn't good. She dropped her head back against the seat, her brain racing. The thought of having the car checked by a mechanic had crossed her mind, but she'd been running late and the salesman had seemed so reputable. Now here she was, in the same old position, needing to be rescued.

There was no way she could call Andy, even though part of her yearned to hear the comfort in his voice. He'd already done more than enough. Besides she didn't want to see the I-told-you-so look in his eyes. That left Dad or Steve. With a heavy weight on her chest, she grabbed her cell phone.

Dad answered on the second ring. "Hello?" Laughter rang in the background. What was going on?

"Dad, my car broke down."

"Where?" His voice took on instant seriousness.

"I'm about a mile outside the city limits on my way to the ranch."

"We'll be there soon."

True to his word, her father and brother pulled up a few minutes later.

"Whose car is this?" Steve gave her a hard stare as he slammed the pickup door, his eyes disappearing behind his scowl.

She raised her chin. "Mine."

"Since when?"

"Since this afternoon when I traded the Suburban."

"You traded your SUV for this?" Dad spoke with an incredulous tone, his bushy gray eyebrows inching upward.

"Relax, Dad. I checked the Blue Book values. I got enough cash to pay off the Suburban and have some left over."

Steve started the car and put it in gear. Nothing. "Transmission's gone."

"Tr-transmission?" Trish hated the quake in her voice. "How much does that cost?"

"A couple of thousand." Steve's mouth flat-lined. "If you're lucky."

Dad stalked off toward the pickup, the fury on his face like a thunderous black cloud.

So much for the extra cash. What she wouldn't give for a hole to crawl into. "At least it gets good gas mileage." The explanation sounded weak and puny to her ears.

"Yeah, especially now." Steve deadpanned the line, but none of them laughed.

Later that night, after paying to have her car towed to Billy Ray's Auto Shop, and after she and Bo made the trip to Miller's Creek in the ranch pickup, Trish stood in the cottage and ogled her artwork with a critical eye. If only she could make a living with her paintings like Andy had mentioned.

Was he just offering encouragement when he'd said she should sell her art, or was it a viable option? She chewed her bottom lip and tumbled the idea in her brain. The monthly Morganville Trade Days were next weekend. Should she take the chance of renting a booth space?

Her imagination took over as she considered the possibility. Well, it wouldn't hurt to try. All of the paintings could go except the one Andy liked best. That would be her farewell gift for all he'd done to help her and Bo.

Andy rolled out of bed on Saturday, still fatigued. He yawned and raked a hand over his whiskers. The past few weeks had been crazy. Besides keeping up with his law practice and t-ball team, he'd monitored the new building's progress and his father's decline. Sleep and relaxation had become a precious commodity.

He moved to the bathroom sink and removed his shaving supplies from the medicine cabinet. The mirror revealed sagging pouches of skin beneath his eyes. More evidence that time was passing.

Even with his father's medical problems, the main thing tormenting him now was Trish's situation. He'd spied her from a distance at church last Sunday, but by the time he'd made it out the door, she and Bo were pulling away in an old pick-up. What had happened to her car? He lathered his face with shaving cream while the sink filled with water.

Yesterday he'd learned from the scuttlebutt at Granny's Kitchen that Trish had been hired to help the summer custodial staff at school, and Dani mentioned that she also planned to sell her artwork today at the Morganville Trade Days. If the tide didn't turn for her, and quick, she'd be gone before summer was up. The thought flooded his body with panic. *Lord, help me know how to help her. And help me know when to let go, if that's Your plan.*

An image of the stacked paintings in her cottage popped into his mind. He needed to find a way to buy her art today without her knowing it. And he knew exactly which painting he wanted.

Half an hour later, shaved and showered, he downed a banana and glass of milk and headed downstairs. Just as he reached the bottom step, his cell phone rang.

"Mr. Tyler, this is New Horizons Nursing Home. We wanted to make you aware of a problem." The woman's voice held a gentle Southern drawl.

He stopped in the foyer of City Hall and ran a hand down his neck. "What kind of problem?"

"Your father had a seizure, and we've transferred him to the hospital."

His heart pounded against his ribs. "I'll be there as soon as possible."

Half an hour later he arrived at Morganville General, parked his car, and hurried inside, the smell of disinfectant burning his nostrils. Within a few minutes, he located his father's room. A doctor and nurse stood at the foot of the bed perusing charts and conversing.

"I'm Andy Tyler, his son." He looked toward the frail man who once intimidated him. "How is he?"

"I'm Dr. Green." The older man with salt and pepper hair shook his hand, concern in his face and voice. "We gave him some medication to stop the seizures, but I'm glad you're here. I need to ask a question."

"Okay."

"Does your father consume large amounts of alcohol?"

"He used to, so I assume he still has a problem." There'd been days when he'd come home from school to find the house littered with empty beer cans. "Why?"

"Because it explains both the dementia and seizures." He no longer made eye contact, his lips pressed into a taut line of disapproval. "I'd like permission to try an experimental drug to see if it controls the seizures a little better. Of course, the nature of an experimental drug is that it is in the early testing stage. We'll need your written permission." He never looked at him directly, but instead stared at his clipboard.

"Of course." Andy battled ancient feelings. Was yet another person shunning him because of his father's problem? Like he was somehow responsible.

The doctor clicked his pen and stuffed it in his shirt pocket. "We'll get the paperwork rounded up for you to sign." He pivoted and hustled from the room with not so much as a "goodbye" or "nice to meet you." The nurse plumped Dad's pillow, sent him a "poor you" smile, then left.

Andy released a sigh and checked his watch. As badly as he wanted to get to Trish, Dad was his responsibility. He wandered down the hall to a chair in the waiting room, picked up a magazine, and tried to distract himself with an article about plants that thrived in hot Texas summers. Fifteen minutes passed. He tossed the unread magazine aside and approached the nurse's station.

A woman in scrubs stared at her computer screen, never glancing his way. "Can I help you?"

"Yes, I'm supposed to sign some papers for Dr. Green concerning my father's medication. I've been here a while—"

"We're working on it." She glanced up, impatience flashing in her eyes. "Our computers are having issues. If you'll have a seat, I'll call you as soon as I have them ready."

He nodded. "I'll be in my father's room."

Back at Dad's bedside, he plopped down in the chair next to beeping machines and stared at the grizzled profile of the man who'd once struck terror in his heart. The man he'd loved desperately—the man who'd never shown love in return. Trying to figure out why was pointless. The best thing to do was accept it for what it was and move on.

A scene from his childhood flashed to his mind. His father had towered over him, his breath thick with booze. "It's all your fault that your mother left!" Andy blinked back the sting in his eyes. For years he'd believed it, and part of him still wondered if—

"Here you go, Mr. Tyler." The nurse entered the room with a clipboard and pen and held it out to Andy. "Thanks for being so patient."

He signed his name and handed it back. "I'll be back later today to check on him."

It wasn't difficult to locate Morganville Trade Days. All he had to do was follow the flow of traffic. Downtown swarmed with people. After several minutes of driving around, he found a parking spot, and joined the hustle and bustle. Historic buildings housed businesses and encircled a turn-of-the century courthouse. The pecan trees surrounding the square were so thick that grass struggled to grow in the shade.

Andy tried to keep a safe distance from both sides of the street. It wouldn't do for Trish to see him. He finally spotted her on the far side of the square, and his heart melted. She stood near the entrance of her booth in a flowered dress that billowed around her knees. Several minutes passed. Her attempts to befriend people who passed appeared futile. No one entered her booth. Only a few accepted the business cards she offered.

He ducked behind a pecan tree to think through his options. He needed an accomplice. An elderly man parked on a nearby bench, the woman with him unloading her packages. "I know you're bored to tears, Henry. Why don't you sit here while I shop?"

The man nodded in relief.

As the woman bustled away, Andy approached. "Excuse me, sir, my name is Andy Tyler. Could I get you to do me a favor?"

The man didn't respond, but just looked skeptical.

"I want to purchase a painting from an artist here, but I don't want her to know I'm the one buying it." Andy pointed toward the stall where Trish's artwork hung on display. "She's right over there."

"Why don't you want her to know?" The old man's tone held wariness.

Andy propped one hand against a pecan tree's rough bark. "Well, it's a long story, but the short version is that she'd think I was doing it just to help her out."

"Is that why you're buying it?"

"Yes and no. I want to help her, but I also really love her artwork."

"You in love with her?" The man cocked his bushy eyebrows in a way that made Andy laugh.

Good question. "Let's just say I care about her."

"Same thing, if you ask me," muttered the old man, "but in that case, I'll do it."

Andy grinned and reached for his wallet. "The painting I want is large and shows a cowboy hat on a fence post with a rocky path and bluebonnets." He withdrew the bills and handed them to the man, who reached for his own wallet. "I want her to have all this money."

The man's bushy brows rose again as he counted the money. "You must love her a lot." He tottered off toward Trish's booth.

Andy hustled to the safe side of a pecan tree to watch. The man located the painting and pointed it out to Trish, but she shook her head no. Andy frowned. Why wouldn't she sell it? The man stuffed the bills back in the wallet, shook her hand, and hurried back across the street.

"She won't sell," he wheezed once he reached the bench.

"Did she say why?"

"Something about how she planned to give the painting to someone, but she'd take orders to paint another one just like it."

Andy peered around a low-hanging branch. Trish looked utterly dejected. Her shoulders slumped and she hung her head. He turned back to the man.

"Let's try again. Let her know you really want the painting, but you need it now. Tell her you'll give her half the money now and send her the other half later."

The man gasped. "The painting's beautiful, but it's not worth that much money."

"It is to me."

The older man's expression changed from incredulity to soft understanding. "I'll do what I can."

Andy watched the scenario unfold from the safety of his pecan tree. His new friend gestured and talked while Trish listened intently.

She hesitated as if mulling over the man's words, then reluctantly nodded. Henry handed her the cash, which she put in a bank bag. Then she gave him a business card and removed the painting from its hanger. The man thanked her and shook her hand before scurrying back.

"Here it is."

"Thanks so much. You'll never know how much I appreciate this." He took the painting then reached out to grasp the man's hand.

"Oh, I think I know."

Andy smiled. "How?"

The man glanced over at the park bench, where his wife unloaded an array of multi-colored bags. His eyes misted and a soft smile curved his mouth. He nodded toward his wife. "That's how."

19

Trish did a double-take when she spied Andy from a block away. He paced outside the developing shell of his new office in a dark suit, his blond curls tousled by the breeze. The sight took her breath away. She could no longer deny her attraction—spiritually, mentally, physically, emotionally—there was nothing about him she didn't like. Even more than her family, he'd been a support system and source of constant encouragement for her and Bo, his Christ-likeness shining like a beacon in a dark storm.

The one traffic light in Miller's Creek flashed to red. She braked to a stop and stifled a cough, the fumes from the diesel pickup directly ahead of her strong enough to choke a horse.

Andy had kept his distance for a couple of weeks, but over the past week, he'd been more attentive, more like the Andy she'd desperately missed. She moistened her lips and rested an elbow on the car door. What made the situation especially difficult to bear was his attraction to her. She felt it every time he was near. Felt his gaze on her. Noticed his tenderly-spoken words and the soft sheen in his eyes. To his credit, he never mentioned his feelings, never once pressured her.

A heavy sigh escaped. She'd love to reveal her own growing attraction, but it wouldn't be fair to offer either one of them the hope of a relationship. Not when everything pointed toward a move to Austin.

Sometimes trusting God meant launching out in faith. And for her that leap of faith possibly included leaving Miller's Creek. She brought a hand up to rub away the tension building behind her eyes. Only one painting had sold in Morganville last weekend—the one she'd planned to give Andy.

At least it had been a big sale. The proceeds had covered the house mortgage and utility bills. Hopefully, with her next paycheck for Andy's job, she'd be able to pay off her debt to Otis and have a little left over for the move.

The light turned green, and she pressed the accelerator. She had no other design jobs lined up, and the mental stress of not being able to provide for Bo was wearing her down. But she refused to become a burden to her family.

As she pulled into the parking lot, Andy met her, his dimpled grin wreaking havoc with her resolve to appear disinterested. He opened the car door. "Well, don't you look all business-like today?" His gaze rested on her hair, which she'd pulled back away from her face.

"That's what I call curb-side service." Trish smiled briefly, then reached for her digital camera, notepad, and measuring tape. She exited the car, sucking in a deep breath to slow her racing pulse.

"Anything for you." He gave a mock bow.

She ignored the gesture and faced the new building. "Shall we?"

He motioned with one arm. "After you."

They traveled from room to room discussing furniture layout, and confirmed the color choices for each space. Andy helped measure the rooms for flooring and the windows for draperies. Within the hour they were finished.

Trish turned toward him. "I think that gives me everything I need. I'll get things started so we can get you moved in before the Chamber banquet."

Andy shifted his weight to the opposite foot and glanced at the floor before peering back up at her. "Could I interest you in lunch at Soldano's?" The words were spoken with slight hesitation.

She searched for a way to say no, but just couldn't bring herself to destroy the hope in his eyes. "Sounds nice."

His face lit up. "Great! I'll give you a ride." He grabbed her hand and led her to his car, her heart pounding so fast she could barely breathe. Why, oh why, hadn't she told him no?

Andy could hardly contain his jubilation as he hustled around the car to open Trish's door. This was his chance. He'd hoped for an opportune moment to tell her how he felt, had prayed for it. He warred with a sudden attack of nerves. He could do this. God had brought him this far and wouldn't desert him now.

Once inside Soldano's, the air awash with the aroma of grilled chicken, enchiladas, and sopapillas, Gracie Soldano led them through an archway and seated them in the front near a large plate glass window that overlooked a lush garden. The lunch crowd had almost dissipated, and they were virtually alone. Perfect.

He pretended to study the menu, knowing full well he'd order the chicken fajitas like he always did. Andy thought through what he wanted and needed to say. While part of him wanted to blurt out his feelings and get it over with, it would be better to wait until after they'd eaten. Maybe by then he could work up his courage.

"So how's your work going?" Trish sipped her iced water.

"Can't complain. More than enough to keep me busy." A solemn expression covered not only her face, but inched its way into her posture and dark eyes. "How about you? Dani told me you entered some of your artwork in a show at Morganville." Sneaking around behind her back to buy the painting still made him feel like a creep—no, make that a creep *and* a stalker.

"Not really a show. It was the Morganville Trade Days."

Gracie swished up in her traditional Mexican dress, plunked down a basket of fresh tortilla chips and salsa, and took their order.

After she left, Andy returned his attention to Trish. "How'd you do?"

"I only sold one painting." She lowered her gaze, her tone flat. "I guess I shouldn't complain. I got a lot for it. The one you really liked."

"Good for you." How could he best encourage her? "Don't be upset, Trish. There are other ways to get your work out there. Keep trusting God."

"I'm trying, but His plans seem to be different from mine." She blinked rapidly, then stared out the window, her mind obviously somewhere else.

The softly-spoken words spawned fresh fear in his heart. What if he bared his soul only to have her disappear like every other woman in his life? He shook off the thought. Love was a risk—a risk he was prepared to take when it came to Trish.

Their meal arrived a few minutes later, and Andy delved into the creamy guacamole. Amid bites of the delicious food, the conversation relaxed into comfortable chatter about various subjects from the baseball team to Trish's one-day stint as a substitute teacher near the end of the school year.

Andy couldn't keep his eyes off her while she relayed the teacher story. The hard edge of disappointment was replaced by animation, and laughter now sparkled in her eyes.

Trish continued to chatter away. "The lesson was on healthy breakfast foods. I asked the first-graders what they liked to eat for breakfast. One little boy raised his hand and said 'blueberry Muppets.'"

They both laughed out loud.

Their eyes met, and Trish shyly lowered her head. "I've really enjoyed our lunch today, Andy. For just a little while it helped me forget my problems, and for that, I thank you."

Andy gulped in a big breath. "I have something I'd like to give you." He reached in his jacket for the gift he'd ordered, pulled the package from his pocket, and pushed it across the table toward her.

She sighed and tucked her lower lip between her teeth, her eyes sad again. "I can't. You've already given me so much."

"Like what?"

"Like my son back. I'm not sure he would've made it through all his psychological problems if it weren't for you. If anyone deserves a gift, it's you."

He laid a hand on top of hers. "It was my privilege and honor to help. I've enjoyed every minute I've spent with both of you."

Again she lowered her eyes, and this time allowed them to rest on the gift. She seemed apprehensive about accepting it.

"Please take it, Trish. It would mean a lot to me."

She met his gaze and attempted a smile, then nodded.

Time slowed as she withdrew her hand from beneath his, carefully undid the tape on the package, and lifted the box lid to reveal the wooden box inside. Carved into the lid was the verse, *"Trust in the LORD with all your heart and lean not into your own understanding. In all your ways acknowledge Him, and He shall direct your paths."*

Trish drew back with a sharp intake of air.

"Something wrong?"

She glanced up, mouth half open, the area above her eyes wrinkled. "No, it's lovely. It's just a special verse to me—one that God seems to keep directing me to."

Andy's breath caught in his throat. Her too?

Her expression still held heavy sorrow. She lifted the lid of the box to uncover the collection of artist's brushes he'd placed inside. Fingers shaking, she gently stroked them. "These are expensive. I'm not sure I can accept them."

"Please. I believe in the God-given ability you have. I-I wanted to encourage you to keep painting and keep trusting."

She studied him a while longer—almost as if memorizing his face—then gave a tentative nod. "Thank you."

His heart galloped, half in joy, half in apprehension. He swallowed hard and reached across the table to take her hands in his own. "Trish, I want you to know how special you are to me. I'd be honored if you'd allow me to . . . to . . ." To what? How did he put into words that he wanted to spend every spare second with her?

Trish yanked her hands away, her chocolate-drop eyes swimming with tears. "Andy, I wish things could be different. I really do. But somehow the timing seems all wrong. Not just because of Doc's death, but because of where I am in my life." A tear escaped and slid down her right cheek. She raised fingertips to swipe it away. "I'm not sure I can make it in Miller's Creek. If something doesn't change soon, I'll be forced to move to Austin. Under those circumstances, it wouldn't be fair to either of us to allow this to progress any further."

20

What a lousy birthday this had turned out to be. Bo's first birthday without his daddy, and Trish hadn't had the time or money to throw a big party.

She peered in the rearview mirror at her son's sad eyes and pouting lips. He hadn't been pleased with either of the gifts she'd given him, and she understood why. Bo had asked for only one thing—a video game—but she didn't have that kind of money. Instead she'd purchased a football and a stuffed horse like the one Dr. Wyse had in her office. Seeing his fallen face had just about done her in.

Now—on this beautiful Saturday afternoon in June when she'd rather be painting—they were on their way to Mama Beth's house for a family birthday party. Ever since Dani had entered the family, it seemed like they were always going to Mama Beth's for some event or celebration.

She steered into the driveway, the gravel crunching beneath the tires of her Yield-sign-yellow rattletrap. In sharp contrast, Andy's sleek silver sports car sparkled in front of her.

Trish frowned and pressed her lips together. She'd managed to keep things on the friendly-slash-professional side since the incident at Soldano's, but rather than the normal easygoing conversation they once shared, everything now felt stilted and awkward. It was difficult enough to be around him during t-ball games and at the job site. Now she had to deal with him at intimate family functions as well? She inhaled a deep breath and let it out slowly. This wouldn't be easy, but she'd somehow muddle through for her son.

"Why are we here?" Bo poked his head up from the back seat.

"It's a surprise."

His face brightened. "What is it?"

"Well, it wouldn't be a surprise if I told you, now would it?"

He released his seat belt, bounded from the car with a whoop, and headed for the picket fence gate. She slammed her car door and followed, attempting to psych herself up for the party, the inevitable move from Miller's Creek also weighing heavy. In spite of months of financial hardship and her memories of the accident and happier times, she still loved this place. Still called it home. And bit by bloody bit, it was being ripped from her grasp. Would life ever be the same once they left?

She trudged to the front door and knocked, Bo already long gone.

"Come on in, Trish." Mama Beth sang out the words, bustled toward the door, and engulfed her in a hug. "How are you, dear?"

"Fine." The familiar lie burst from her lips, but she didn't know what else to say that wouldn't cause her to dissolve in tears.

The older woman skewed her lips to one side and studied her through narrowed blue eyes. "Everyone's in the kitchen," she said kindly.

Trish stepped toward the back room, the pine floors creaking beneath her feet, the scent of a fresh-baked cake in the air. Even this old house was a part of her heritage—a part of who she was. How much of her would be left with all the pieces she'd leave behind once they moved to Austin?

Dad met her at the doorway to the large eat-in kitchen and hugged her neck. “There’s my beautiful daughter.” He crooned the words, rocked back and forth with her still in his embrace, and kissed her cheek.

Dani and Steve were close behind to greet her and give her a hug.

Andy stood on the far side of the table, his frank green-eyed perusal sending off shivers down her bare arms. He sent a half-smile and wave, which she returned with an equal lack of enthusiasm.

Mama Beth clapped her hands to get everyone’s attention. “Y’all have a seat and help me sing ‘Happy Birthday’ to the birthday boy.”

Little Bo’s face beamed with the force of a thousand suns as they sang, and Mama Beth placed a towering chocolate cake with six candles on the table. He smiled at the people he loved. The people who loved him.

The bittersweet moment brought tears to Trish’s eyes. This might well be his last birthday party in Miller’s Creek. She reached up a hand to dab the tears, glancing around to make sure no one noticed.

Andy’s gaze was trained on her, his expression solemn, his eyes troubled and stormy.

“Happy Birthday to you!” The song ended and Bo blew out all the candles in one breath, his face a study in triumph.

Trish snapped a photograph. Maybe one day she could paint the picture with the new brushes Andy had given her. She longed to sneak a peek at Andy, but dared not. Instead she turned toward her father.

The sight before her sucked air from the room. Dad’s hand covered Mama Beth’s, and the look in his eyes was one of unadulterated love.

Rage bubbled inside. When had this happened? And why? Mom had been dead less than a year, and Dad was already in love. With Mama Beth. And judging by the happy glow on her face, she loved him, too. No wonder she hadn't seen much of him lately.

She swallowed against the rush of emotion and focused on her son, trying to erase the image of Dad and Mama Beth from her mind.

Bo giggled as he reached for the first gift and opened it, then squealed with glee. "Just what I wanted!" He held up the video game he'd asked her for, jumped from the ladder-back chair, and hurled himself into her brother's lap. "Thanks, Uncle Steve."

"You're welcome, tiger. Aunt Dani picked it out."

Bo peered over Steve's shoulder and shot Dani a huge grin. "Thanks, Aunt Dani."

She smiled back and patted his arm, then allowed her hand to rest on Steve's shoulder. "You're welcome, sweet pea."

Jealousy and resentment swirled and mingled in Trish's insides. She was tired of not being able to give her son what he wanted. Tired of trying to make ends meet in a place that had no use for interior designers. Tired of happy couples. She bit her lip and battled more threatening tears. Why had God deserted her?

The rest of the party passed in a fog, as if everything had been tainted by a gray wash she could no longer paint over with high hopes and pipe dreams. Even Mama Beth's delicious chocolate cake and her son's laughter couldn't pull her from the mist. Darkness had descended with Doc's death, and now enshrouded her with such intensity she doubted she could ever escape.

Dad cornered her a few minutes later. "You okay, honey?"

She tried to muster a feeble smile, but instead, bitterness spilled from her in words designed to hurt. "Obviously not as good as you." She growled the comment as angry tears plopped to her cheeks.

His eyes and mouth widened, revealing the pain her sharp tone inflicted. "What do you mean?"

"What's with you and Mama Beth? And why am I the last to know?" She sounded selfish and small, but didn't care one whit.

"I didn't know how to tell you. I was afraid you would react, well, like this."

"Didn't know how to tell me what?"

Dad lowered his gaze and took a deep breath. "I love her, Trish."

"What about Mom? It hasn't even been a year—"

"I'll always love your mother. You know that." He rubbed her arm.

Trish's throat cinched up so much she could barely speak. "Well, you have a strange way of showing it."

Mama Beth waddled over, her expression etched with alarm. "Is everything okay?"

Unable to contain the spitefulness that reigned within, Trish spun around to face her, fists clenched at her side. "How long have you been waiting for my mother to die?"

The color drained from Mama Beth's face, but she said nothing.

"Thanks." Trish spat out the word. "You just confirmed my suspicions."

"Trish!" Dad spoke the word with censure she hadn't heard since she was a teenager.

She hastily gathered the presents Bo loved more than the ones she'd given him. Avoiding Andy's concerned gaze, she flew out the door and across the yard to get Little Bo. Next stop, the grocery store, to pick up moving boxes.

Andy sauntered away from the futon he'd slept on for the past two months to get a closer look at the painting he'd just hung on the wall. The small studio apartment didn't do Trish's artwork justice. He couldn't wait to hang the painting in his new home. Maybe things would eventually work out with Trish, and he could hang it where she could see how much he loved her. Then again, maybe not.

His thoughts returned to last weekend's birthday party. Though he hadn't heard the words Trish leveled at her father and Mama Beth, their strained faces and Trish's quick departure had spoken loud and clear. Yet one more reason for her to leave. *Lord, help me find a way to reach her.*

He studied the precise detail in the painting more carefully. Her gift was undeniable. A gift she seemed determined to ignore in favor of an interior design career. He sensed she loved painting more, so why was she so focused on the Austin job?

Andy's mind wandered to their lunch together, her face animated as she'd excitedly relayed stories about the kids at school. He shook his head in exasperation and eyed the clock. Time to get to the ball field. If nothing else, maybe it would allow him extra time with Bo and Trish.

Out of nowhere, an idea popped into his head. *Yes, that might just work.*

A smiled wiggled onto his face. He grabbed the bat bag and his baseball cap, then headed out the door singing the electric guitar lick from an old Eagles' song.

Once at the ball field, he went to work to get everything ready for the game. The Eagles had settled into a comfortable routine now, and the team had gone undefeated. After everything was set, he moved to the fence to wait for Trish and Bo.

A few minutes later they pulled up, the knock of the car engine sounding from a block away. That junker couldn't last much longer. Not without a pile of money spent on repairs. They parked, and Bo ran toward him, his face lit with a happy smile.

Andy scooped him up in his arms, remembering the sad-faced little boy from a few weeks ago. "Hey, buddy, how have you been?"

"Good. When are we going horseback riding again?"

"Well, I came out the other afternoon just for that very thing, but no one answered the door."

With solemn eyes Bo glanced around, his words hushed. "I know. Mom wouldn't let me. She's very sad right now."

Trish approached, her gait slow and lifeless. She barely acknowledged his presence with a tight tilt of her lips. Her face was pale and drawn, and in contrast, her eyes seemed especially large and luminous.

"Hi, Trish."

"Hey. You need help in the dugout? If not, I'm headed to the stands."

Andy shook his head, his heart aching at her pain. "I don't need help, but if you don't mind I'd like to talk to you alone."

She stopped, released a tired sigh, and turned weary eyes his way. "Okay."

Andy slid Bo out of his arms. "Go sit in the dugout, buddy. I'll be there in a second."

"'kay." The boy bounded off with a smile.

"I thought of an idea I'd like to run by you." He tried his best to inject his tone with enthusiasm, but it was difficult when her face was as hard and unyielding as a towering brick wall.

"What?" She looked eager to escape.

"Well, after hearing your stories about your teaching experience, I got to thinking. You love painting. You love kids. Why not teach art lessons?"

Her flat expression remained in place. “Yeah, maybe. We’ll see.” She gave a noncommittal shrug and pivoted toward the stands, her shoulders slumped. “I’ll think about it. Thanks.”

As she shuffled away, his heart dropped to his stomach. She’d given up hope. Had he already lost her?

The rest of the evening went downhill from there. The Pirates had improved since the first game of the season, and played as if invincible, while his team regressed to stupid mistakes. During the last inning, the Pirates led 8-7, with two Eagle players on base, and one out.

Andy stuffed a handful of salty sunflower seeds in his mouth while Brody Clark headed to the batter’s box. Little Bo waved from first base, his smile revealing a toothless gap. A sudden wave of resentment washed over him. The son of his heart was growing up before his very eyes.

Brody swung and missed.

“Stre-ike One!” The ump’s heavy Texas drawl split the air.

His thoughts traveled to the weeks he’d spent caring for his dad. Almost every evening, except for game nights, he’d gone to sit with him. His dementia had worsened, as had the seizures. The doctors offered no hope of improvement.

“Stre-ike two!” called out the umpire.

C’mon, Andy. Keep your head in the game. He glanced over his shoulder at Trish. She hunched over, one arm curled around her waist, the other hand propping up her chin, while she stared off into the distance.

Crack! The bat made contact, and Andy snapped his head around to see what had happened. Brody raced full out toward first base, where Little Bo stood, frozen in one spot.

“Run, Bo!” Andy yelled at the top of his lungs, but it was too late.

The first baseman scooped up the ball, stepped on the bag then tagged Little Bo for a double play.

Game over.

Andy came unglued. He stomped toward Little Bo, the frustration taking over. “What were you thinking? How many times have I told you to pay attention to what’s going on around you?”

Bo’s bottom lip quivered, and his eyes filled with tears. “I was paying ‘tention.”

“No you weren’t. If you’d been paying attention, you’d have run to second base like you were supposed to. What were you looking at anyway?”

“You and Mom.” Tears spilled over onto his chubby cheeks.

Sharp-edged slivers of guilt imbedded themselves in his heart. Andy dropped to one knee and took Bo in his arms. An odd mixture of sweat and baby shampoo made its way to his nose. “I’m sorry, buddy. I shouldn’t have lost my temper. Why were you looking at us?”

Sobs erupted from the boy and his tiny shoulders began to shake. “I’m just tired of seeing you both so sad.”

21

"*Against You, and You only, have I sinned.*" Trish read the words from her Bible again, their startling clarity winding their way throughout her being. She *had* sinned. Sinned by neglecting to be grateful for what God had given her. Even worse, she'd blamed God and allowed bitterness to take root in her heart.

God, forgive me and help me do better. She thought back to her behavior over the past couple of weeks. Shame washed over her. How had she allowed herself to slide down the slippery slope of depression? While it was true she couldn't control the situation, she did have a choice in how she reacted. It all came down to her choice. She could choose not to allow the horrid and difficult circumstances to get her down. After all, God was still in control, and she belonged to Him.

Trish glanced at the words she'd penned before sitting down to read her Bible.

Art Lessons Available
Taught by Trish James at the
Community Center
Call 555-5273 to enroll.

Would Andy's suggestion work? Part of her wanted to believe the idea was a good one, but the hurt part of herself—the part that had seen disappointment after disappointment—cautioned against getting her hopes up.

"Bo, are you ready for practice?" Trish called out, then stood and meandered from the sofa toward his room.

Bo met her in the hallway, cap and glove in his hands. "Ready." He grinned up at her, his eyes twinkling with excitement.

The bittersweet moment hit full force, and she caught her breath. Her baby was growing up. She marveled at the difference she saw in him after only a few weeks. Andy deserved all the credit. His influence was the gentle drip of love on the grieving heart of a little boy without a daddy.

As they drove into town, Trish thought of Andy again, and her heart overflowed. A realization had taken place over the past few days. She loved him. Not a first love like what she'd shared with Doc, but something just as deep and just as intense. She pressed her lips together. This wasn't something she could allow herself to consider at this point. Until she knew whether the art lessons would garner enough interest for her to make a living, it just wouldn't be fair to any of them. But maybe one day.

Maybe one day. Her new mantra.

She parked in front of the Miller's Creek Crier newspaper office, cracked the windows, and turned off the ignition. Swiveling in her seat, she faced her son. "I need to run this ad into the newspaper office. Unbuckle and come in with me."

"'kay." He didn't argue, just unclipped his seatbelt and opened the door. More of Andy's influence.

Trish and Bo entered the building to the smell of fresh ink and stale coffee.

Janet Beecher perched behind the counter, her fingers flying over the computer keyboard. She glanced up. "Hi."

Trish slid the paper across the counter. “Hi, Janet. I need to run this ad for a couple of weeks.”

The older woman scanned the words. “Really? You’re going to give art lessons?” Was she excited or only curious?

“I thought I’d give it a try.” Trish lowered her gaze. If this flopped, people would consider her the biggest fool in town. How many different ways had she attempted to make a living for her and her son over the past few months? She sighed. More than she cared to count.

“Wonderful. My group of ladies were mentioning the other day how we needed something like this. I might be interested.”

Trish’s mouth dropped open, but she quickly closed it with a smile. “Just let me know what day and time will work best for you, and I’ll put you down.”

“I’m off on Mondays.”

By the time they made their way back out to the car a few minutes later, Trish had managed to set a firm time for an art lesson the following week—Monday afternoon at 2:30. She slammed the car door behind her, snagged a notepad from her purse, and wrote down the appointment with a feeling of satisfaction. A spark of hope ignited in her heart. *Maybe one day.*

Her next stop brought her to Soldano’s. This should be the best time to drop in. It was still too early for the evening crowd. There were only a few cars in the parking lot, so hopefully they weren’t too busy yet. Trish hurried inside, Little Bo’s hand tucked safely in hers. Juan Soldano met her at the counter.

“Welcome, Meez Trish. Table for two, *sí*?” The Hispanic man smiled, a gold-capped tooth winking from his grin.

“No, Juan. I’m not here to eat. I wanted to see if . . .” She paused, unsure of how to ask, finally just opting to plow ahead. “You wouldn’t need any help during the lunch hour by any chance?” She peered up at him and waited for the expected “no.”

His coal-colored eyes widened. "*Si,* we do need help. Especially since Graciela has gone to work for Señor Tyler."

"Gracie's working for Andy?"

"*Si, si.* She is answering the phone and filing and learning about how to become a lawyer. Señor Tyler is such a good man. He is going to pay for part of her schooling. Such a good man."

A tender smile made its way to her face. "Yes, he is."

"Could you work from eleven until two, Monday through Saturday?"

Trish nodded. Perfect. She'd work on Andy's interior design project on the mornings she wasn't working at school, then she could work her shift at Soldano's and go straight to art lessons. She caught herself. It was only one lesson at this point. *But maybe, just maybe, one day . . .*

"Bo let's try you at short stop." Andy motioned him to the spot between second and third base. "If someone hits the ball to you, where do you throw it?" he asked as Bo trotted to his new position.

"The base ahead of the lead runner."

Andy followed behind him and gave him a high-five. "Atta boy!" Little Bo grinned up at him and Andy's heart turned to mush. He'd fallen so quickly for the brown-eyed fellow who looked just like his mama. Andy glanced to where Trish stood, dressed in a pair of cut-offs and a T-shirt, her fingers entwined in the chain link fence behind home plate. With her hair pulled back in a ponytail, she looked more like a teenager than a mom. She seemed better somehow. Stronger. He sauntered toward home to hit balls to the team and prayed it was true.

"Pretend there's a runner headed to third." Andy tossed the ball into the air and nudged it with a soft tap toward first base.

Brody fielded the ball, tagged the bag, and threw the ball to the third baseman, who pretended to tag the runner.

"Good job, Brody!" Carla Clark bellowed from the stands.

"Now pretend there's a runner headed home." Andy hit a grounder to Bo, who fielded it, but threw the ball to first.

"He said home, you moron." Brody snagged the pitch and threw the ball back to Andy.

"That's okay, Brody," yelled his mother. "You're good enough for the both of you."

Bo started to swell up like an old toad, and Andy yanked his head around to glare at Carla. His attention was sidetracked by Trish. She had Bo's full attention and held up one finger at a time, counting.

Bo shot her a snaggle-toothed grin. Her lips curved upward in response.

Good for them. They were both learning to deal with adversity. Did that mean they didn't need him anymore?

Andy continued to hit balls to the team, his thoughts on the scene he'd witnessed after the last game. On his way toward his apartment on the second floor of the City Hall building, he'd seen Trish and Little Bo behind the grocery store, picking up boxes. He released a sigh and pounded a ball to center field where one boy plopped in the grass to tie his shoelaces.

Lord, I feel like I'm missing something here. There's gotta be a way to keep them in Miller's Creek. Show me how.

Only as the team ran their after-practice laps, did another idea germinate and take root in his mind. After the visit with his father tomorrow night, he'd head to Dallas with Trish's painting in tow.

Andy strode toward the upscale Dallas art studio on Saturday morning with Trish's painting tucked under one arm. It had been several months since he'd seen the woman who would've been his mother-in-law. His skin crawled as nerves took over. Their last meeting had been the night of the wedding rehearsal right before he'd discovered Sheila in the arms of her supposedly ex-boyfriend.

Claire Windsor poised like an elegant bird behind the counter of the posh Dallas studio, the air saturated with cloying perfume. When she saw him, her perfectly made-up face took on a hard edge. "You have a lot of nerve coming here." Her voice held venom.

"Hello to you, too, Claire."

She didn't acknowledge or respond to his greeting. Instead she glared, her eyes searing a hole straight through his head.

How was he supposed to cut through her anger to show her Trish's work? "Look, I know this is awkward."

"Awkward? You back out of a very expensive wedding the day before it's to take place and have the nerve to call this awkward?"

Hadn't Sheila told her the truth? And if not, how was he supposed to tell her what had happened without looking like he was making excuses? "Didn't she tell you?"

"Tell me what?"

"She was still seeing Brad. I found them kissing after the rehearsal."

Her eyes widened.

So Sheila hadn't mentioned it. So like her.

Claire pursed her lips in thoughtful repose. Finally she spoke, her tone demanding. "Why are you here?"

Andy pulled the large-scaled painting from beneath his arm and rotated it to show her. "I have a friend who painted this, and wanted to see if you'd be interested in a showing of her work."

Claire's dark-lined eyes scanned the picture and took on a glint.

Ha! He had her hooked.

"It's good. Very good." She tilted her head his way. "And where is the artist?" She glanced down at the signature, a wry smirk curling one corner of her dark lipstick. "Where is Trish James?"

Andy ignored the subtle hint in her voice. "Let's just say she doesn't have a whole lot of confidence in her work or herself."

Claire arched one perfect eyebrow. "She paints like this and has no confidence?" She narrowed her eyes into cat-like slits. "Why did you choose me?" Her tone was all business now.

"Because I believe you'll treat her fairly."

Her expression softened. "You always know the right thing to say, don't you, Andy?"

He handed her a card with Trish's contact information and raised his shoulders in a slight shrug. "It's still your choice, Claire. Here's where she can be reached." He pivoted and headed to the door, turning back to face her before he left. "Oh, and please don't tell her I had anything to do with this."

"I'll do what I can, but no promises."

Andy heaved a sigh and returned to his car with the painting. He'd done all he could. The rest was up to God.

22

The old wood and glass door squeaked and then slammed. Andy glanced up from his desk as a very nervous Gracie followed Otis Thacker into his office. "I'm sorry, Andy, but Mr. Thacker needs to see you."

Demanded to see him was more like it. He sent her a reassuring smile. "Thanks, Gracie." She let herself out the door as Andy stood and offered a hand. "Nice to see you again, Mr. Thacker."

Thacker set his bulldog jaws and harrumphed, completely ignoring his outstretched hand.

Andy's eyebrows rose in spite of his attempt to keep his expression under control. He motioned to the two leather chairs positioned in front of his desk. "Please have a seat. Would you like some water or coffee?"

"I didn't come here for happy hour. I came to talk business." The older man groused the words, then shuffled to the chair and creaked his way into it. He rested both hands on his cane and glared.

Andy brought a hand to his nose. That cologne Otis doused himself with must be left over from the 1960s. "What can I do for you, sir?"

"Well, since you're charging me an arm and a leg in retainer fees, I figured it was time to put you to work."

"Okay. What are we looking at?"

Otis jutted out his jaw, his mouth arching downward in a grouchy rainbow. "I'd like to file suit against a tenant who broke lease. And I wanna get more than what they owe since I haven't been able to lease the building on such short notice."

"Sorry to hear that. We'll do all we can to make sure you receive full compensation."

"I certainly hope so since that's what I'm paying you for. How much is all this gonna cost me anyway?" Thacker's voice came out in a gravelly growl.

Andy took a sip of coffee and cleared his throat. "Well, sir, counting the time to draft the necessary legal documents and any court time involved, I would guess I'll be spending several hours—"

Whack! Thacker brought his walking cane down hard on the corner of the desk. "Enough of the legal mumbo-jumbo! How much?"

"Roughly a thousand dollars." Andy reached up and tugged on the tie which had suddenly cinched tighter.

Thacker's face turned purple, and his eyes bugged out like a bullfrog on steroids. "A thousand? Why, that's highway robbery! I've been paying you five hundred a month since you got here, and haven't used your services once. Now you're gonna charge me a thousand? You might get that out of some of those city dudes in Dallas, but you ain't gonna get it outta me!" He creaked out of his chair and tottered toward the door.

Andy's pulse escalated, and he hurried to his side. "I'm sure we can work something out, Mr. Thacker. Please have a seat and let's talk through this."

Thacker squinted, then released a grunt. "Oh, all right." He waddled back to the chair, his cane raised. "But I'm not paying you a penny more than five hundred."

Andy returned to his seat mulling the matter over in his mind. The old codger had him in between a rock and a hard place and knew it. As an influential member of Miller's Creek, he had the power to make or break his stay as the city attorney. "Tell you what, since you've already paid five hundred this month, we'll make the total owed five hundred." Andy once more positioned himself in the chair and rolled it under the desk, grabbing a pencil and a legal pad. "Now how much does your client owe in back rent?"

"Three months worth. Three thousand dollars."

Thacker was getting a thousand bucks a month in rent and choking on paying him? There weren't any houses in Miller's Creek nice enough to qualify for that kind of lease price. "And where is this house located?"

"House? I never said it was a house."

"What is it then? A building?"

"Yep, and renovated recently."

So Otis owned part of downtown Miller's Creek. Probably didn't pay a penny for the renovation, thanks to Dani's generous donation. "How many more months remained on the lease?" He tried to keep his voice on an even keel.

"Eight."

Andy scribbled some notes on the legal pad. "You been in contact with this person?"

"Yep. Phoned 'em several times, but now they won't answer my calls."

No surprise there. "And did the lessee mention why they were behind and why they were breaking lease?"

Otis waved a dismissive hand in the air. "Ah, some sob story about not getting enough business and needing the money for something else. Said they'd pay as they could, but I haven't seen one red dime."

Andy's radar went up. "Um, who is this person?"

"Steve's sister, Trish James."

Otis' words pushed him back against the seat. How was he going to explain this? "Sorry Mr. Thacker, but I can't represent you."

Otis' face screwed up. "Why's that? I have you on retainer."

"It's called conflict of interest. I've hired Trish to help me with my new office, and I coach her son's t-ball team."

"Doesn't sound like a conflict to me."

He squirmed in his seat, suddenly feeling like a catfish on a hook. Out of the water. Flopping around on the creek bank. "Uh, this is confidential, but we've . . . er . . . also considered a relationship." Well, he'd considered it anyway.

The older man's uni-brow rose and fell before curving into a scowl. "You don't waste any time, do you, young man? What's wrong? Not enough pretty women in the city for you, so you move here to hit on our young widows?" He rose to his feet and made his way to the door, slamming it behind him.

Andy's blood pressure climbed to the stratosphere. So much for making a good impression on Thacker. This would most likely be the latest fodder for the grapevine, and there was absolutely nothing he could do about it.

Trish signed out at Soldano's, shucked the apron covered with smiling maraca-shaking chili peppers, and hurried to the car she'd not-so-affectionately nicknamed The Lemon. Her shift had run late again today, leaving her fifteen minutes to set up for afternoon art lessons. Her two students barely made teaching worth the effort, though she enjoyed it more than she'd ever imagined possible.

She crawled into the car, heat blasting her in the face. Summer obviously wasn't the best time to open a private art studio. Several people had expressed an interest, but wanted to wait until fall to begin. To make matters worse, the money she'd made off lessons had been eaten up by childcare expenses.

With a toss of her head, she made her way to the Community Center. Oh well, things worked out the way they did for a reason. It must be part of God's plan, even though God's plans sometimes made no sense to her.

The cell phone buzzed and she grabbed it from the console. Steve. She punched the talk button. "What's up?"

"Hey, I have something I think you should know." The warning in his tone sent shivers down her spine.

"What?"

"I ate lunch with the geezers at Granny's. Otis was shooting off his mouth about filing suit against you for being delinquent on your payments and breaking your lease."

Her mind went numb. Then hot anger flared, coupled with embarrassment. "You've got to be kidding!" Now that Steve knew this detail of her financial situation, it wouldn't be long until Dad found out.

"There's more." Her brother paused, an ominous silence filling the void. "He said he'd hired Andy Tyler for the job."

Her stomach grew queasy, and her mouth dropped open. Andy? Not noticing the red light until it was too late, she plowed right through the intersection.

23

Trish balanced the tray of drinks and soft-stepped toward table five, praying she wouldn't trip. The lunch shift had been busy, and her tip apron now held a nice bulge.

She passed out drinks to the people at table five and jotted down their food order. As she reached the kitchen door, a loud throat-clearing sounded from the booth to her left. Trish yanked her head in the direction of the noise. How long had she been sitting there?

Carla parked at the table, a scowl embedded on her face. "I've been here almost ten minutes, and no one has taken my order."

"Sorry, I didn't see you. What can I get you to drink?"

"I'll have iced tea with two lemons and the blue plate special, cut the salad and add a guacamole." She barked out her order then tossed the menu. "Bring the blue sweetener. I don't like the pink stuff."

Trish quickly scribbled down the order and managed a polite "thank you."

She returned a few minutes later with Carla's tea, basket of chips, and ramekin of salsa, trying to disregard the delicious smells swirling around her and setting off a rumble in her belly.

Dani, Steve, Mama Beth, and Dad rounded the corner and seated themselves at a nearby table, their faces registering shock. Trish sucked in a deep breath. Had they forgiven her birthday party outburst? She squelched the animosity she still felt over the relationship between Dad and Mama Beth. Nothing good could come from stewing over it. She was an adult, and it was high time she acted like one.

Trish sidled over to her family. “Hi, y’all.” After their returned greetings, an awkward silence ensued. “What can I get you to drink?”

“Why?” Her father’s voice was gruff.

“Why what?” Trish steeled herself.

“You know what.” His expression held reproach. “We would’ve helped. All you had to do was ask.”

“I’m a grown-up now, Dad. I can take care of myself.”

He started to speak again, but Mama Beth laid a hand on his arm. He met her gaze, then clamped his lips in a taut line.

Mama Beth made direct eye contact, her light blue eyes sincere. “Trish, I know you’re busy, but could we set up some time to talk—just the two of us?”

Trish shifted uncomfortably. “Sure.” Though she hated confrontation, it *would* be better to clear the air instead of letting frustrations build. “I’ll stop by later this afternoon.”

A soft smile of appreciation curved Mama Beth’s lips. “Thank you, sweetie. I’d like a glass of unsweetened tea, please.”

Trish took their food orders, then made her way to the drink station, her thoughts on Dad’s reaction. Why was he so upset? Surely he favored her taking a job in town as opposed to moving to Austin. Or did he? Trish filled glasses with ice and gave her head an angry shake. *Snap out of it, Trish. Prove that you’ve got what it takes.*

Surprisingly, she was able to do just that, and responded calmly to Carla a few minutes later when the food wasn’t to her liking. And when her family left the restaurant, she sent them off with a smile. As the clock inched toward two, she breathed easier. Even after a couple of big challenges, her day had gone pretty smoothly.

But when she neared table two, her breath caught in her throat. Andy lounged at the table studying a menu. Was it true that he was going to file suit against her, or was that information just another nugget of geezer gossip? She steadied her nerves and approached his table. "Let me guess, chicken fajitas?"

He looked up, his mouth agape at first, then it widened to an infectious grin. "Good to see you, Trish. For your information, I thought I'd step outside my box today and try the chicken fajita nachos."

She laughed and wrote down his order. "Bold move." His friendly response was just the balm her spirit needed. No lectures, no accusations, just the same old Andy. "And to drink?"

"What do you recommend?"

"We make a mean glass of sweet tea."

"So I've heard. Sounds good."

As she moved to pick up the menu, Andy placed his hand on hers, his sea-green eyes no longer teasing. "Nice to see you smile again, Trish."

"It feels good from my perspective, too."

"I'm sure it does. You mind my asking what brought it on?" His eyes held . . . what was it? Hope?

"Well, this job for one, and I have a couple of art lessons this afternoon."

His face brightened. "Good for you."

"It was your idea." She pulled the menu and her hand from beneath his grasp. "I'll be right back with your tea."

After she delivered Andy's tea and helped bus a few tables, she returned to the kitchen to wait for his order. Her cell phone buzzed in her apron, and she checked the digital readout. Not a number she recognized. "Hello?"

"Is this Trish James?"

Please not another bill collector. Didn't they know she was doing her best? "Yes. May I ask who's calling?"

"My name is Claire Windsor." The elegant voice dripped money and culture. "I own an art studio in Dallas and host an art show on the third weekend of every month to highlight Texas artists and their work. Would you be interested in a show in September?"

The room seemed suddenly devoid of air. "You've seen my work?"

"Yes. You have talent, Mrs. James. Based on the painting I saw, I think your work will not only sell, but sell well."

Her pulse careened through her veins, and she brought a hand to her face. "Th-thanks. I'd love the opportunity."

The woman gave her a website address to check out for the details and promised to stay in touch.

Trish managed a mumbled word of thanks, then clicked the phone shut, her mind reeling. There was so much work to do between now and September. And why had she forgotten to ask where the woman had seen one of her paintings?

"Order up for table two." Rafael, the middle Soldano son, let his bass voice ring out, then flashed a winning smile the Soldano men were famous for. "You have stars in your eyes, señora."

She told him her good news as she loaded Andy's order on a tray.

When she reached the stainless steel swinging doors, Rafael's hearty congratulations sounded. She swiveled to smile at him, and backed her way out of the kitchen. As she cleared the doors, Trish turned and collided with a broad chest. The lunch platter slid down the man's suit and landed with a clank on the floor.

Trish backed away, eyeing globs of sour cream, guacamole, and pico de gallo on the man's shirt and tie. Her foot landed in a pile of something slippery. She tried to keep her balance, but the room shifted as she hurtled toward the floor.

Two strong arms reached out to save her, then pulled her toward a food-splattered chest. The moment passed, and she looked up into familiar green eyes and a dimpled grin. "I know you're eager to paint, but did you have to start with my suit and what I presume was my lunch?"

God, help me not to say anything I shouldn't, and help me listen more than I talk. Please give me answers.

Trish stepped from her car into Mama Beth's gravel driveway and made her way to the picket fence gate. The fragrance of roses wafted from the white rose arbor that framed the cobblestone path.

She repositioned a stray strand of hair, her pulse throbbing in her throat. While she'd never felt fear when it came to Mama Beth, she had a feeling this conversation wouldn't be easy. She'd always loved the woman and looked up to her, but the relationship between her and Dad made this uncertain ground.

Trish wearily climbed the wooden steps to the wraparound porch and tapped lightly on the screen door.

"Come on in." Mama Beth squeaked open the door, then reached up and hugged her neck.

"I can't stay long."

The older woman pulled away and blinked, her blue eyes taking on hurt. "Sorry if I'm keeping you from your time with Bo, but I wanted to explain a few things. I couldn't stand this distance between us."

Trish nodded, then lowered her head to stare at her hands. "I apologize for losing my temper at the birthday party. It had been a rough day."

"You've had a lot of rough days here lately. That's another thing I wanted to talk about."

She raised her head, her eyebrows on the climb. Was she about to endure another lecture on how to cope with losing a spouse? And from someone who'd never even been married?

"Have a seat." Mama Beth motioned to the sofa. "Can I get you something to drink?"

"No, thanks." Trish moved to the overstuffed couch and sank into it, longing for the world to go away so she could relax and sleep.

The older woman shuffled to the other end and plopped down, her eyebrows crinkled. "I'm not sure how to even begin this story, but I know you're in a hurry so I'll just start. You probably know your dad and I graduated together and dated all through high school."

She nodded. Mom had never let any of them forget it, constantly harping about Mama Beth, her jealousy deep and unforgiving.

"He went off to college while I stayed in Miller's Creek to work. We weren't engaged, but there was a promise between us." Mama Beth's voice hitched. She paused as her shoulders rose and then settled. "When he came back home with a wife and child, I thought I'd die from the pain. But I didn't. I got up, put one foot in front of the other like you're doing now, and made a life. But I never stopped loving him."

Trish's heart beat faster, but she didn't answer. Couldn't answer.

"But contrary to what you said the other day, I haven't been waiting for your mother to die. I gave up hope that I'd ever have a relationship with Bo when he came back to Miller's Creek with a family."

A frown wiggled on to Trish's face. "Why didn't you ever marry?"

"I never found anyone else I loved." Her voice decreased to a hurt whisper. "So even though I never lost a husband, I do know a thing or two about loss. I can't promise your heartbreak will go away, but it does get easier to bear."

Trish swallowed a wad of grief. At least with Doc, she didn't have to suffer through knowing he belonged to someone else. "I-I'm sorry. I never knew all the facts. I didn't mean to be so cruel the other day, but it hasn't even been a year since . . ."

Mama Beth scooted closer and wrapped her in a hug. "I know, sweetie. Just remember that for your dad, the woman he loved and married died a long time ago."

True. Alzheimer's made it that way for all of them. They missed her, but were glad she didn't have to suffer anymore. "I want Dad to be happy. I really do. And I want that for you, too." Trish pulled away and used the heels of her hands to swipe at the tears spilling onto her cheeks. She released a frustrated groan. "Sorry I'm crying. I'm so sick of tears."

"There are plenty of people willing to help, you know."

Please not again. Trish rose to her feet and drifted to the tall front windows, rubbing her arms. "I'm just trying to cope. I'm not asking for help.'

Mama Beth let out a tired sigh. "I understand. I really do, but make sure your pride isn't getting in the way." A long moment of silence passed. "Forgive me if I'm sticking my nose where it's not wanted, but I've seen the way you look at Andy and the way he looks at you. He loves Little Bo as if he were his own son."

Trish froze, her feet rooted to the floor. How could she have noticed? She licked her lips. "It's much too soon to even think abou—"

"Not if you love him. Have you stopped to consider that God may have purposely brought Andy into your life for this moment in time?"

Yes, but only as a friend. Right?

"I love you, Trish. I hope you know that." Mama Beth stood and shuffled over to stand beside her. "But I see you struggling so hard to do things on your own when God may have another plan."

Trish brought both hands to her cheeks. "There's just so much to think about. I don't feel ready to add a relationship to the mix.'

"I'm not trying to rush you. I just want you to consider the options. Remember the story of Joseph?"

She let her hands drop to her sides and faced Mama Beth. "What does that have to do with this?"

"Think about all he suffered. His brothers hated him and sold him into slavery. For thirteen years he endured prison and hardships. Then, when God's timing was right, he became a leader in Egypt and was responsible for saving many lives." Growing confidence resonated from her tone and her face glowed. "God doesn't waste any hurt you endure, Trish. What He allows into your life—even something as painful as Doc's death—He'll use for the days ahead. I know it's hard to see past the pain, but try to view the situation from an eternal perspective. And make sure you don't miss out on something wonderful because of fear and pride."

Fire blazed in her veins. Everything she did was for her son. *Everything*. Now Mama Beth had the nerve to call her proud and afraid? Her fists clenched, then went limp. Mama Beth was right. She was proud and afraid. Was she right about Andy, too?

24

Trish hurriedly wiped down tables and chairs at Soldano's in anticipation of an afternoon with Bo. Between all her jobs, she'd barely had time to breathe, much less spend time with him. She released a tired sigh between her lips. Just another fringe benefit of being a single parent.

At least she had Andy to fall back on. After last night's ball game, he'd kindly offered to keep Bo today, since the daycare wasn't open on Saturdays, and since Dad and Mama Beth had plans. Of course, her son had been giddy at the prospect of riding horses and playing catch with Coach Andy.

She counted her tip money. Not as good as last week, but every little bit was appreciated and needed. Worry gnawed at her. She'd heard nothing about any legal action since Steve's phone call. Apparently Otis had decided to let her overdue payment slide. Maybe he'd just been loose in the lips the day he'd spouted off to her brother. The check she'd mailed yesterday should keep him at bay a while longer.

Heading for the back, she untied her apron strings. Juan caught her as she passed the glass checkout counter, his dark eyes a-twinkle. "You have customers at booth four."

Trish checked the clock and gulped. Already ten after two. If she made Andy late to an appointment, he'd be furious. She retied her apron and hurried to booth four, her pen and pad in hand. Her mouth fell open.

Bo giggled. "Hi, Mom."

"Hi, Mom," reiterated Andy with a catchy laugh.

Her pulse quickened at the sight of his handsome face. *Careful, Trish.* A smile curved her lips before she could contain it, but she quickly assumed her waitress persona. "What can I get for you two gentlemen?"

Bo chortled at the charade. "We want ice cream."

"Ice cream?" she asked in mock surprise.

"You heard the man." Andy laughed again and sent her a wink. "The biggest bowl you can find with lots of hot fudge sauce. Oh, and bring three spoons."

"One extra-large hot-fudge sundae coming up." She laid a finger on the tip of her son's upturned nose.

Andy made a move to stand. "While you get the sundae, I'll ask Juan to let you clock out. You look bushed."

Mr. Fix-It to the rescue again, but he'd get no objections today. "That would be awesome. My feet are killing me."

Minutes later Trish returned with the ice cream and sank into the booth beside Bo. She dipped her spoon into the fudgy, melting ice cream and scooped a bite into her mouth, closing her eyes in rapture. Ice cream, her son, money in her pocket, and a wonderful friend—what more could she ask for? God continued to provide. Now if He could just do it a little faster.

"So what's on your agenda this afternoon?" Andy's friendly question intruded into her thoughts.

She opened her eyes. "Well, first I wanna hug my son. I've missed him all day." Trish reached toward Bo.

He wrapped his arms around her neck and planted a sticky kiss on her cheek.

Her heart melted. "Have you had a good day, sweetie?"

"I had a great day!" Her son resumed his dig into the ice cream sundae.

Like a big overgrown kid, Andy delved in for his own bite. "Okay, you have your hug, now what?"

"There's a garage sale I want to check out, then I'm headed to the ranch. Bo's gonna help me organize my studio."

"Mo-o-om!"

"Mind if I tag along?" Andy's eyes held tentative hope.

How could she refuse after all he'd done for her and Bo? "Not at all, but I hope you're not afraid of work."

"I wouldn't have asked if I were."

A little later, Trish led the way to the garage sale, while the guys followed in Andy's car. She pulled up in front of a brick house and parked. Carla and Brody stood at a table full of toys. She breathed a quick prayer that God would guide her words, thoughts, and actions, and climbed from the car.

Andy accompanied Bo to the toy table while she headed to a rack of boys' clothing. Good. There was still a big selection. Bo would need school clothes in another month or so. She picked out several pairs of shorts and a few shirts, handed the woman a five, and headed over to Andy and Bo.

"I had that first." Brody's belligerent voice rose above the soft conversation of other shoppers, and he grabbed for the toy truck tucked in Bo's arms.

Mother-bear fury raged inside. She quickened her pace. *Count, Trish. One, two . . .*

Bo glanced up as she approached, his brown eyes full of questions.

Time to set a good example. She smiled at him, then turned her attention to Carla and Brody. "You did a great job at last night's game, Brody. You're quite a ball player."

Brody's glare turned to confusion. "Thanks."

"Yeah, you did super," added Bo.

Pride swelled in her heart at her son's kindness. He'd come so far. She placed a hand on his shoulder. "You must be so proud of him, Carla."

The woman's mouth hung open in disbelief. "Yeah."

Bo handed the truck over. "Here. You can have it."

Andy caught her attention. His eyes shone like emeralds, and his lips turned up softly at the corners.

A burst of emotion threatened to swallow her whole. It wouldn't do for her to get lost in those eyes of his. She turned back to Carla. "Well, we'd best be going. Brody, if you'd like to play with Bo tomorrow, we could pick you up for church and take you back home tomorrow night."

"Yeah, we could play video games and catch." Bo actually sounded excited.

"Sure, I guess. Would that be okay, Mom?"

Carla smiled at Trish. "That'd be nice. What time do I need to have him ready?"

"We'll be there at 9:30. You're welcome to come with us."

She lowered her head. "Maybe some other time."

"The invitation always stands. See you in the morning." Trish herded Little Bo toward the two cars, Andy in step beside them.

After he helped Bo into his seat and slammed the door, Andy faced her. "That was pretty awesome to watch."

"Thanks." Heat rose in her cheeks, and a nervous laugh fell from her lips. "Well, I guess we should head on out to the ranch."

"See you there." Andy smiled and trailed fingers down her arm.

Trish climbed in The Lemon and started the engine, her heart bouncing in her chest. If everything went well with the art classes and show in Dallas, then she could consider the option Mama Beth mentioned.

Andy steered into the driveway of Trish's house right behind her. First, time with Bo, now time with both of them. And if things went according to plan, later he'd have time alone with Trish.

She climbed from her car and used a hip to shut the door. "Hope you're ready to work."

"It's what I live for."

"What? Work?"

"No, helping you."

"Haven't we already had this discussion?" Trish's aggravated tone matched her scowl.

Andy held up both hands in surrender. "Sorry, my mistake. Now I remember. You don't like to be helped." He sent a teasing grin as he sauntered closer.

Her pursed lips curved upward. "And don't forget it." She spoke the threat softly, handed him the garage sale sack, then pivoted toward the house. "You can lay that on the kitchen counter for now. I've gotta change clothes." The soft scent of perfume trailed behind her.

One minute telling him not to help, the next bossing him around like some domestic diva. He shook his head, peered down at Bo, and let out a chuckle. "Just like a woman. She tells you one thing, then does something completely opposite."

Bo's face took on disgust. "Yeah, I know."

Andy's eyebrows inched up. "You do?"

"Yep."

"Like how?"

Bo made his way to the door, and Andy followed. "Mary Simpson at school."

Girl trouble in Kindergarten? "Who's Mary Simpson?"

"This girl." Bo swung open the door for both of them, then slammed it after Andy passed.

"Yeah, I gathered that. What about her?"

"She told me she liked me, then pushed me down in the dirt."

Laughter poured from Andy. He plopped the bag on the counter and squatted in front of Bo. "See, I think Mary pushed you down 'cause she likes you." He tickled the boy's ribs.

Bo didn't laugh. Instead he pulled away, one corner of his mouth hiked up on his darkened face. "Yuck! I'm staying away from all girls!"

"Trust me, buddy, you'll change your mind one of these days." Andy patted his shoulder and stood. "Speaking of girls, would you mind paying a visit to your Papaw later so I can spend some time alone with your Mom?"

"You like Mom?"

Andy grinned. No beating around the bush with this boy. "Yeah, as a matter of fact, I do. Is that okay?"

He shrugged. "I guess. Does she like you back?"

Trish's footsteps sounded down the hall. Andy skewed his lips and brought a hand up to scratch his cheek. "That's what I'm trying to figure out." She'd been sending off mixed signals for weeks.

Even in cut-offs and a T-shirt, her hair swept back in a silky pony tail, Trish looked gorgeous.

She glided to the back door. "Okay, guys, let's get this done in record time so I can have some time to rest before dinner."

An hour later, she stood in the middle of the cottage floor, arms crossed, and viewed the space. "There. That's much better."

Andy sauntered over beside her, wiping sweat from his forehead. The room no longer held the smell of dust, but the fragrance of fresh flowers Trish had picked from her now-weeded garden. "You weren't kidding when you said you were gonna put me to work. I didn't know you were gonna rearrange the whole cottage."

"That'll teach you to volunteer." She sent a teasing smile that tugged at his heart.

Bo yanked on Andy's fingers and looked up at him with a impish grin, then turned his focus to Trish. "Mom, can I go over to Papaw's for a while?"

A frown wrinkled her forehead. "I guess so, but call first to make sure he's home."

"'kay." He raced out the screen door, letting it slam behind him.

She scrunched her eyebrows together again, staring after him. "I wonder what he's up to."

"What do you mean?"

"He's acting a little odd, like he's up to something."

"Probably just wants to spend time with his grandpa." Andy plodded to the overstuffed sofa and sank into the cushion. "So how's the painting coming along?"

"Not as fast as I'd like. I'm worried that I won't have enough paintings for the art show in Dallas." She raised a hand to her mouth and nibbled at her thumbnail.

His pulse quickened. So far she seemed oblivious to the fact that he'd arranged the showing. "I'm sure you'll do fine. Have any completed?" He scanned the far corner of the room where they'd set up her easel.

Trish shook her head, a brooding look on her face. "No, I just haven't had time. Between trying to get stuff done for your office, my art lessons, and the job at Soldano's, I'm snowed under right now."

"Mom, he's there!" Bo hollered the words from the house.

She traipsed to the doorway and waved. "Okay, have fun!"

Andy cleared his throat. "What can I do to make things easier for you?"

Her head cocked to one side, Trish studied him with her dark brown eyes. “Nothing. I wasn’t complaining. I was just stating fact. I’ve already planned to start staying up a couple of hours later than usual after Bo goes to bed.”

“I don’t think that’s wise.”

“I don’t think it’s any of your business.” She grabbed a rag and started dusting a table that had already been dusted.

Hmm, best if he didn’t respond.

A moment later Trish stopped and looked his way. “I’m sorry, Andy. You didn’t deserve that.”

He patted the cushy couch. “Come here.”

Trish dropped the rag, made her way to the sofa, and plopped down beside him with a tired sigh. “Things are going so much better right now, but I’m so afraid of doing something to mess it up.”

Fear. How many times had he done battle with it himself? “I feel that way sometimes, too, but fear isn’t from God.”

Trish nodded. “You’re right, but it’s hard not to be afraid. I need these jobs to support myself and Bo, but I also need to be painting. I’d like to set up a website to showcase my art, but there’s not enough ti—”

Bingo! That was it! “Let me help.”

An exasperated grunt fell from her lips. “There you go again, bu—”

“Wait, hear me out. I built my website, so I already know how to do it. The only cost will be the domain name. I can take pictures of your art to add to the site.”

“I just told you I don’t have anything painted.”

He leaned forward and tweaked her button nose. “Yes, but according to your brother you have paintings all over town. I could probably knock on any door in town and find a Trish James painting.”

She sent him a dubious smile. “I’m not sure they’re good enough, and when will you have time? Sounds like a lot of work.”

“I’ll make time.” Even as the hope-laced words sounded, he knew it would mean losing a couple of hours’ sleep for a week or so. So what? If it kept her in Miller’s Creek, it was worth it.

“I don’t want to overload you. And what if I get so many orders I can’t keep up?”

“Stop being such a worrywart.” He grabbed her hand. “We’ll cross that bridge when we come to it.”

She didn’t pull her hand away, and a flicker of hope sparked in her eyes. “I owe you so much for how you’ve helped Bo and me. How can I thank you?”

Andy inhaled deeply. Put up or shut up time. “Let me take you to dinner.”

“I’m sure Bo would be delighted. Thanks for the invi—”

His pulse roared in his ears and his mouth went dry. “No. I mean just you and me.”

25

"Delaine, I've already told you, I don't have an answer yet." Frustration crept into her tone. "Right now, things are going well. I won't know about the move for a few more weeks."

"How can you say things are going okay when you're still just scraping by?"

Trish eyed the digital alarm clock. Andy would be here in a half hour to take her to dinner, and she still needed to get ready. "I may just be scraping by, but I'm happy. And more importantly, Bo's happy."

"Have you gotten any orders from your website yet?"

Fresh anxiety attacked. She hated that Andy had worked so hard for nothing. "No, but it's only been up a week. Andy says it takes a while for the search engines to start picking you up."

"Andy says." Delaine's voice took on a mocking quality. Trish could imagine a similar expression on her face. "It seems to me that you're putting a little too much stock in what Andy says."

Her backbone stiffened. "He's done a lot for me, Delaine."

"No need to defend him, but if you ask me, he's escorting you straight to the poorhouse."

"Look, I've gotta get ready. Can we talk about this later?"

Delaine huffed a sigh through the phone. "Okay, but Francesca needs an answer soon. I can't keep putting her off forever." Without even saying good-bye, she hung up.

Trish massaged her stiff neck. Delaine had always been overly dramatic, but she'd also been right on target when it came to business advice. *Lord, I don't know who to listen to anymore. Show me what I'm supposed to do.*

Part of the verse that had been on her heart for months made its way to her thoughts—***don't lean on your own understanding.***

Trish brought both hands to her face and peered at the clock. She'd better kick it into high gear if she expected to be ready by the time Andy arrived. Now if she could only figure out how to lean on God instead of her own understanding. That, and figure out what to wear.

Fifteen minutes later she stood in front of the full-length mirror and examined her reflection, wishing she had a nicer dress. The slightly faded sundress was more than a little outdated, but would have to do.

Her stomach did a saucy pirouette and deposited a sour taste to her tongue. Moving a hand to her abdomen, she took a gulp of air and let it out slowly. Why did she feel so frazzled? She'd shared a meal with Andy before, but this time it felt like a date.

The doorbell sounded, and her pulse ratcheted up a few notches. She forced her legs to move slowly to the front door. No sense in getting all bothered about one evening.

But one look at Andy's face made her fears return. Excitement bounced in his eyes, and a grin wider than the Brazos lit his face.

Trish wet her lips and sent a shaky smile. How she wished she could share in his excitement, but she couldn't. One of them had to keep their feet on the ground. She couldn't allow things to move too quickly. Not while there were still so many unknowns.

"You look stunning. Here, these are for you." He pulled a bouquet of sunflowers from behind his back, the pungent smell wafting to her nose.

"How'd you know I like sunflowers?"

His broad grin widened even more. "Lucky guess."

"Let me put these in water, and then we can go."

Andy closed the door behind him. "Can I see the painting you finished?"

"It's over by the fireplace."

He moved in the direction of her pointing finger and picked up the canvas. When she returned from putting the sunflowers in water, Andy still stood in the same position, perusing the painting.

She wiped her sweaty palms against her sundress. "Well, what do you think?"

"It's beautiful. You've outdone yourself." His voice was low and throaty.

"I'm glad you like it. I really struggled with getting the creek just right. I'm still not sure it's all that gr—"

"Stop it, Trish." The words almost sounded angry, but then his expression softened. "Stop being so hard on yourself. You asked my opinion and I gave it. I love the painting."

"Thanks." She pressed her lips together, unsure of what to say.

Andy leaned the painting against the stone fireplace, then grabbed her hand. "Sorry if I sounded harsh. I just wish you could see your art the way I see it."

"That's hard to do when you've struggled to make it just right."

"I'm sure it is, but when someone gives you a compliment, take it and keep your critical thoughts to yourself." He ended his lecture with a playful tug at her fingers.

Trish pulled her hand away and forced a laugh, wishing again that she'd declined his dinner invitation.

Andy took in the stunning sight. Bathed in the light of a glorious Texas sunset, Trish stood perfectly still, like a golden-hued statue carved from the finest marble.

"This is your boat?" She stared ahead, her mouth half open as they walked side-by-side down the pier, their shoes thudding against the grayed wood.

He chuckled. "Not hardly. I borrowed it from a judge friend of mine."

"You went to all this trouble for me." The words were half-comment, half-question as her gaze danced across the scene.

"It was no trouble. I enjoyed it, and you deserve it."

"But it *was* troub—"

He held a finger to her lips, and she turned her doe-like eyes his way. "Don't ruin it, pretty lady. I wanted to do this for you." He grabbed her hand and climbed in, helping her into the boat. "Watch your step." The boat bobbed a bit, and he gripped her hand to make sure she didn't lose her balance.

Trish glanced toward the skirted table, set with flowers and fancy dishes. "I still can't believe you did this."

"Why not?"

She laughed and shook her head. Her silky brown hair bounced around her tanned shoulders. "It's not that I doubt your ability to do it, I just don't understand why."

He wrapped an arm around her waist. "For you. That's all you need to know." He delivered a stern look to let her know this line of discussion was closed. "Allow me to escort you to our table."

As if on cue, Hector Soldano, Juan's oldest son, moved from beneath the canopy to the table, balancing a tray loaded with bread, cheese, fruit, and salad. He positioned the tray near the table. "*Buenos noches*," he said in his thick Hispanic accent as he pulled out a chair for Trish.

"You're in on this, too?" The incredulous look on her face was priceless.

"*Si, señora*. Enjoy the starter course." He placed the items from the tray on the table. "I'll bring out the entrée when we reach our destination."

"Destination?" Trish arched both eyebrows inquisitively.

Andy couldn't help but laugh. "This may be a boat, but there'll be no fishing tonight, especially when it comes to any of the details of this evening. Thanks, Hector."

Hector started the boat engine and set a slow, but steady course toward the sunset.

Trish carved off a piece of the fresh-baked bread and buttered it, then took a dainty bite. "I still can't believe—"

"Hush. Just relax and enjoy."

She did as he asked, to the point that the only sound was the soft purr of the motor and the water lapping against the edge of the boat. "So do you have ideas for more paintings?" He sipped sparkling grape juice from the crystal goblet.

"More than I can possibly ever paint," she replied drolly. "I've done a few sketches. Now I just have to . . ." She hesitated, as if not quite sure how to voice her thoughts.

"Have to what?" Andy sliced a piece of Swiss cheese from the block and layered it on the warm rye bread, then bit into it.

"Would it be possible for me to get an advance to buy canvases and paints?" Trish's face was drawn and tight, like it was killing her to have to ask.

Andy paused in mid-chew. "Of course. You can't exactly paint without supplies, can you?"

She shook her head, her gaze trained on her plate.

He took her hand, forcing eye contact. "Don't feel bad about asking, Trish. I'm excited that you have this opportunity."

"It's so important for the show to go well. I know I need to swallow my pride, but I can't help but feel bad. I feel like such a loser having to depend on others."

"You shouldn't. We all need outside help from time to time." His mind instantly turned to his father, and the words he'd just spoken attacked his conscience. If he'd taken his own advice a little sooner would it have made a difference in his father's medical condition?

"Where'd you go?" Trish's question broke through his muddled thoughts.

"Hmm?"

"You kinda zoned out on me there, like Bo does when he's watching cartoons."

Andy wiped his mouth on the cloth napkin. "Just thinking about something."

"Which is a nice way of telling me to mind my own business. Okay, I'll choose a different topic. I still don't know anything about your family except you have a younger brother. Matt, isn't it?"

"Yeah. Wow, look at that sunset."

Trish faced the sinking orange orb, and her face softened. She gave a slow blink as the breeze tousled her hair. "It's lovely. I wish I had my paints and a canvas. Maybe if I stare at it long enough, it'll become etched on my memory."

Amazing how her words echoed his sentiments. Only it wasn't the sunset that swiped his breath.

She swiveled toward him. "I don't deserve this, Andy, but thank you. It really is delightful."

The smile she sent reduced him to a puddle of goo, and words eluded him. Rare occurrence for a lawyer.

"So how's business?" Trish lifted a strawberry from the fruit plate.

He shook himself and took a quick drink. "Better than expected. In fact, when I got back from the construction site today, I noticed my answering machine is full of messages." He just hoped one of them wasn't from Otis. Hopefully, the man would take his advice to wait a while longer until Trish had a chance to get back on her feet.

"Speaking of the construction site, when will they be ready for me to take over the inside?"

"Probably week after next." The boat slowed, and Andy glanced around. Good. They had the place to themselves.

"Where are we?" Trish sounded eager and excited, like a child discovering uncharted territory.

"This is Eagle Island. Apparently eagles nest here in the winter." The soft strains of jazz music began to waft from the speakers.

Her tawny eyes widened, gold-flecked in the light. "I've lived near here all my life and never knew this place existed."

"Really? Then we'll have to come back in the winter to scout for eagles. My favorite verse is the one from Isaiah that mentions how 'those who wait on the Lord will mount up with wings like eagles.'"

A faraway look nestled on her face. "Waiting's so hard, isn't it? Sometimes it seems like I'm in a holding pattern. Then at other times I feel like I'm about to do a nosedive."

A pang of hurt pounded through his chest. "Don't give up, Trish. God won't let you fall."

She smiled sadly. "I'm trying to hang on. I really am."

"I know." He'd never seen anyone try so hard. Andy reached across the table and caressed her cheek. "I want to help."

"You already have. More than you know."

Behind them, Hector cleared his throat.

Trish pulled back and fidgeted with her napkin.

"Hope you like seafood." Hector placed a covered tray on the table, and Andy lifted the lid to reveal boiled shrimp and grilled amberjack.

"I love it, but there's no way I can eat that much." She turned to Hector. "I didn't know you knew how to cook seafood, too."

An approaching motor boat garnered their attention.

"Looks like my ride is here," announced Hector. "Can I get you anything before I go?"

Andy smiled and shook Hector's hand. "No thanks. I think we can handle it from here."

Hector waved and climbed onto the other boat. As it sped away, Trish squirmed in her seat, her discomfort obvious. Andy did all he could to lighten the mood. Finally, he got her to relax by sharing some of Bo's antics during their horse ride the previous day.

The rest of the meal was filled with great conversation and laughter. Finally, Trish leaned back, both hands on her stomach, and groaned. "I can't eat another bite."

"Me either." Andy wiped his hands and mouth, then laid the linen napkin beside his plate. "Mind if I ask you a question?"

"Of course not."

"You mentioned once that you felt like God sent me your way. You still feel that way?"

She frowned. "In some ways."

His heart lurched. "What do you mean?"

"I do believe He sent you our way. I'm just not sure how far our friendship is supposed to go." She moistened her lips and looked at him directly. "I enjoy your company. You've been wonderful for Bo. I just can't get past the fact that it hasn't even been a year since Doc died."

"Your dad and Mama Beth—"

"That's a completely different situation."

He longed to tell her that it was indeed a different situation. She had a son who needed a daddy.

Trish sighed. "I just wish I knew what God wanted."

How could he get through to her? "That's what I like about that verse on the box I gave you. We don't have to know, or question why. We just have to trust."

"I wish it were that simple."

"It is simple. We're the ones who make it complex." He turned her chin to face him, taking a moment to search her eyes. "Earlier tonight when I was looking at your painting, you said something about staying with a work until you got it just right. That's one of a thousand things I love about you."

She pulled away, rested her elbows on the table, and laid her chin on top of laced fingers, her lips curved up ever so slightly.

"God's the same way with us, Trish. He's always working to make things just right. He's the One painting the picture."

Her dark eyes took on a soft glow, one he could get lost in if he weren't careful. He reached up to capture a strand of her hair and rubbed its silkiness between his fingers. "You feel up to a boat ride?"

She nodded.

Andy stood and held out a hand. She latched on and rose to her feet. He led her to the cockpit and nestled her in beside him while they boated around the lake, now molten gold in the ebbing sunlight.

Neither of them spoke, but Trish gave a contented sigh and relaxed into his embrace, resting her head against his shoulder. He longed to glance at her, but was too afraid of breaking the spell.

An hour later, the stars began to peek through the darkened sky. He made his way back across the lake and motored up to the dock. "I hope you've enjoyed this as much as I did."

"Very much." She laid a hand on his arm, her chocolate eyes peering into his. "I can't remember the last time I enjoyed something this much."

"My pleasure." His gaze traveled to her full lips, and the next thing he knew he kissed her—a soft, sweet kiss, which she returned.

Then just as quickly as it began, she pulled away. "I'm so sorry," she said, bringing trembling fingers to her lips. "I didn't mean to kiss you."

He caressed her arms. "Hey, it's okay. And for the record, I kissed you."

Trish's smile disappeared. "Andy, I'm not sure about this. I mean, I don't even know if I'll be staying in Miller's Creek, and it's so soon after Doc's death . . ."

"Shh." Andy pulled her to his chest, hugging her tightly, his cheek resting on her strawberry-scented hair. He refused to ruin this perfect evening with the thought of losing her. "I promise not to rush you. We'll just take one day at a time and see where God leads."

She peered up at him, uncertainty inscribed on her features, studying his face for a long minute before she nodded her head.

As Andy arrived back at his modest apartment above City Hall later that night, his mind reeling with the events of the day, he offered up a prayer of thanksgiving and praise to God for the wonderful evening with Trish. Things weren't perfect, and there were still obstacles to overcome, but at the very least, they'd made great strides forward.

He removed his dinner jacket, wandered to the answering machine, and pushed the play button, jotting down the messages on a legal pad. The last one in particular caught his attention and sent fear speeding through his veins.

"Otis Thacker here. I've decided to go ahead with the lawsuit against Trish."

26

Trish dabbed the last brush stroke on the over-sized painting and imagined the dimpled grin on Andy's face when she presented it to him. It would look perfect hanging in his new office. Though time had been scarce because of work and getting ready for the Dallas exhibit, she'd pulled two weeks of long days to copy the painting she'd sold in Morganville.

She stood back and viewed the piece in the last rays of daylight. It was the best she'd done yet and the very least she could do for the man who'd made such a difference in Bo's life. The change in her son was nothing less than miraculous, and it was all because of Andy.

The memory of the evening they'd spent at the lake flooded to the front of her mind, sending warmth throughout her body as she remembered his kiss. He'd been true to his promise and hadn't tried to kiss her again. Disappointment flooded her heart, and she released a heavy sigh. It was for the best.

An unexpected clap of thunder broke her reverie. She peered out the long expanse of windows toward the meadow. A black cloud hung low and ominous. If it were April or May, she'd be headed to Dad's basement.

Hurrying to the door, she flung it open and stepped out into stifling summer heat. Grayish-green clouds swirled above her head. Everything was perfectly still. Too still. Leaves hung limp from the trees, with not even the slightest of breezes to make them dance, and the mockingbirds had hushed their incessant copycat cries.

Trish started for the house. She had to call Andy to warn him, then she needed to get to him and Little Bo before the storm broke.

As she made her way to the door, pea-sized hailstones and heavy raindrops pounded to the dusty earth, sending up puffs of dirt and releasing the familiar musky scent of a Texas rainstorm. Covering her head with her arms, she sprinted the rest of the way and headed straight for the phone, raindrops sliding down her face into her mouth.

Andy picked up on the first ring, unleashing a torrent of words. "Where have you been? I've been trying to call you for the past half hour. We're under a tornado warning."

"Sorry, I didn't take my cell phone out to the cottage." Then his words sank in. "But it's not the right time of year for a tornado."

"That tropical storm that hit the coast this morning is spawning them all across the state."

The hail banged louder against the metal roof. She raised her voice. "Are you and Bo okay?"

"We're fine. We headed to the church basement along with the rest of the town when the sirens started to blow. You need to take cover now."

But what if Bo needed her? "I'll be fine. I'm coming to town. Bo is terrified of storms."

"No!" Andy's shout sounded above the racket the hail stones made on the steel roof. "Stay put and take cover. Do not get out in this storm. Understand?"

Trish started to argue, but the phone went dead, and a howling wail rumbled through the house like a freight train. She dashed toward the hall bathroom, her heart ricocheting in her chest. *Lord, protect us.*

Just as she closed the door behind her, the house groaned and creaked, the pounding so loud she thought the roof might cave. Her leg muscles liquefied, and she sank to the floor. The walls shook, like a giant hand had closed around the house and wiggled it back and forth.

From outside, the sound of trees snapping and glass breaking accented the horrific roar. The lighthouse picture Doc had bought on their honeymoon crashed to the floor beside her, and a shard of glass slashed into her arm, blood spurting from the open wound. The lights flickered off, leaving her in total darkness. Trish tucked her head between her knees and prayed.

Then, just as suddenly as it hit, it was over. She rose, her knees still weak and wobbly, and peeked out the bathroom door. Except for broken window panes and fallen pictures and knick-knacks, the house looked miraculously the same. From the treacherous racket, she'd been convinced that not a stick would be left standing. She cautiously moved to the back door and opened it.

The blood rushed from her head, and she leaned against the door frame to keep from falling. Debris littered the area, trees snapped in two like toothpicks, their branches stripped bare. Where the cottage once stood, only a gray expanse of concrete remained, and scattered across the backyard were her cottage and paintings—the last remnants of her attempt to stay in Miller's Creek—the last shreds of her shattered hope.

Trish battled tears as she swerved to avoid the massive live oaks blocking part of the road in front of the main ranch house. Their exposed roots were gnarled hands clawing the sky, while holes gaped nearby like giant wounds upon the land. She loved those old oaks. Losing them was like losing childhood friends.

Her thoughts turned to Bo. Surely he and Andy were safe. After all, they'd been in the church basement. Dad wasn't at home, which meant he was with Mama Beth. She'd tried calling all of them on her cell phone, but only received the pleasant voice of a woman telling her that all circuits were currently busy and to please try again.

Fresh doubts surfaced and sent panic to tap dance in her stomach. What if the church had been hit and the basement had caved in? What if Bo and Andy were trapped beneath the rubble? Her throat cinched, and she floored the accelerator.

As she reached Miller's Creek, fear nipped at her mind and her jaw hung slack. Trees crushed houses. Cars looked like toys tossed to the ground by a careless child. She had to get to Bo and Andy. *Now!*

A minute later she braked to a hurried halt outside the church, which appeared undamaged. People huddled in groups, obviously in a state of shock. Steve met her at the curb, engulfing her in a bear hug. "Sis, I'm so glad you're okay."

Trish pulled away, her trembling hands finding their way to her face. "Bo. Where's Bo?" Her voice elevated with each word.

"Relax. He's fine. Andy took him to check on you since there's no phone service. They may have stopped by his new office on their way. Supposedly that side of town took a pretty hard hit." He looked down at her cut arm. "You need to get that tended to. I'll go see if I can find something." He raced toward the church.

She didn't have time to wait. Instead, she climbed in her car and tore out for the other side of town, her heart in her throat. Until she saw Bo and Andy with her own eyes, she couldn't rest. As she neared the downtown area, the destruction before her eyes stole her breath, and it became evident she'd have to abandon her car and travel on foot.

Ernie, the town policeman, stood nearby holding back traffic. She tried to sneak past, but Ernie saw her. “Trish, this area is blocked off for emergency personnel only. There are electrical lines down.” In high alert mode, he barked out the words.

“I have to find Little Bo. He’s in there.” Without waiting for permission, she raced ahead. Steering clear of downed electrical lines, her feet pounded against the pavement as she dodged debris. But when she turned the corner, she came to an abrupt stop.

A shiver ran down her arms and spine. The new office looked almost as bad as her now non-existent cottage. Were they still here? The milling crowds separated, and Andy came into view, Bo clinging to his neck.

In a heartbeat, she found herself in Andy’s embrace, with no recollection of how she got there.

He hugged her tightly, his breath hot against her cheek. “Thank you, God.” His voice trembled with suppressed emotion.

She could hold back no longer, and wails ripped from her throat. The depth of her fierce love for Bo and Andy burned like fire in her stomach. She could’ve easily lost them both.

Andy hugged her close again and kissed her cheek. “Shh, it’s okay. You know I wouldn’t let anything happen to Bo.”

Trish nodded, too embarrassed and shocked to tell him her tears weren’t only for her son. She pulled away, wiping her eyes with her palms. “I know. Thanks for taking such good care of him.”

Bo released his death grip on Andy and fell into her arms, snuggling his head under her chin. She planted a kiss on his silky hair, the citrusy scent of his shampoo pouring into her senses. More tears streamed down her cheeks.

"We need to doctor that arm." Andy removed a clean handkerchief from his back pocket and gently wrapped it around the cut and secured it with a knot. "That ought to do for now."

"How bad is the damage to your office?"

His face clouded. "Pretty bad. The roof sustained structural damage." He pointed to one corner that looked like a tyrannosaurus had taken a bite. "It's a good thing you've finished so many paintings, 'cause I'll need your help if I'm gonna get this office opened before the Chamber Banquet like I've advertised."

An ache pierced her chest. She couldn't tell him there were no longer any paintings. If he knew, he'd insist she spend all her time getting ready for the show. Well, that wouldn't happen now. She couldn't let him down. He'd done so much for her when she needed him the most. Now was her chance to return the favor. But at what cost?

Andy scraped fingernails down his neck and leaned back in his leather office chair. If something didn't let up soon, he was gonna blow a gasket! In the week since the tornado, he'd spent more time handling his caseload than working on his new office, and it was taking every bit of strength he had to continually talk Otis out of the lawsuit. He'd been tempted to pay the man himself, but considering Trish's desire to do things on her own, had thought better of it. Once the building was complete, he'd give her a hefty bonus and wouldn't take no for an answer.

He rubbed a hand across his mouth, trying to focus on the computer screen, but the lines of legal research ran together. Trish had been such a God-send. She'd taken his continual absence in stride and worked pretty much non-stop with the rebuilding of his office, taking care of Bo, working at Soldano's, and helping others clean up from the tornado. When did she find time to paint? Two in the morning?

His phone trilled, drawing his thoughts back to his too-hectic life. He almost didn't answer, but changed his mind after further thought. He couldn't afford to turn clients away right now. The phone shrilled again, and he snatched it from its cradle. "Tyler Law Firm, Andy here."

"Answering your own phone these days?" Claire Windsor's cool words sliced through him like a blowtorch through butter.

Andy took a breath and released it slowly. "Hello, Claire." He pictured her sitting behind an ornate mahogany desk, not one hair daring to step out of place. "May I help you?"

"That remains to be seen. I thought you'd want to know your friend cancelled her appearance in the exhibit next month."

He sat up ramrod straight. Trish had backed out of the show? Why? He thought fast, his law training kicking into gear. "I'm sure there's been some misunderstanding. Please keep her on the schedule, and I'll do what I can from this end."

"You must really care about her." Claire's voice held an uncustomary softness.

"What do you mean?"

"For one thing, you're answering your own phone in a back-roads Texas town when you had a thriving practice in Dallas. Then you took the time to drive here with one of her paintings. Now you're going a step further when she clearly has no interest in her art career."

"She's had a rough road. I'm just trying to help. Besides, I truly believe she *is* interested in her art career."

"The line she fed me was that she didn't have time to paint. In case you haven't heard, painting is required to be a painter."

The words slapped him in the face. Trish told him she had several paintings ready to go. Had she lied?

"Are you still there?"

“I’ll check into this, Claire, but please keep her on the schedule. I know several people who have one of her painti—”

“Okay, whatever. But if you let me down on this little deal, it will be the last time. Understand?”

“Yeah.” He clenched his lips and hung up the phone. Trish would have her art exhibit one way or another. Now he just had to find a way to bring up the subject without her knowing he’d been the one to approach Claire in the first place.

27

"For someone who doesn't like people to be late, you're sure doing a lot of it yourself here lately." Trish blurted out the words in a huff, then turned away from Andy to gather the supplies to paint the office. They'd had no choice but to do the work themselves, since crews were in short supply in the aftermath of the tornado. Finding a time when both of them could be here had been almost impossible. Thank goodness Steve had invited Little Bo to go fishing with him for the day.

Andy sent an apologetic grin. "Sorry I'm late, but things are just hectic right now. Let me change clothes and we'll get started. By the way, thanks for cleaning up the place. It looks better every time I see it."

Through narrowed eyes, Trish watched him stride down the hall. Not once since the tornado had he asked about her art. Instead, he seemed restless and distracted. Whenever she questioned him about it, he deftly changed the subject.

She tightened her ponytail. He might have a lot on his plate right now, but so did she. The clock was ticking. School started in two short weeks. Trish nibbled the inside of her cheek. She had to finish this job as soon as possible so she'd have time to handle the details of the move to Austin—packing, locating a house and school, and most importantly, securing a job.

Andy's cheery whistle sounded down the hallway, and with his usual loose-limbed gait he swaggered up to where she knelt beside the paint cans. "So speaking of painting, how's it been going?"

She turned her head away. Now was a fine time for him to ask.

His cell phone jangled, and he removed it from the holster. "Sorry, Trish, I gotta take this." He strode back down the hall and leaned against an unpainted wall.

Trish studied him. She couldn't tell what he was saying, but his hushed voice and waving arms screamed agitation.

A few minutes later, Andy clicked his phone shut and shoved it back in the holster at his hip, striding toward her with a dark thundercloud on his face. "Sorry, but I gotta go. I'll be back as soon as I can." Without a further word of explanation, he strode out the door leaving her alone. Again.

Her frustration mounted, but she shoved it down. No sense in getting upset. The work had to be done, and it was her responsibility—the job he'd paid her to do. With a sigh, she popped open the lid on the bucket of slate gray and poured it in the tray, the room immediately flooded with the heady odor of fresh paint. She moved to the focal wall in Andy's new office. First she cut in around the crown molding and baseboard, then readied two rollers in case Andy made it back.

She'd just layered her roller with paint when a voice she didn't recognize called out from the front door. "Hello. Anyone here?"

"I'm in the back."

A younger, stockier version of Andy lumbered into the room with the same loose-limbed gait and golden curls. He gave her a wide grin, his cheeks cherubic. "Wow, Andy, you've changed!"

Trish laughed and rose to her feet. She moved toward him with an outstretched hand, the paint roller in the other hand. "I'm Trish. You must be Andy's brother."

"Matt." He eyed her paint roller. "Most women try to dye their hair to cover the gray. Not the other way around."

"I'm sorry?"

"Your roller is dripping gray paint in your hair."

Her free hand jerked to her head and landed in something wet. Just great. She laid the roller on the edge of the tray and grabbed a nearby roll of paper towels. "Are you always so witty?"

"Andy was born with the looks, so I compensated for it with a sharp mind."

Laughter erupted from her while she attempted to remove the paint from her hair with a paper towel.

He surveyed the room. "Nice space. Andy left you to do this all alone?"

Trish sobered. Alone seemed to be her new mode of operation. "Yeah, he took a phone call and then left."

"Here, let me help. Maybe we can laugh our way through it."

"Thanks." She handed him the roller she'd intended for Andy. "Is your brother expecting you?"

"Nah, I'm not a control freak like he is. I just show up when I feel like it."

"Ah, the free spirit type."

Matt struck a thoughtful pose, his fingers stroking his chin. "Yeah, that pretty much sums it up." He resumed painting. "Doesn't appear to do much good being any other way. Too much stress."

"Pretty astute observation for a young guy like you. Oh, but I forgot, must be more of that sharp mind."

He let out a hearty laugh.

They both grew quiet, and the only sound was the rollers against the wall. Trish searched for words to fill the void. Andy had mentioned something about Matt being in school at Austin. "You're still in school at the University of Texas, right?"

"I'm growing to hate that word 'still,' but, yeah, to answer your question."

"Sorry, I didn—"

He waved a hand. "Forget it. I was being sarcastic again." His shoulders hiked up. "I like school. I see nothing wrong with being a perpetual student."

Trish raised her eyebrows. Spoken like someone who wasn't the one doling out the money. "If you can afford it."

"Ouch. Now you sound like Andy. My first love is actually music, but it's hard to make a go of that, so I'm also working on a counseling degree. That way I can help others and support my music career."

"Smart move and one I totally understand. I love to paint, but I'm not sure it's a good way to pay the bills."

Matt peered over at her. "Cool. I take it you paint pictures, not just walls?"

Trish giggled. "I don't mind walls, but I much prefer a canvas. Walls are my way to make ends meet, though that doesn't seem to be working too well either." She frowned. Why had she brought that up?

He loaded more paint on his roller. "So if you don't mind my asking, do you work for my brother, or is there some special relationship between you two that he hasn't clued me in on?"

Loaded question, and she wasn't about to go there. Kinda hard to have a relationship with one party missing in action. "I'm his designer. We had a tornado here a few weeks ago—"

"Tornado? Nice of him to keep me informed."

So she wasn't the only one being left out of the picture. "In his defense, he seems to be really distracted lately."

He stopped painting, a troubled look in his eyes. "Could be something to do with Dad." His heavy sigh deflated his shoulders.

"Your dad?" But Andy had said he was no longer in the picture. "Is something wrong?"

"Guess you could say that. We haven't seen him much over the past few years and just learned he has alcohol-related dementia. If I know my brother, he's killing himself trying to fix things."

Heavy disappointment draped her heart. So that's why Andy had been so busy. Mr. Fix-It to the rescue again, only this time it wasn't her he had to rescue. And for some reason, he didn't trust her enough to tell her the truth. The realization sliced through her. "Sounds like y'all had a rough childhood."

Matt nodded, a sour expression on his face. "Our Mom left when I was just a baby. Andy's been the grown-up in the family since he was seven years old."

Now heartache replaced the disappointment, and tears swam in her eyes. She pictured a child-sized version of Andy crying for his mom while trying to care for his drunken dad and baby brother. Mama Beth's words about Joseph rang in her mind. They certainly proved true in this case. Andy had endured an awful lot of hurt and suffering to become the man he was today. But why had he felt the need to hide it?

Later that day, Trish unloaded the last of the boxes she'd picked up from behind the grocery store, shut the trunk, and hurried inside to deposit them in the hallway. Hopefully, she'd have time to pack a few things later tonight. She wandered back to the kitchen and grabbed a banana to replace the lunch she missed while painting Andy's office. He'd finally returned just as she and Matt had finished painting, and she'd made her exit to allow them time together.

After one bite of the banana, a car pulled up outside, followed by two door slams. She moved to the garage door and opened it to see Steve and one very happy little boy making their way up the driveway.

"Look what I caught, Mom!" Bo held up a stringer with four large-mouthed bass.

Ugh. Smelly fish to clean. Trish resisted the urge to pinch her nostrils shut. "That's my little man, bringing home supper. Go put them in the sink and I'll clean them while you clean you."

His face fell. "Aw, Mom, why do I have to take a bath?"

Trish laughed. "Number one, because you smell like fish and dirty little boy. Number two, because I said so."

"You always say that."

She patted his cheek, one of the few areas not covered with grime. "That's 'cause I'm your mom, and that's what moms always say."

As he scooted into the house, she faced her brother with a grateful smile. "Thanks, Steve. You made his day and mine. This allowed me to get some things crossed off my to-do list."

"My pleasure." Steve tipped his hat. "He's a great kid, Sis. Sorry I haven't been around much. I'll try to do better."

Trish felt her smile fade. "That's kind of you, but we're fine." She considered telling him about the more-than-likely move, but changed her mind, pretty certain he wouldn't take the news well. "Come in and I'll fix you something to drink."

"I can't. I gotta get on back to the house. Dani's been by herself all day."

Jealousy crested in her chest. How she missed having Doc come home to her at the end of a long day. "I understand. Give her my love, and thanks again." As he sauntered away, his boots scuffing against the concrete, she shut the door and leaned against it briefly before moving to the kitchen to deal with the fish.

"Mo-om!" Bo hollered down the hallway then appeared, wrapped in a towel, and his hair tousled and wet.

"You weren't in there long. Are you sure you got clean?"

"Yep, I even washed behind my ears. See?" He pushed an ear forward as evidence.

A smile tugged at her lips. "Very good. Now what did you want?"

"Oh yeah, why are all those boxes in the hall? I thought the tornado blowed them all away."

Her muscles froze. The moment she'd dreaded. "These are new boxes I picked up today." Trish laid down the fillet knife and knelt in front of him, placing her hands on his still-damp arms. "Honey, you remember when we took the trip to Austin to see Delaine?"

He nodded. "Yep, we had lots of fun at the water park and playing video games and eating pizza."

She released a shaky breath and followed it with a smile. This was gonna be easier than she'd originally thought. "We sure did. How would you like it if we moved to Austin so we could go to that water park whenever we wan—"

Bo yanked away and bolted for his room, slamming the door behind him.

Trish followed and opened the door. He lay on his bed, his shoulders shaking with sobs. Her heart ached. What could she say to make him understand? "Oh, honey, it's gonna be all right." She perched on the bed next to him and rubbed his back.

"No, it's not. Nothing will ever be all right again!" He jerked to a sitting position, tears streaking down his chubby cheeks. "I don't wanna leave here." His shoulders still shook, the result of hard crying, and he sniffed.

"I know, honey. I've tried really hard to keep us here, but there's no work I can do in Miller's Creek to give us enough money to live."

"But here's where Domino and Papaw and Mama Beth and Uncle Steve and Aunt Dani live." More tears brimmed in his big brown eyes. "But I 'specially don't wanna leave Andy, 'cause then we won't have nobody and he won't either." He threw himself back on the bed, face to the pillow, and sobbed like his heart was broken.

28

Andy forced his eyelids apart and sat up in the king-sized bed, uncertain where he was. Once his eyes adjusted to the darkened room and his brain started functioning, he remembered. His new place. He allowed himself a brief sense of accomplishment. Finally, he could put down roots in Miller's Creek instead of living out of a suitcase in the cramped apartment above City Hall.

Truthfully though, he'd done very little except unpack and hang pictures. Trish had taken care of the rest while he'd handled his heavy caseload and looked in on his dad. He released a weary sigh and scratched his face, still bothered by the fact that she wouldn't take the bonus money he'd offered. She'd given some lame excuse about all he'd done for her and Bo, then had waved and driven off, not giving him the chance to ask if she'd like to go out again sometime.

A subtle, but definite, chill hung between them, brought on most likely by his absence the past few weeks. The uneasy feeling had kept him praying until the early morning hours, and what little sleep he'd managed to get had been restless.

He untangled his legs from the maroon bed sheet and padded to the bathroom, impressed as always by Trish's careful attention to detail. The floor, cool beneath his feet, was a tasteful combination of tan and taupe diagonally-laid tiles that flowed up the side walls of the shower. A beautiful space.

Just as he reached to turn on the tap, the phone rang. He retraced his steps.

"Hi, it's Trish. Sorry to bother you on a Saturday, but I . . . um . . . have a favor to ask."

"Okay."

"I wouldn't have called, but everyone else is busy."

Hurt bubbled up inside. Was he supposed to be grateful that he was last on her list of people to call when she needed help? He clenched his jaw.

"I had an unexpected appointment pop up in Morganville this morning. Would you mind watching Bo for me?"

"Not a problem, but I have an afternoon meeting with a client. What time will you be finished?" Otis had called last night demanding to see him. Just what he needed—another battle with Otis.

"I should be back by two at the latest."

"That'll work. Would you mind dropping him by here dressed in something to go fishing in?"

"I'm sorry, I didn't even ask if you had other plans."

"I can still fish. It'll be great to have Bo's company." Come to think of it, why couldn't she take Bo with her? It wasn't like he was any trouble. "I'll even take him to my afternoon appointment if I need to. I'm sure he'd play quietly until the meeting was over." His words held the intended accusation.

A tense silence now hung between them. "I could take him with me, too, but—"

"No need to explain." He huffed a frustrated breath through his nostrils. "I'll see you in a little while."

Half an hour later, they arrived. "Andy!" Bo squealed out his greeting, then launched himself into Andy's arms.

"Hey, kiddo. Missed you!" He gave him a squeeze.

"I missed you, too! When you gonna take me riding again?"

Andy glanced at Trish. She was dressed in a pink business suit, with her face made up, and her nails done. The look was topped off with an expensive-smelling perfume. He'd seen enough businesswomen in Dallas to know that something was up. She quickly looked away and pretended to search for something in her purse. "You'll have to ask your mom."

"When, Mom?"

Trish looked up nervously, a terse smile pasted in place. "We'll talk about it later, sweetie. Mama has to go to her appointment right now."

Bo's face fell. "'kay."

Poor kid. Andy lowered him to the floor tickling his ribs on the way down. "Ready to do some fishing?"

"Yep!" His smile returned.

"Where do I need to pick him up?" Trish spoke softly, and still refused to make eye contact.

"After we go fishing, we'll grab a bite to eat and head out to your house, if that's okay."

She nodded and gave Bo a quick hug. "See you later. You have fun and mind Andy." Her lips clamped together briefly before she turned and let herself out the door.

An acidic taste landed in his mouth. What was up with her? He puffed out his cheeks with air and released the breath between pursed lips. Better to forget it and enjoy this time with Bo.

The day was unusually cool for August, so they fished until late morning. After stopping for chili-cheese burgers at Granny's Kitchen, they made their way to the ranch. Andy's mouth gaped open at the destruction. "Man, I didn't know the tornado left this much damage out here."

Bo pointed to the blank space in front of the main ranch house. "Yeah, it blowed over all those big trees in front of Papaw's house."

"What about your house? Is it okay?"

"Mom cried the other day. She said the tornado hurt our house and it was gonna cost a lot of money and time to fix. Plus it blowed away her painting place."

Andy's heart pounded. "The cottage?"

"Yep."

The news socked him in the gut. No wonder she'd cancelled the art show and been so withdrawn. He'd been so consumed with work that he'd let Trish handle the details of fixing up his office and house. She'd sacrificed the art exhibit to help him. Though the thought hurt, it also sowed hope in his heart. Maybe she cared about him after all.

A second later they pulled in front of Trish's house, and his jaw flopped open. In several places, the long front porch sagged. The jagged edge of broken tree branches made the house feel deserted. Why hadn't she said anything? Better yet, why hadn't he thought to ask?

His chest tightened with knife-like remorse. After his meeting this afternoon, he'd come back out to see if he could repair the damage—not just to the house—but to their broken friendship.

Bo let him in the garage door with the key he wore around his neck, an item of jewelry that bothered Andy to no end. A bucket was propped next to the back door, the ceiling above it stained.

"Can we go riding now?"

Andy squatted in front of him. "Tell you what. I'll saddle the horses while you take a nap. You were yawning all over the place today. Don't you know cowboys have to be rested up before they saddle up?"

Bo giggled and grinned, sending warmth coursing through Andy's veins. "'kay."

As soon as Bo disappeared into his room, Andy sauntered to the barn behind the main ranch house and saddled the horses, then returned to the house. He moved to the back door and peered outside. Trish's cottage was completely demolished. Piles of debris littered the back yard where someone had made an attempt to clean up. He imagined Trish courageously trying to rake up her shattered dreams, tears streaming down her face.

Andy raked a hand through his hair, his insides churning. How could he ever make it up to her? Sobs and sniffles sounded from Bo's room. Frowning, he hurried down the hallway and opened the door. "Bo, you okay?"

The boy's cheeks were wet. "No. I'm very, very sad."

"How come?" Andy perched on the edge of the bed.

Wiping his eyes with his fists, Bo scooted back against the wagon-wheel headboard. "Mom says we have to move to Austin."

The news jabbed him in the stomach. So it was true. She *was* leaving. No wonder she'd erected a barrier between them.

"But I don't wanna go. I'll miss you and Domino and Papaw—" His sobs started afresh.

Andy yanked him into his lap and rocked back and forth. "Shhh, it's okay."

"It's all my fault." Bo whimpered the words.

The all-too-familiar words sent alarm drag-racing through his veins. He set Bo back at arm's length to make eye contact. "What's your fault?"

"Everything. Mom moving . . ." He started crying again, but this time it was harder, his face screwed up in intense pain. "But 'specially Daddy dying. I should've minded him, but I didn't."

"Bo, it's not your fault." Andy hugged him to his chest, an achy feeling shooting through his entire body. He knew exactly how he felt. The drunken words his Dad had spoken after Mom left had haunted him for years. "It was an accident, Bo, not your fault."

The boy's cries softened, but he continued to sniff.

Mind a-whirl, Andy searched for words. What could he say to offer comfort? I'll talk to your mom and see if she'll change her mind? You'll like living in Austin away from everyone you know and love? His cell phone vibrated at his waist. One arm wrapped around Bo, he pulled the phone from its holster. Otis Thacker.

He sat Bo on the bed and stood, one hand in the air. "Bo, I have to take this call, but I'll be right back, okay?"

The boy shook his head slowly, his eyes full of sorrow.

Andy cringed as he hurried from the room. Poor little guy. He had no way to understand everything that was happening. After this phone call, he'd sit down with him and try to explain.

The call took longer than expected. When Otis got a bee in his bonnet, there was no moving quickly. Afterward, Andy made his way back to Bo's room, expecting to find him waiting patiently. Instead, the boy hunkered down under the dark blue comforter, a big lump, snoozing away.

It was for the best. After Bo was rested, the situation would be easier to explain. Andy quietly closed the door and moved to the living room to catch some ESPN, and for the first time noticed the bulging boxes stacked in the dining room.

Trish navigated the rutted ranch road as quickly as possible, her mind staggering with all that had transpired. Francesca had driven all the way from Austin to meet with her, and the meeting had gone extremely well. The job was hers, but the woman wanted her to start Monday morning. She combed a hand through her hair, then removed the heavy silver loops from her ears and dropped them into the console cup holder. Did she not realize how difficult it was for a single mother to move at the drop of a hat? Still it must be what God wanted. Especially since everything had fallen into place.

She released a breath, willing her mind and heart to slow their quickened pace. Somehow she had to find time to get Bo enrolled in a new school. Thankfully, Delaine had already agreed they could crash at her place until they found a place to live. That wouldn't be easy on any of them, but it couldn't be helped. At least she had a high-paying job now, and once she proved herself, she might qualify for a raise that would provide a very nice life for Bo.

Heaviness descended on her heart. Andy deserved to know about the move, and she needed for him to understand why. *God, give me the strength and the words. And while You're at it, could You help my family understand, too?*

She grabbed her cell phone to call Steve. "Hey, I need to talk to you and Dad and Dani about something. Will y'all be around later this afternoon?"

In the background lively chatter erupted and Steve chuckled in response. Sounded like they were having a good time. "Actually, we're all headed to the lake. What about tomorrow?"

The news that they were once more on an outing without her and Bo knifed into her. "Yeah, that'll work. I'll talk to you then. Bye." She clicked the phone shut and tossed it to the passenger seat, and ache in her heart. The house came into view and she checked the dashboard clock. Thirty minutes late. Hopefully, it wouldn't make Andy overdue for his appointment.

His mad dash out the garage door said otherwise. He held up a hand. "Sorry I have to leave like this, but I'm running behind. Bo's taking a nap."

"Sorry I made you late." Trish stood on one foot, the other one still inside her car.

"Not a problem. Listen, I need to talk to you, so I'll be back after my meeting."

No asking if it was okay. He was telling, not asking. "I have something to tell you, too."

He hopped in his car, the engine roaring to life. The car spun out of the driveway, sending up a cloud behind him that showered her and her car with a layer of dust. She coughed against the fine powder and entered the house.

While Bo was asleep, she'd clean house and pack. That way they could leave early tomorrow morning. She'd have to deal with the house repairs and moving the furniture another time. Trish tossed her keys on the kitchen counter where they landed with a clank, then tiptoed past Little Bo's room. She changed into shorts and a t-shirt, then pulled her hair into a ponytail.

An hour and a half later, she gazed around the-cleaned house, which now smelled like the amaretto candle she'd lit. Tears stung. How could she leave this place and all the fond memories it held? *Stop it, Trish. You have no choice.* A better question was how could she stay? She'd tried everything else. God had a reason for the way things worked out. He just had a different path than the one she'd hoped for, and it did no good to question why.

Trish spied the clock and frowned. How long had Bo been asleep? She'd better wake him or he wouldn't sleep tonight, and the last thing she needed on the trip to Austin was a cranky boy. Quietly, she opened the door and moved to the opposite side of the bed, positioning herself next to him and peeling back the covers.

Her heart pounded into overdrive. Instead of her son's face, a pillow stared back at her. Frantic with fear, she raced from the room, yelling Bo's name as she went. Searching the house turned up nothing. He wasn't hiding under any beds or in the closets. She sprinted outside, still calling him, the August heat merciless as sweat poured from her, drenching her clothes.

Panic clamped her throat shut. What if he'd gone to the horses? She tore out to the barn behind the main ranch house, salty tears streaming down her face and into her mouth. A quick scan of the horses sent fresh terror coursing through her veins. Domino was missing!

With no one in sight, she hurried to the ranch house and pounded on the door. No one answered. Her mind whirled, and she brought both hands to her head. *Think, Trish, think!*

Andy. She'd call Andy. He'd know what to do.

She ripped the cell phone from her pocket. After several rings, he picked up. "Hey, can I call you back later? I'm in the middle of—"

"Bo's missing!" She screamed the words, then gave into the sobs she'd been holding back.

"Trish, calm down so I can understand you. What do you mean, he's missing?"

"I thought he was asleep. When I checked on him, I found a pillow he'd stuffed under the sheets. I've looked everywhere, and Domino's gone." Her voice elevated in pitch and volume. "Andy, help me. I don't know what to do."

"I'll call the police, then I'll be right there."

Trish hung up, pacing back and forth down the road that led to her house until Andy arrived a few minutes later, concern etched on his pale face. "Have you found him?"

She shook her head, then fell to her knees and started sobbing.

Andy was at her side in a split second, his arms around her. "C'mon, Trish, we'll find him."

She looked into his face, his eyes soft and loving.

"Trust me."

Trish nodded and swallowed, then pushed herself to her feet. Falling to pieces wouldn't help find Bo. Andy stood at the same time and removed his coat and tie.

"What are you doing?"

"I'm gonna get on Biscuit and go looking for him."

A horse whinnied behind them. They turned in tandem.

The blood rushed from her head, and the world started to turn in slow motion. Domino hobbled toward them, still saddled and reins dragging, a bloody gash snaking down one leg.

29

God, I know I don't deserve Your help, but please bring back my little boy. And don't let anything happen to him. I couldn't bear it. Trish buried her face into Bo's Sponge Bob pillow. Oh, it smelled like her baby. She released a wail that robbed her of breath, rocking back and forth as she clutched Bo's pillow to her chest. Hadn't she endured enough?

She scrambled from the bed and raced to the front door to peer out. Nothing. No one. Andy had been gone almost an hour. Ernie, the town policeman, had joined the search a few minutes ago with the promise that the county sheriff and his mounted search and rescue team would be there shortly. What was taking them so long? Didn't they realize she needed to be out looking for Bo instead of waiting on them?

Oh God, let them find him. Alive. More grief slid down her face and deposited salty tears on her lips.

As she turned to move to the back door to look out for the hundredth time, her cell phone buzzed. She flipped it open without even checking the display. Maybe Andy had found him.

"Sis?" Steve's voice held a panicked edge. "We just heard an APB on the radio that Little Bo is missing. When did it happen and why didn't you call?"

Her gaze moved to the mantle clock, and she brought trembling fingers to her face. How long had it been? When had Bo slipped out of the house without Andy's knowledge? "I—I don't know." Her voice trembled. "I'm sorry. I'm not thinking too clearly right now." Shock. She'd gone through it before when Doc died.

"We headed back as soon as we heard the news. We'll be there shortly."

Trish clicked the phone shut, then turned and stumbled down the hallway. A new wave of panic flooded over her at the sight of Bo's empty bed. She gasped for air. They just had to find him!

Several minutes later, a car door slammed, and she scurried to the door, guessing that the sheriff's mounted team had arrived. Instead, Steve and Dani hurried toward the house, followed by Dad and Mama Beth. She swung the door open.

Her brother's long legs had already closed the distance between the driveway and house. "What happened?" His voice thundered.

Dani rushed around him and engulfed Trish in a hug, opening another floodgate of tears. "It's okay, we'll find him. He's a tough little boy."

No. He used to be tough. Now he was a hurting little boy who was missing. And it was her fault. Her knees buckled beneath her, but Steve caught her and ushered her inside to the couch.

Mama Beth bustled up a minute later, a glass of water in her hand. "Here, drink this. It'll make you feel better." A shiny new engagement ring winked from her finger.

Better? Nothing could make her feel better except getting Bo back safely. Trish's hands shook as she took the glass. "Nice ring."

Mama Beth's face paled. She covered the ring with the opposite hand and peered at the other three. "Oh—I—I didn't think . . ."

Dad eased to the couch beside her, his eyes solemn. "We were gonna tell you, honey, but we thought you needed more time."

She released a laugh that sounded anything but happy and held up one hand. "Don't worry about it. That's the least of my concern right now." Her laughter turned to sobs and she doubled over.

Dani knelt, her hands resting on Trish's knees, her big blue eyes soft and kind. "Tell us what happened, Trish, so we can know how to help."

She relayed the story, skipping over the fact that she'd been in Morganville for a job interview, and ended with the news that Andy had borrowed Steve's horse to search for Bo.

"How long ago did Ernie tell you the mounted search and rescue team would be here?" Steve's voice was more kind and controlled now.

"About a half hour ago."

Dad glanced at Steve. "They have to come from all over the county, son, but they're used to responding quickly. They should be here soon, and then we can join the rescue team."

Trish stood. "I want to come with you."

"No." Steve's expression held bullish resolve.

"He's *my* son." Her fists clenched at her sides.

Dad pulled himself to a standing position and laid an arm across her shoulders. "Honey, it's best if you stay here."

She suddenly felt like an eight-year-old, in trouble for doing something she wasn't supposed to do. Something that once again made them come to her rescue.

Dani grabbed Trish's hand. "Don't you want to be here in case Bo comes back?"

Trish closed her eyes, pulled her hand from Dani's grasp, and raised it to rub her forehead, too numb to think or argue. "You're right. I guess it makes more sense to stay here.

"I'd like to say a prayer first, if you don't mind." Mama Beth stepped forward and latched on to Trish's arm. "Dear Lord, we pray Your protection over Little Bo. We also pray for peace of mind for Trish and the rest of us, knowing that You are Sovereign God, and Bo is in Your care. For those searching and about to join the search, we pray for wisdom, guidance, and skill. We pray all this in the name of Jesus. Amen."

Outside, tires crunched against gravel and sent them all rushing for the door. Dust billowed around the caravan of pickups and inched into Trish's nostrils and eyes.

A tall man in jeans and boots climbed from his truck and made his way toward them.

Steve extended a hand. "Hey, Sheriff."

"Hi, Steve. The little boy that's missing is kin to you?"

"My nephew. Dad and I would like to join the search."

The sheriff's handlebar moustache reminded her of Doc. It bounced as he shook hands with Dad. "Mr. Miller." He turned his attention back to Steve. "I think that's a great idea. Y'all know the land better than the rest of us."

All around them, cowboys unloaded their saddled horses from trailers, and from the backseat of an extended cab pickup, a pack of bloodhounds began to whine and bark.

The sheriff faced her. "You the boy's mother?"

"Yes."

"I need to ask you a few questions, and we'll also need an article of clothing or a toy with your son's scent on it for the dogs."

Steve's mouth set in a grim line. "Go ahead and ask your questions. I'll get the toy so we can get started."

Trish wrapped her arms around her waist and once again told the story, while Steve stepped past her and entered the house. A few minutes later he returned with Bo's stuffed horse clutched in one hand. He turned it over to the sheriff, who promptly headed toward the gathered men.

Dad turned and shuffled toward the barn. "Let's saddle up."

"Right behind you, Dad." Steve turned to Trish, his cinnamon eyes full of questions. "Planning a trip?"

Her breath caught. He must have seen the suitcases and boxes. "I'll tell you later. Find my son."

Andy opened the canteen and took a tiny sip, grateful he'd remembered to get some water before he'd set out on his search. He swished the cool drops around his tongue before they rolled down his parched throat. No more for now. Bo might need it.

Images of Bo's injured body floated across his mind and sent tears to his eyes, but he shoved the scene away and nudged Biscuit forward, a constant prayer flowing.

God, help me find him and keep him safe.

He used his forearm to swipe away the sweat that rolled off his face, then peered into the late August sun that lowered by inches rather than degrees. It would be dark soon. How was he supposed to know where to look on a ranch of well over a thousand acres?

Think like a scared little boy.

The words washed into his consciousness, and he immediately offered up thanks. He tugged Biscuit's reins and turned into an open meadow, allowing the horse to lead as a childhood memory flashed to the front of his mind—the note on the kitchen table from Mama saying she needed to go away. He'd been the first to find it and couldn't bear the thought of her leaving without him.

He'd cried as he ran after her. How far had the seven-year-old version of him walked? It had seemed like hours. Exhausted, he'd searched for a place to rest and had headed into a wooded area to lay down in the cool shade. It was dark when he'd awakened, and the trees had seemed like giant monsters with outstretched arms.

Biscuit whinnied and slowed to a stop.

Andy inhaled a deep breath in an effort to dispel the remains of the haunting memory. The Appaloosa snorted and danced to the right, where a trail disappeared into a grove of oaks and cedar. His pulse quickened. He had no choice. Horses had unbelievable instincts, and Bo might be in there. Andy swallowed his fear, and nudged the horse down the shadowy path. "Let's go, Biscuit."

Once under the cover of the trees, it grew dark quickly. His heart pounded against his ribs at a furious pace. Funny how something that happened so long ago still affected him this way. But he had to find Bo and take him back to Trish, no matter how scared he was.

He breathed easier when he emerged from the trees a half hour later. Only enough light remained to barely make out the edge of a rocky bluff. The hair on the back of his neck stood up. Fresh horse tracks lay in the powder-dry dirt beneath him. "Whoa, boy." He pulled back hard on the reins and sat silently in the saddle, his ears trained for the tiniest of sounds. A brief breeze rattled the oak leaves behind him, then stilled. From the dark pit to his right came the faint whimper of a child.

"Bo?" His voice echoed off the boulders in front of him. Biscuit spooked and pranced a bit, sending a spray of gravel over the sharp drop-off.

"I'm down here, Andy. Help me."

He bolted from the horse, wrapped the reins around a gnarled mesquite tree, and crawled to the edge of the bluff, peering carefully over the side. Bo huddled on a narrow ledge about fifteen feet down, clutching a scrawny oak growing out of the rock with both hands. "Hey, buddy, are you okay? Can you move your arms and legs?"

"I think I'm just scratched from sliding down here."

"Good. I'm gonna get a rope to throw down to you, okay?"

"'kay." His hoarse voice trembled.

While Andy scrambled for a rope and knotted it into a loop, he attempted to ease Bo's fears. "You sure are being brave. Wanna tell me what happened?"

Bo sniffled. "Domino slipped on the rocks and I fell off."

"That crazy old horse sure loves you a lot. He came to the house to let us know to look for you."

"He did?" Bo's voice strengthened.

"Yep." Andy tied the other end of the rope around the mesquite tree, then moved back to the cliff. "I'm gonna lower this rope down to you, and I want you to be very careful. Put the noose over your shoulders and under your arms. Then tighten it. Can you do that?"

"Yes, sir."

"Good boy." He sent a quick prayer heavenward and dropped the rope down gently, landing it right beside Bo.

Bo grabbed the rope a little too quickly, sending loose stones tumbling down the steep mountainside.

"Don't move so fast, Bo. Slow down."

The boy did as he said, securing the rope under his arms, but each second that ticked by felt like an eternity. At last he tugged on the rope. "'kay, I'm ready."

Andy's pulse roared in his ears. He breathed a prayer for God's help. "I'm gonna pull you up real slow. When you get close to the top, use your hands and feet to pull yourself over the ledge."

Perspiration trickled down his face as he hoisted Bo up the mountain. One wrong move would . . . *no!* He couldn't think that way. Instead he breathed deeply and focused on drawing the rope with no jerky movements.

But with no warning, the ground beneath his feet began to crumble. His foot slipped against the loose rocks, sending him perilously close to the edge. Bo screamed at the lurch, and started to cry.

Andy fell to the ground and scooted backwards, digging his dress shoes into the rocky soil. "I gotcha, buddy."

After several tense moments, Little Bo's fingers appeared at the edge of the cliff and dug into the gravelly dirt. Andy gave one final tug and pulled Little Bo into his arms. The scent of sweaty little boy was the sweetest smell he'd ever breathed. For a moment, they clung to each other, then Andy's shoulders began to shake. He managed to hold back his cries, but not his tears.

Bo, his face streaked with dirt, wiggled out of the embrace. "You crying?"

Andy laughed. "Yeah, I guess I am. You had me a little scared."

"I was scared, too, but I only cried a little bit." Bo's eyebrows crinkled. "But don't tell. 'Specially don't tell Mary Simpson."

Andy chuckled. "Your secret's safe with me. Guess we'd better get you back home."

"Yeah, I miss Mom."

The boy needed to know that what he'd done was wrong. "She's very worried about you."

Bo hung his head. "I know. I'm sorry. I shouldn't have run away, but . . ."

"But what?"

"I did it 'cause I didn't want to move to Austin."

Andy knelt in front of him. "Listen to me, Bo. Your mama's just trying to do what she thinks is right for you. You may not like it, but she wouldn't do it if she thought it was wrong."

"I know. Can we go now, so I can tell her I'm sorry?" His eyes, though fatigued, held a hint of a sparkle. "And something else."

"'What?" Andy tousled his hair.

"I'm really, really hungry."

Andy laughed and scooped him up in both arms, then hauled them both up onto Biscuit's back. "You're always hungry."

Bo let out a hoarse laugh. "Yeah, I know."

They made their way together through the woods, now completely dark. Once they reached the clearing, Andy spotted several flashlights. He gave a loud whistle, and was instantly surrounded by several men on horseback, including Steve and Bo Miller.

A half hour later they arrived home, every window in the house aglow with light. Trish met them as they sauntered up on their horses, ran toward them and snatched Bo into her arms, sobbing. Andy turned his head to keep from bursting into tears himself.

Dani hurried over as he dismounted. "Andy, thank you so much for finding him."

Andy could only nod, emotion still squeezing his throat. He made his way to Trish and Bo. She stood, her tear-streaked face lit by moonlight and her tawny eyes full of unspoken words.

"Thank you," she whispered, her lips trembling.

"You're welcome." Andy brushed away a tear that trickled down her soft cheek then patted Bo's head. He glanced around. The area was swarming with people. Now wasn't a good time. He turned back to Trish. "I know we need to talk, but we're all pretty worn out right now. I'll see you at church in the morning. Maybe we can eat lunch together and talk about it then."

A brief wrinkle appeared between her eyebrows, then disappeared as she nodded and lowered her gaze.

30

Andy jerked awake and bolted to a sitting position, raking a hand over his opened mouth as he sucked in air. *Something was wrong!* He puzzled over the emotions flooding his system. Maybe he'd just had a bad dream. But if that was true why couldn't he remember it?

He flopped back onto the bed and tried to relax into the cool, soft sheets, but the longer he lay there, the more unsettled he became. *God, I don't know exactly what I'm experiencing here, but all I know to do is pray. I don't even know who to pray for.*

Trish and Bo.

His heart pounded faster. He rolled over to his side to check the digital alarm clock. It wasn't even five o-clock in the morning. They were probably both still asleep, and after yesterday's ordeal, he wasn't about to call and wake them up.

Lord, keep them safe. You know how much I love them. Help them feel Your presence. Make their paths straight, Lord, and help Trish trust You completely.

Familiar peace drifted over him, but sleep still wouldn't come. He lugged himself to his feet and padded to the kitchen to make coffee, the fragrant aroma teasing his senses as the machine gurgled and dripped. When it finished, he headed outside to the deck, a steaming cup of coffee in one hand. The outdoor space had been Trish's suggestion, and he was glad he'd agreed to it. How many hours had he already spent out here praising God for His night sky handiwork and praying—most of the time for Trish and Bo?

He sipped coffee and stared at the stars. The birds stirred in the trees and shrubbery surrounding him and began to twitter, the only sound except for an approaching car. It slowed a moment, then drove straight past and headed out of town, the tail lights oddly familiar.

Trish! He jumped to his feet drizzling hot coffee down his t-shirt and pajama bottoms. Surely he'd been mistaken, but what if it *was* her? Panic sent a cold chill down his spine. What if she and Bo were leaving? He paced to the kitchen and deposited his coffee cup in the sink. There was no way he could rest until he knew for sure.

He unplugged his cell phone from its charger and called Trish. It went directly to her voice mail.

"Hey, it's me. I know it's early, but I thought I saw your car go by. I was worried something might be wrong. I want you to know that I . . . well, I . . ." No, he couldn't say it for the first time over the phone. "Call me back."

Next he punched in Steve's number. No answer.

Now what? There wasn't a second to waste. He laid the phone on the counter and trotted to the bedroom to change clothes. Just as he reached the closet door, his cell phone rang out. As he turned to retrace his steps, he caught his toe on the nightstand. Pain throbbed in his big toe, and the bedside lamp toppled to the floor with a crash. He didn't bother to pick it up, but hurdled over it and half-ran, half-hopped, to the kitchen counter. The phone's song was replaced by silence just as he reached for it.

A missed call from Steve. He quickly redialed the number.

"It's Andy."

"Hey, Andy. Sorry I missed your call." His voice sounded groggy.

"I think I just saw Trish's car drive by, and she didn't answer her phone. Is something going on?"

"I thought you probably already knew."

"Knew what?"

"She's moving to Austin."

The same ache he'd known as a child pierced through him. Yet another woman had chosen a career over him.

Trish dropped the phone to her lap, and brought a hand to her cheek. The car tires droned against the pavement as she approached Morganville, the eastern sky now edged in pale purple. Like murky floodwaters, questions boiled in her brain. What had Andy left unsaid? In his message, he'd been about to say something and changed his mind.

What had he wanted to tell her? That moving to Austin was a big mistake? That he was sorry about Bo's disappearance? That he cared about her?

She squeezed her eyes shut for a brief moment before refocusing them on the road. Andy's tired and strained face from the previous night sent a cloak of guilt to enshroud her heart. He'd been so good to her and Bo, but if he truly loved her, he'd had plenty of opportunity to say it and hadn't. And even if he'd said it, she couldn't go there. Not yet. Not until she figured out if God wanted her in Austin.

It had been dark when she'd left town, eager to start this new adventure. But now that they'd put a few miles between them and Miller's Creek, doubts started to rise. This was the right choice, wasn't it? It was the only move that made sense. The only one that allowed her to make a living for her and her son. Her chance to prove she could make it without help from Dad or Steve or . . . or anyone else.

Lord, am I making the right decision?

Trust in Me with all your heart, and don't lean on your own understanding.

There it was again—the same verse from Dani and Steve's wedding and stitched on Dad's old bookmark. The one carved on the box of brushes Andy had given her. A verse she'd known since childhood. What was God trying to tell her? That she wasn't trusting Him? She gave her head a shake. *Nonsense, Trish.* The move to Austin proved she trusted Him. It was a huge leap of faith.

In all your ways acknowledge Me. I will direct your path.

Trish released a sigh. That settled it. Didn't her prayers acknowledge Him as God? He would direct her path. This was nothing but nerves. Except for college, she'd never lived away from Miller's Creek. It was only natural to be a little apprehensive.

Bo, still in his pajamas, stirred in the backseat, then raised himself to a sitting position, his eyes squinting. "Where are we?"

"Almost in Morganville. Want some McDonald's?"

He glanced at the box of toys beside him and his face took on an immediate scowl. "We're going to Austin today?"

"Yes, sweetie. I didn't have a chance to tell you with everything that happened yesterday, but I got the job. My new boss wants me to start tomorrow."

A big tear rolled off his cheek and plopped onto his chest. "But I didn't get to tell anyone goodbye."

"We'll be going back to Miller's Creek on the weekends until we can get everything mov—"

"Did you tell Papaw and Uncle Steve we were leaving?" The words sounded more like an accusation than a question. Bo's lips turned down at the corners.

"Yes, I talked to them last night after you went to bed." They had taken the news much better than expected, but she knew they were hurt. Dad hugged her, his eyes sad, and told her she had his full support. Her throat knotted at the memory. Dad had also been kind enough to agree to pay Otis, and she'd promised to pay him back once she started bringing in a steady income. That was the last option she wanted to take, but she didn't have much choice.

"Did you call Andy and tell him?"

"No, why would I do that?" Trish kept her eyes on the road, but chewed the inside of her cheek.

"'Cause you promised you'd see him at church this morning."

"No, I didn't."

"You nodded, and nodding is the same thing as saying yes."

She searched for words, but everything that came to mind sounded like a lame excuse.

"You lied to Andy."

Trish huffed out her exasperation. "Good grief, Bo, I didn't exactly lie to him. It's complicated, and you're too young to understand."

"I'm not too young to understand that it's wrong to lie.

His words stabbed at her. Trish pulled into the drive-through line at McDonald's. "Speaking of lying, that's exactly what you did when you tucked a pillow under the covers and then took off on Domino."

"Welcome to McDonald's! I'll take your order when you're ready!" The over-exuberant voice blared through the crackling speaker, enough to make even non-coffee drinkers beg for a cup.

She looked at Bo in the rearview mirror. "Would you like a sausage biscuit?"

"And a hash brown." Resignation and disappointment resonated in his tone and expression. Normally breakfast at

McDonald's would have him bouncing off the seats in excitement. Not today.

"I'll take a sausage biscuit, a hash brown, and a milk."

"One sausage biscuit, one hash brown, and one milk, coming up! Pull around to the next window, please, and have a good morning!"

Trish pressed both hands over her ears until the blaring voice stopped, then released the brake and pulled up as far as she could, counting four cars in front.

"Aren't you gonna get something to eat?" Bo's eyes held a knowing look.

"Nope, I'm really not that hungry. I might take a bite of yours, but that's all I want."

He studied her a while longer, then turned his head away.

Now was as good a time as any to discuss yesterday's episode. "Wanna tell me why you ran away?"

His eyes filled with tears, and his mouth worked like he wanted to speak but couldn't. Finally the words spilled from him. "'Cause I'd rather live outside on the ranch by myself than move to Austin." He dissolved into tears.

Trish pulled up to the payment window, choking on his words. She somehow managed to count out the right change and take the bag from the woman.

"Thank ya much! Come back and see us!" The woman sent a toothy grin that Trish didn't even try to return.

Instead of pulling out of the parking lot, she yanked the car into an empty slot near the highway and buried her head in her hands, loud sobs pouring from her. Bo could have been killed in yesterday's ordeal, and it was her fault.

31

Andy gave his head a shake, then rubbed his eyes and yawned, forcing his attention from the mesmerizing center stripe on the pavement to the early morning lights of Morganville. It didn't help matters that he'd spilled his earlier cup of coffee down his shirt instead of into his stomach.

Another yawn escaped. If he expected to catch Trish on her trek to Austin, he had to wake up. A strong dose of caffeine would do the trick, but did he dare take the time knowing that Trish and Bo were somewhere on the road in front of him? He ran a hand over his whiskered chin. If it kept him from falling asleep at the wheel, a few minutes' delay to grab some coffee would be well worth it.

He zipped the Z-3 under the golden arches and into the drive-through line, his teeth immediately set on edge by the blaring speaker. Okay, nobody had a right to be that peppy before six a.m. Inching forward behind the cars in front, he prayed for the millionth time. *Lord, help me find them.*

At the pick-up window, he reached for the cup with one hand and gave Happy Woman a five with the other, trying to infuse his tone with a friendliness he didn't feel. "Keep the change."

"Thank ya much! Come back and see us!"

Don't count on it, lady. Andy eased forward enough to let the car behind him reach the window, then braked and cracked open the coffee lid. The aroma filled the confines of his sports car. He added two packets of sugar, stirred, and took a sip, feeling instantly revived. Too bad you couldn't get this stuff as an IV drip. As he deposited the coffee cup in the holder on the console, his eyes widened in surprise at the sight before him. A lemon-yellow car sat in the last parking spot. Surely there wasn't another car that same gosh-awful color. It had to be Trish.

His heart pounding, he steered into the only available space, then climbed from the car, praying for wisdom. He hurried to the driver's side, then halted, a knife lodged in his gut.

Trish hunched over, her head covered by her hands, and her shoulders shaking.

Andy rapped gently on the car window.

She yanked her head toward him, her eyes red from crying, her mouth half-open, and her face streaked with tears.

From the backseat came an excited cry. "Andy! Andy!"

When the car window lowered, Andy reached into the backseat and grabbed Bo's hand. "Hey, buddy!" He turned back to Trish, his heart breaking at the sorrow in her brown eyes. "Hi, Trish."

She opened her mouth like she wanted to speak, then clamped her lips together and faced forward.

He lowered his head and released a sigh. How long would he have to fight this battle with her? "Don't worry, Trish, I'm not here to rescue you."

"That's too bad." She whispered the words, and then sniffled.

"What does that mean?"

"I could really use rescuing right now." She choked out the words, then buried her head in her hands and sobbed some more.

In less than a heartbeat, Andy yanked open the car door and pulled her into his arms. She clung to him and cried. He caressed her hair with one hand, while his other arm held her close. Now was the time to say it. "I love you, Trish. Please let me help."

She tore herself from his embrace, using her fingertips to swab at the tears on her cheeks. “Quite honestly, I could use a little help, but I’m not sure you’re ready.”

How could she say that? Didn’t the past few months prove how ready he was? Didn’t chasing her across Texas at an ungodly hour show her how he felt? “What are you talking about?”

Trish pointed to his pants. “I’m a little embarrassed to take help from a grown man who . . . ” She pulled both lips between her teeth, as if trying not to laugh, her amused gaze travelling over him.

Andy glanced down, fiery heat creeping up his torso, neck and face. In his haste to chase after them, he’d left Miller’s Creek in his green plaid pajama bottoms and coffee-stained t-shirt.

Trish leaned back in the passenger seat of her car and peered over at Andy. One arm draped the steering wheel as he chatted easily with her very excited little boy. Even in pajamas, with his sandy curls plastered to his head and his jaw covered with stubble, the sight of Andy sent a ribbon of delight spiraling through her insides. This felt so . . . so right, but was it?

It might not be right, but neither was moving to Austin. Not if it made Bo so miserable that he would run away to avoid it.

Andy pulled into a parking space at Walmart and turned off the engine, then faced her with that killer dimpled grin of his. “Hurry up, woman. I need some clothes if I’m gonna treat y’all to pancakes.”

“Yay for pancakes!” Bo raised both fists in the air, a different kid from the glum child who’d been in his place only a half hour earlier.

Trish smirked and reached for the door handle. "Well, if you guys would learn how to dress yourselves, we wouldn't be making this little side trip."

Laughter burst from Andy, a contagious sound that seemed to saturate every ounce of air in the car. He removed several bills from his wallet. "Point taken. Just grab a large button-down shirt, size 11 tennis shoes, and a pair of jeans, size 34-36."

"And if those sizes aren't available?"

"Then I guess I'll play the penguin part again like I did at Steve and Dani's wedding."

Now it was her turn to laugh. "In that case, I think I'll buy a camera while I'm at it." She unbuckled the seatbelt and sat up on her knees to rifle through the box in the back seat. A minute later she found what she was looking for and handed Bo a pair of shorts and a matching shirt. "Here, kiddo. Unbuckle and change into these while I'm in the store."

As she traipsed across the mostly-empty parking lot, her thoughts turned to Andy, and she couldn't help but notice the warm feeling flooding through her veins. All this wasted time. God had surely sent him their way, not just this morning, but back in April when he'd burst through the back doors of the church, messing with her decorations and her carefully-laid plans.

And now, wonder of all wonders, he'd told her that he loved her. *Loved her*.

She pulled a green button-up shirt from the rack. This would match his eyes perfectly. As she made her way to the men's jeans, she thought about her own selfish reaction to Andy. In her pride, she'd done nothing but push him away, choosing to believe she had to do it on her own. But he hadn't given up on her—or on her son. Andy knew better than anyone how to handle Bo—how to make him smile when he was grouchy, how to make him mind without shattering his fragile heart.

Trish grabbed a pair of size 11 white tennis shoes from the shoe department and made her way to the check-out. A few minutes later, she was back in the car.

"Wow, you're fast!"

No, she was incredibly slow. Too slow. Especially when it came to catching on to what might have been God's plan all along. Trish sent a wry smile. "Yeah, well, it helps when it's early on a Sunday morning. The store was deserted."

His eyes took on a scheming gleam. "How about going to church in Morganville after breakfast? Then we'll grab a bucket of chicken and find a shady park at the lake for a picnic, so Bo can play and we can talk."

She smiled her approval.

After locating an outdoor public restroom where he changed clothes, Andy treated them to a tasty sit-down breakfast at the local waffle house. Feasting on pancakes loaded with butter and blueberries, they spent the time laughing about their early morning adventure. With their bellies full, they opted to walk across the road to a small stone church for the worship service.

As they seated themselves, an elderly lady, her skin translucent and her eyes reflecting an inner light, turned around to shake their hands and introduce herself. "What a beautiful family you have."

At that moment the music minister had everyone rise to sing, so Trish had no opportunity to correct the woman. Not that she wanted to. The early morning sun streamed through stained glass windows, and left a pattern of dappled light on the forest green carpet and maple-colored woodwork. Soon the preacher, a rotund, balding man, made his way to the pulpit. "Turn to Proverbs, chapter three, please."

Trish's heart fluttered. The chapter with the verses about trusting God. Was this some kind of sign? Could it be that God had been trying to get her attention since Dani and Steve's wedding? The sound of turning pages whispered across the room. Trish located the passage and positioned her Bible so Andy could look on.

"Trust in the Lord with all your heart, and lean not on your own understanding. In all your ways acknowledge Him, and He shall direct your paths."

Trish felt Andy's eyes on her. She turned to meet his gaze. The look that passed between them possessed an electric energy that zapped its way through her and landed in a tingle in her toes. She inhaled a deep breath and focused her attention on the pastor.

"Trusting God is easy to say, but not so easy to do."

How many times had she considered that very thought?

"I can say that I trust this pulpit to hold me up, but that's not really trust. Trust is active. Only when I lean my weight against the pulpit is my trust proved. It's the same with God. Only when we lean against Him—and not our own understanding—is our faith proved."

Trish pressed her lips together and lowered her gaze to the velvety pew cushion. Had she trusted God over the past few months or fought against Him? Had she leaned the weight of her worries against Him or her own understanding?

The pastor's gentle voice lulled her back into the sermon. "We're sensory creatures. We tend to base our decisions on what we can see, hear, smell, taste, and touch. But as children of the kingdom, we have another dimension to consider—a spiritual dimension—where God reigns and often moves in ways that are beyond our ability to understand."

Her heart pounded faster, and she rubbed her arms to erase the chill bumps that gathered. God's thoughts and ways *were* far above hers. Had His plan involved Andy all along? If so, she'd ignored all the signs, intent on finding her own way, sure that it was much too soon to give herself to another man.

"His timing is often puzzling to us, but once we put our trust in Him completely, with all our heart, we later can look back and see how He wove situations and days and moments and people together in a way that gives direction to our lives."

Andy reached over and grabbed her hand, entwining his fingers with hers. She raised her gaze in utter amazement at what was taking place. He held her hand for the rest of the service and all the way to the car, then helped her and Bo into their seats. Soon they were on their way to the lake, the delicious aroma of fried chicken wafting from the large bucket they'd picked up on their way out of town.

As soon as lunch was over, Bo high-tailed it to the playground while the lake gently lapped against the shore. Trish watched his retreating back, then turned to Andy with a smile. "I don't know what we would've done had you not showed up when you did."

He frowned and concentrated his gaze on the ground. "I had to know you were okay. I—I wanted you to know how I felt before you left for Austin."

Her heart pounded. His words proved how much he cared, but also revealed his vulnerability. He intentionally put himself in a vulnerable place, a place where his heart could get broken. Showered with shame, she gulped down her fear. "I'm so sorry for how I've acted over the past few months, Andy. I was just so confu—"

He held up one hand, his ocean eyes stormy and troubled. "You don't have to explain. I know you're still grieving your husband."

Andy's chest heaved. "I shouldn't have pressured you so much. I moved too fast, and I'm sorry."

"Can I ask you a question?" Trish chewed the inside of her cheek. The last thing she wanted to do was offend him, but she had to know.

"Anything." His direct gaze sent a shiver down her spine.

"Do you think you're just enamored with the idea of family, or do you . . . is it . . .?"

"How can you even ask me that, Trish?" The wounded expression on his face stabbed her heart. "Do you see me acting this way with other single women and their children?"

Her mind flitted to Carla and Brody. "I see you being kind to them."

"Kind, yes, but do you see me pouring my life and heart into helping them?"

"No."

"I'm not saying that to pressure you. I know you might not feel the same, that it might still be too early after your husband's death for you to even consider it. I know you have other things you want to do with your life, besides—"

"No, I don't."

Andy looked up, the surprise on his face echoing her own. "What?"

"All I ever wanted to be is a wife and mother. Everything else is secondary."

"But your design work. You're so talented."

"Maybe so, maybe not. My degree was something I did to appease my parents." She hesitated, searching for words, while a mockingbird belted out his song from a nearby pole. "The truth is that I enjoy sharing my art skills with others, whether I get paid or not. If anything, trying to make a living off of it has made it less enjoyable."

He studied her, and she allowed it, not feeling the least bit uncomfortable.

"There's something I need to tell you." His words came out throaty and husky with emotion. "I've been afraid to mention it. Afraid it would be one more wedge between us. I didn't come from a great family like the one you have. My dad . . ." He blinked rapidly. "My dad is an alcoholic. He's in a nursing home here in Morganville."

"I know."

"You do?"

"Yes, Matt told me when he came to town. Why didn't you tell me sooner?"

A brief coolness descended on his face. "I don't know. I guess because my past really has nothing to do with who I am today."

"It has everything to do with who you are, and it's nothing to be ashamed of." She reached across the concrete picnic table and grabbed his hand, drawing his attention. "Don't you see that it's made you the wonderful man you are today?"

He ducked his head, but continued to hold her hand. Finally he looked back up at her. "I guess I was afraid you'd dismiss me as suitable partner material if you knew. Sounds crazy now, but that's how I felt."

A breeze danced through the branches of the willow tree that stood beside the lake, and then caressed her face. She relished it for a moment, then did a quick scan of the playground to check on Bo. "We all deceive ourselves." Just like she'd deceived herself into thinking she couldn't accept help from others. It had taken a lot of courage for him to tell her the truth. One more thing to add to her list of things she admired about this man sitting across from her. "In all honesty, I wasn't completely truthful with you, either. I didn't want anyone to know how bad my financial situation was."

"It wasn't too hard to figure out."

Trish laughed in spite of the seriousness of the conversation. "I'm sure it wasn't, but at the time it felt like something I needed to keep hidden. Something no one could know. Something to be ashamed of."

In a flurry, he moved around the table and straddled the bench next to her. He grabbed her shoulders, his eyes inches from hers. Her pulse pounded in her throat. "Trish, I'm tired of holding back, tired of not being completely honest with each other. I love you and I love Bo. I'm willing to wait if that's what you want and need, but I refuse to continue to pretend I don't care."

Her heart melted at the sincerity in his eyes. She brought a hand to cup his cheek. "Andy, I care about you, too. I'm so grateful God sent you to me and Bo."

The next thing she knew, his lips were on hers. His kiss was tender, but revealed the emotion he'd bottled for so long. She couldn't be sure how long the kiss lasted, a moment or several minutes, but it ended when she felt Bo's hand on her knee.

They both looked at him at the same time, a snaggle-toothed grin spread across his chubby-cheeked face. "Does this mean you like each other?"

32

Trish leaned against the red brick of Miller's Creek Community Church, checked her watch, and huffed out a disgruntled sigh. What was keeping Andy so long? He should've been here a half hour ago to help with the fall decorations for Dad and Mama Beth's last-minute wedding. A stickler for punctuality, Andy had fallen into the habit of being late. Especially, it seemed, when he was supposed to meet her.

The past few weeks since her return to Miller's Creek, his attention had been constant, as if he were somehow trying to prove himself. Her emotions did battle within. Doubts, fears, and insecurities wanted her to believe Andy didn't care as much as he professed. She did her best to push the imposters aside and replace them with an image of Andy's loving eyes and kind heart.

Her cell phone vibrated in her hand. Andy. "Where are you? I need your help unloading the wedding decorations."

"I know, Trish. I'm so sorry. I got hung up in court, and there are a few other things I'm trying to take care of as well."

"What things?"

"That's for me to know and you to find out." A cocky smugness resonated in his tone.

Why was he being so secretive? Doubts returned. *Enough.* She didn't have time for this insecurity. Nor did she have time to wait on him. "Where are you?"

"I'm on my way. I should be there in five minutes."

"Fine." Feeling more than a little snarky, she clicked the phone shut, grabbed a box that wasn't too heavy, and lugged it through the double wooden doors of the church. She'd done this on her own before. No reason why she couldn't do it again.

On her own. Trish shook her head. Was she doomed to repeat the mistakes of the past? Would she ever move past her foolish tendency toward pride? She plopped down on the front pew and bowed her head. *Lord, thank You for making me recognize when I start to wander from Your path. Forgive me for these fears, and help me to do better.*

The side door swung open, and Andy sauntered in, his face lit with a grin that vanished when he saw her sitting there. He hurried to her side. "Sorry I'm late, sweetheart." He sat down beside her and plunked a kiss on her forehead. "Will you forgive me?"

She sent him a sideways mock glare. "Only if you'll tell me what you're up to."

He chuckled. "Nice try, but not gonna happen. You'll just have to trust me."

"You, more than anyone, should know I have trust issues."

A teasing smirk landed on his face. "Just think of it as practice."

Trish glanced at the clock. "Yikes!" She jumped to her feet and headed toward the door. "We've got to get this decorating done. I already feel about two years behind, and my to-do list is out the door."

Andy latched on to her hand and spun her around. "Hey, slow down. You don't have to be in such a mad dash."

Her frustration mounted. "I don't think you realize how much I have to do. In addition to this wedding, I have five internet orders to fill. The Dallas Art Show—which may I remind you, you got me into—is coming up, and I want to have a booth at the Autumn Daze festival. I don't know when I'm supposed to get all this d—"

He clamped a palm over her mouth. "Shhh. Chill out, Trish. Remember our pact?"

She breathed in deep. Only after she calmed down did he remove his hand. Trish repeated the words that they'd prayed over together. "Trust that God is only going to give us what we can handle. Anything else is our struggle to do it on our own."

His eyes took on that loving look that made her go weak in the knees. The one that made her question her resolve to move slowly in this relationship. "I love you, Trish James, and I'm so glad God allowed our paths to collide. I don't want to take this journey with anyone but you."

Trish swallowed and lowered her head. Why was this moving so fast? The more determined she was to pull back, the more determined Andy seemed to break down her feeble barriers.

He must have sensed her indecision, because he pulled her to him and sealed his words with a kiss. "Now, let's go get that stuff and get it thrown into place."

Trish laughed and plopped a kiss on the end of his nose. "As I recall, that was your method of decorating at the last wedding you helped me with." She shot off the comment, then noting the mischievous look on Andy's face, she screamed and raced away from his grasp.

He caught her before she reached the door, and she wasn't sorry.

The next day, Trish stood at the back of the church and viewed the decorations, chiding herself for her frantic behavior the day before. Andy had proved to be a capable helper, able to somehow anticipate what needed to be done, and they'd finished time. Now gold, orange, and fiery-red leaves, along ...es and sunflowers, decorated the podium and spilled over onto the pew decorations. The fragrance of cinnamon apples and pumpkin rose from lit candles that decorated the perimeter of the sanctuary. The results were even more stunning than Steve and Dani's wedding.

She shook off a chill that seemed to work its way out from a cold place inside her. Her Dad would marry Mama Beth in a few minutes, a reality she still struggled with. Her head knew Dad had no intention of replacing her mother with a new wife, but her heart still ached for Mom.

Once again, all of Miller's Creek had turned out for the wedding, the friendly chatter in the church louder than the soft music that spilled from the speakers. Dani sidled up and put an arm around her shoulder. "Trish, you've outdone yourself again. It's beautiful." She paused, her blue eyes full of concern. "I know this isn't easy for you, but I want you to know how much Mama Beth loves your dad."

Trish ducked her head to hide the tears that stung her eyes. "I know she does."

"She'd like to speak with you alone before the wedding, if you feel up to it."

A knot formed in her throat. This was something she needed to do. Dad loved Mama Beth, and it was important that she felt welcomed into the family. She gave Dani a nod, then made her way to the bride's room.

Mama Beth stood near the window, dressed in a knee-length gown of ivory lace, and turned to face Trish as she entered the room. "I was afraid you wouldn't come."

Trish walked over to give her a hug. "You look beautiful."

"Thank you, dear." A hand flitted nervously to the cameo at the base of her throat. "Can we sit and talk for a few minutes?"

"Sure."

They moved to a pair of Queen Anne chairs. Mama Beth studied her with kind, wise eyes. "I know I've already told you this, but I wanted to say it again. I've loved your father my entire life. During high school, we both dreamed of the day we'd be grown and married with children." Her voice caught, and she lowered her head to gather control. "But God had other plans. For reasons no one knows, God's plan for your father was to marry someone else."

Trish thought through the information, realizing again how much this woman had endured, her dreams and expectations for life bound up in a man who took a different road. "I'm sorry for how painful that must have been."

Mama Beth smiled sadly. "For a very long time I questioned why God allowed my path to be so painful, just as I've seen you ask Him the very same questions."

It was true. She'd never seen the path of widowhood coming.

The older woman stood and made her way to a small package nearby and brought it back to Trish. "I made a gift for your father a very long time ago, while we were still in high school. I made another one for you."

Trish took the package and gently removed the wrapping to reveal a hand-stitched bookmark engraved with the words: *"Trust in the LORD with all you heart and lean not on your own understanding; in all your ways acknowledge Him, and He shall direct your paths."* Tears slipped down Trish's cheeks unbidden. Mama Beth had no way of knowing how much this very verse had impacted her life over the past few months.

"I'm sorry, Trish. I didn't mean to make you cry."

Trish smiled up at her. "I'm okay. It's just that this verse has become very special to me. I think this bookmark is God's way of telling me my relationship with you is going to be very special as well." She lifted her purse and opened it, removing the matching bookmark Dad had given her—the one worn with time and prayers—the one she always carried with her no matter what.

Mama Beth gasped. "He gave it to you?"

"Loaned might be a better word."

A tender smile crossed Mama Beth's face. "Isn't it amazing how God intersects and weaves our paths together?"

"Andy and I have talked about that before."

"Speaking of Andy." Mama Beth laid a hand on hers. "How are things going?"

Trish frowned. "He's wonderful, but . . ."

"But what?"

"I just can't get past how quickly this has all happened."

"I understand your reservations, Trish, but I believe God brought that young man into your life for a reason." Her kind blue eyes held wisdom. "Trust Him."

Lord, show me how. She faced Mama Beth again, and held out Dad's worn bookmark. "Would you like to carry this as your 'something old'?"

Mama Beth's eyes flooded with tears and she wrapped Trish in a hug. "I'd be honored, dear."

A few minutes later, Trish and Andy met beneath a twinkling arch of fall leaves and berries to once again head down the aisle.

"This seems vaguely familiar," Andy muttered under his breath as they headed down the aisle to camera flashes.

"At least your tux fits this time."

His left dimple winked at her from his cheeky grin. "I like walking down the aisle with you."

Trish's heart bounced in her chest as they reached the steps leading to the platform. Words eluded her. All she could do was send him a brief smile and move to the taped "x" on the floor, praying God would continue to direct her path toward Andy Tyler.

Trish crawled from bed, bleary-eyed, and pulled on her robe over her pajamas. Who was banging at the door so early on a Saturday morning? And didn't they realize she was up late the night before cleaning up after the wedding? She stumbled down the hallway toward the front door, but Bo passed her and opened it right as she got there.

Andy entered carrying two white bags, the accompanying aroma teasing her nose. "Anyone around here like donuts?" He sang the words, then pecked her on the cheek as he passed.

"I do, I do." Bo giggled with delight.

Trish slammed the door and followed them to the dining room. "Are you always so sunny and chipper this early in the morning?"

Andy laughed. "Are you always so grumpy?"

"Yep." Bo sank his teeth into a chocolate-covered donut.

"Thanks a lot, traitor." She moved toward the kitchen to make a pot of coffee. A big one.

But again Andy passed her by. "I'll make the coffee. You go get in the shower."

"Why?"

"'Cause we've got things to do, people to see, life to explore. Time's a-wasting. Hop to it, chick!" He barked the order like an over-exuberant cheerleader.

"Why is it that when I'm in a hurry, you tell me to chill, but when you're in a hurry, you tell me to hop to it?"

He shrugged, laughed, and planted a kiss on her lips. "'Cause what I have to do is more important."

She jutted out her left hip and crossed her arms. "How could it be more important than getting some paintings done for the art show and Autumn Daze Festival? I told you yesterday how far behind I am. I don't have time for fun and games today."

Andy pulled her into an embrace. "For someone who's a non-lawyer type, you sure are argumentative."

Trish glared at him, his early morning pep rally starting to grate on her last nerve.

A goofy grin crossed his face, his eyes half open. "You, my dear, are just gonna have to trust me."

She pulled away and headed down the hallway. "I seem to be doing a lot of that lately."

One hour, two donuts, and three cups of coffee later, Andy escorted her and Bo to his car, almost giddy. "Your coach awaits, princess." He opened the door, held out one arm, and bowed.

"I still don't understand why you can't tell me where we're going."

Exasperation covered his face. "Because it's a secret."

Bo chimed in from the back seat. "Yeah, and everyone knows you're not s'posed to tell a secret."

Trish wrinkled her brows. "You know about this, too?"

"Yep." A smug smile turned up the corners of his mouth.

All the way to town, Andy and Bo sang silly songs and laughed. Trish tried her best to enter their fun, but the thought of all she should be doing kept her from enjoying the time. When they pulled into the parking lot of his home and office, Andy let out a cheery "We're here!" and exited the car, coming around to her side to open the door.

"You got me up this early in the morning to come to your *office*?" Her previous aggravation elevated to anger.

He held up one finger. "Remember. Trust me." He held a hand out as Bo passed. "Blind-fold, please."

Bo slapped a red bandana onto Andy's opened palm. "Check."

Her radar went up. "Oh no, you don't. I'm not going anywhere blind-folded with you two."

"Why?" Andy's expression was one of mock hurt.

"Because I don't tr—"

"You don't trust me." He finished the statement, and let his eyes take on the puppy dog look she could never refuse.

"Okay. Fine." She twirled around, putting her back to Andy, so he could tie the blindfold, then held her hands out to make sure they didn't run her into bushes or buildings.

Andy's lips brushed her ear. "You still don't trust me, do you?"

"What was your first clue?"

"Shame on you, Trish James." He held her hand tightly. "Okay, we're going down the stairs."

"You got your basement finished! That's the big surprise, isn't it?"

"Party pooper."

They arrived at the bottom of the stairs.

"Just a few more steps, Mom."

"Okay, this should do." Andy brought her to a stop. "Take the blindfold off."

She pulled the bandana down around her neck. The basement had been finished in a blah-beige from the carpet to the ceiling. Recessed lighting spotlighted empty walls, and there wasn't a stick of furniture.

"Well, what do you think?" Andy's voice held excitement.

Was he serious? He'd painted the whole room beige and made a big deal over bringing her here to see his lack of design skills? The room was nothing but a blank canvas. How could she express her opinion without completely destroying the joy in his eyes? "Um, it's very nice, Andy, but why is it empty?"

"It's not empty. Oh, I have you facing the wrong way." He grabbed her shoulders and spun her around.

On the wall in front of her was one painting—the one she'd wanted to give him—but had sold at the festival in Morganville. "Where did you get that painting?"

"I bought it."

"No, you didn't it. I sold it to a charming old gentleman. I remember because at first I told him it wasn't for sale, but he offered me so much I couldn't refuse."

Andy nodded. "Which made me pay a ridiculous amount."

Realization dawned. "You mean he . . ."

"Yep. He bought it for me." He crowed the words triumphantly.

"But why?"

He slid his hands down her arms. "Because I wanted to help you, but you wouldn't let me. Because I love the painting. But mostly because I love you."

There it was again, that look of love and utter devotion that made her tremble inside. Suddenly familiar voices sounded upstairs. One by one, her Miller's Creek friends clunked down the steps carrying large frames. Her breath caught in her throat, and she brought both hands to her face.

J.C. was first in line, his kind eyes shimmering, his head lowered bashfully. "Here's the painting you did of the home place where I grew up, Miss Trish." J.C. showed the painting, then moved to one of the spotlights and hung it on the wall.

Wanda Cates, the city secretary, was next. "I've had this painting you made of my prize rosebush hanging in my living room all these years. I'm happy to put it in your exhibit, but only on loan." Her nasally voice called out over her shoulder as she moved to yet another spotlight and positioned the art.

"And I love this picture you did of my old '67 Mustang." Coot trumpeted the drawled-out words in a burst of bad breath, then joined his friends.

In what seemed like an endless line, people brought the work she'd painted over the years, quickly filling up the once bare walls. Last were Dani and Steve. Her brother deposited a pile of paintings at his feet, then stood and glared at Andy. "Next time you plan something like this, would you mind doing it when Dad and Mama Beth are in town?"

"Oh, don't mind him," said Dani, hugging Trish's neck. "We're happy to bring their paintings to add to your exhibit." Then she winked at Andy and stooped to help Steve pick up the pile of artwork at their feet.

Then, to the shouts of the crowd, Mama Beth and Dad came trouncing down the steps.

Trish's mouth flew open. "Y'all are supposed to be on your honeymoon!"

"When Andy told us his plan, we delayed our flight." Mama Beth embraced her.

"I wasn't about to miss this day." Dad choked out the words and planted a kiss on her forehead.

But it wasn't a big enough deal for them to miss their honeymoon! Tears inching down her cheeks and her mouth agape, Trish turned and looked around the room, now filled with the people she loved. The bare walls were now covered with her paintings. Her friends were generously loaning their artwork for her upcoming exhibits, and Andy had been behind it all. She faced him, blinking back more tears. "I don't know what to say. Thank you doesn't seem like enough. I'm sorry I ever doubted you."

Andy looked at Bo, huge grins plastered across both their faces. "Would you help me remember she said that, buddy?"

Bo nodded. "Yep."

Trish wiped away tears and turned to face the crowd. "I'm incredibly blessed to have friends like you. Words can't express how much I love you."

Then in a move that took her breath away, Andy went down on one knee in front of her, a hand stretched toward Little Bo. "Ring, please."

Bo pulled a black velvet box from his pocket and placed it in Andy's hand. "Check."

Chuckles sounded around the room, and Andy's eyes went soft. "Trish James, I want to travel all of life's paths with you. I want to share thousands of sunsets and horse rides. I want to walk down the aisle with you again and again and again. Will you marry me?"

She tried to speak, but words wouldn't come. Instead, she raised both hands to her cheeks and nodded her head.

Bo stepped up to Andy and patted him on the shoulder. "That's her way of saying she's really, really happy, and yes, we'll marry you."

Trish joined them on the floor for a family-sized hug, and the room broke out in cheers.

There was no longer any doubt that this unexpected path had been God's plan all along. She'd spent far too long trying to forge her own path, but it wasn't up to her to paint this picture. Instead, they'd continue to trust God, and He would direct their paths.

Dear friends,

Trish's spiritual journey in the story—as is usually the case in my writing—came from my own quest for God's direction in my life. How many times have I prayed for God's direction, when it clearly states in His Word that if we trust Him with all our heart, He will direct our paths?

When we walk by sight, our journey through this earth to our heavenly home can be so confusing. But these earthly eyes are limited and temporal. They see only a small fraction of reality. A bigger reality is being played out all around us on a daily basis. If we rely only on our finite senses, we miss so much!

A faith-walk is challenging to be sure, but also exhilarating and liberating. When we place our complete trust in the One who loves us perfectly—the One who knows us better than we know ourselves—each step becomes part of a marvelous adventure directed by the very hand of God.

Walking by faith,
Cathy

About the Author

Cathy Bryant is a former public school teacher who handed in her chalk for a private music studio and writing career. Her passion is to write heart-stirring stories that show God's life-changing grace. Her debut novel, *Texas Roads* (a 2009 ACFW Genesis finalist) released in early 2010. *A Path Less Traveled*, the second book in the Miller's Creek novels, was launched in the fall of 2010. *The Way of Grace* (book three in the series) will be available in 2011.

Cathy is the owner and editor of the popular blog, WordVessel, and has written devotions for *The Upper Room* devotional magazine, and for two devotional books, *Spirit & Heart: A 30-Day Devotional Journey* and *Faith & Finance: In God We Trust*. She's the wife of a music minister, the mother of two grown sons and a beautiful daughter-in-love, and the Nana of Harrisen. A Texas gal since birth, she lives in a century-old Texas farmhouse with her husband and a phobia-ridden cat.

Visit her website at www.CatBryant.com.

Book Club Discussion Questions

1. Personal hardships often make celebrations difficult to bear, as we see in the opening of the story. How does Dani and Steve's wedding affect Trish? Can you relate to Trish's struggle? How?

2. Most of us have lies from the past that haunt us. What is Andy's lie? What is Trish's lie? How do lies from your past affect you? How has God's truth helped you overcome Satan's lies?

3. Trish covers up her financial difficulties with little white lies. Is it ever okay to lie? Why or why not? What are some of the consequences for Trish's lies?

4. Post-traumatic stress disorder is usually associated with soldiers returning from battle, but it can also affect anyone who's experienced a devastating trauma. What symptoms of PTSD does little Bo exhibit?

5. What signs of grief do you see manifested in Trish's life? How does having a traumatized child to care for affect her grieving process? How do you think witnessing the accident and her husband's vegetative state affected the process?

6. How do baseball and horses become a healing factor and point of connection for Andy, Trish, and Bo?

7. How do Trish's paintings, interior design work, and cottage serve as symbols of her life? What other symbols in the story are metaphorical in relation to Trish's struggle?

8. What incident in the story serves as a metaphor for Andy's fear of being hurt? Could any of your fears serve as a metaphor for your life?

9. It's often difficult to know how to interact with those who have suffered a devastating loss. Why? Can you think of specific examples in the story where others related to Trish and Bo in a positive way? Negative way?

10. Why does Trish assume that the path God wants her to take involves her interior design career? How does our human understanding of a situation sometimes contradict God's plan for our lives? What is the remedy?

11. How does Andy's desire to fix things cause conflict between him and Trish? Where do you think this desire comes from?

12. It's hard to understand why innocent children are subjected to difficult situations. How did Andy's childhood shape his character? What role did others play in influencing his life? Can you think of a role model or mentor who has influenced you? Can you think of a child who needs your influence?

13. Trish is determined to make it on her own. How does asserting her independence affect her relationship with God, Andy, and her family?

14. Much of Trish's dilemma deals with God's timing. Name examples where Trish should wait on God, but moves ahead on her own. Name examples where her fear keeps her from stepping out in faith. How does God's timing come into play with Trish's opposition to the relationship between her father and Mama Beth?

15. Our lives rarely turn out the way we plan. How has Trish's life turned out differently in both negative and positive ways? Andy's life? Your life?

16. How does Trish struggle with allowing God to direct her path? Why does she struggle? Why is it difficult to relinquish control of our paths to God? Why do we sometimes miss His path?

17. Hindsight is always 20/20, but our lives are spent stepping out into the unknown. Looking back on your life, do you see specific examples of your baby steps of faith and God directing your path?

COMING IN 2011

the way of Grace

A MILLER'S CREEK NOVEL

Book Three

When freewheeling Matt Tyler moves to Miller's Creek, he throws Grace Soldano's perfect world into a tailspin. Caught between a dream and a nightmare—and between law and grace—which of them will become her reality?

ALSO AVAILABLE:

Book One in the Miller's Creek novels

2009 ACFW Genesis Finalist

One secret kept, another uncovered . . .

Dani Davis longs for a place to call home. With quirky residents, quaint country charm, and loads of business potential, Miller's Creek Texas seems like the perfect place to start over . . . except for the cowboy who gives her a ride into town. Then malicious rumors and a devastating discovery propel her down a road she never expected to travel.

Available at Amazon.com
& other leading retailers

LaVergne, TN USA
18 February 2011
217055LV00001B/101/P

9 780984 431120

What Readers Are Saying . . .

"*Texas Roads* is a wonderful book that is like a comfy pair of pj's. I fell in love with the characters and town and wish I lived in a town like Millers Creek . . . . The book will make you laugh, shed a few tears, and hug those you love a little tighter."

~Vicki at Reading At The Beach

"Cathy Bryant has written a solid debut novel . . . . A hint of romance, a closely-guarded secret, and a bit of mystery provide dimension in this story that reminds us that our inner longings will only be satisfied by God's presence. Take a journey along the *Texas Roads*!"

~Linda at Mocha with Linda

"For a debut novel *Texas Roads* is an absolute gem! I really loved every bit of it, from the crazy hairdresser to the hunky rancher/mayor Steve, and even the 'old geezers.'"

~Renee at Black 'n Gold Girl's Book Spot

"*Texas Roads* is a wonderful debut novel by Cathy Bryant . . . . You'll enjoy the well-rounded characters, a godly message, and some good, clean romance when reading this book! This is a definite 5-star read and I am anxiously awaiting her next novel . . ."

~Tammy at Tammy's Book Parlor

"Beautiful description, poignant characters, chuckle-worthy humor, and a heart-healing message make *Texas Roads* a not-to-be missed read."

~Julia at Dark Glass Ponderings

"I have to give kudos to Cathy on her debut novel! What a beautifully written story about faith, compassion, and perseverance."

~Freda at Freda's Voice

"I really loved this simple little story; it was more than a romance, it was about a woman finding herself, finding family, and most importantly—finding home . . . . This is truly a quality book that I'd recommend to any fan of Christian fiction."

~Kate at The Book Buff

"Cathy Bryant has made my 'New-Authors-to-keep-an-eye-on' list! Her writing was flowing, easy to read, and captivating."

~Verlina at What You Reading Now?

"I love a book that makes me laugh out loud and Cathy's wonderful use of humor in this book had me laughing out loud frequently. She blends the humor, suspense, and romance into a thoroughly enjoyable read! The story is full of meaning, and paints a beautiful picture of God's love and salvation . . . . The characters became like family. I'm so excited there are more books to come in this series. I can't wait for the next book. And I wish I could move to Miller's Creek!"

~Michelle at My Life in Review

"*Texas Roads* is a delightful story of heartache, romance, and home. I fell in love with the characters of Miller's Creek and cannot wait to read the sequel to this touching book."

~Cami Checketts at Cami's Books

For more reader's comments, visit www.CatBryant.com